**DO NOT REMOVE**
**CARDS FROM POCKET**

# TO AN EASY
# GRAVE

# TO AN EASY
# GRAVE

## ALEXANDER LAW

A THOMAS·DUNNE BOOK

St. Martin's Press
New York

*Design by Amy Ruth Bernstein*

Library of Congress Cataloging-in-Publication Data

Law, Alexander, 1947–
    To an easy grave.

    I. Title.
PR9199.3.L333T6   1986      813'.54      86-13871
ISBN 0-312-80623-X

First Edition

10 9 8 7 6 5 4 3 2 1

*To Sue, sine qua non.*
*And Joanne.*
*Not forgetting John,*
*for finally catching on*
*and firing me.*

# TO AN EASY
# GRAVE

SEAN DENBY SMILED OUT AT ME ABOUT
twenty-four times and I knew he was dead.
I was on Avenue Road, about a mile south
of Highway 401 on the last leg of a five-hour
drive from Detroit to Toronto. I'd been looking around as I
waited for a red light to change. The October air had looked
good through the windows of my glass and sheet-metal co-
coon, so I'd rolled one down—just a little, so as not to let
anything in but the night air.

Silly man, acting as if I could keep the world out for long if
it wanted in. And it wanted in—with a vengeance.

Sean's still, wary face looked out at me from the two dozen
screens in the window of a TV rental store. I was used to
seeing him on TV sports shows, but not on the national news.

I shivered in the chilly night air, sorry I'd opened the
window.

Sean's faces were soon replaced by the same number of a
TV newscaster's. His faces were familiar, mobile and grim.
He was standing in front of some chaos I could not make
out. The pictures changed again, to twenty-four images of
some unhappy cops running interference for two white suits
rolling a gurney. It was full and covered by a sheet. Twenty-
four times the white suits loaded it into an ambulance. Again
the picture changed, this time to Sean Denby dropping back
to throw twenty-four simultaneous touchdown passes for the
Toronto Metros.

1

When the reporter came back on for his wrap-up on the story, I turned away from the TV screens.

My friend Sean was dead, no doubt about it. He'd have to be to get that kind of coverage on the national news, pro football star or not.

"Sean, too," I thought. The superstition about bad news coming in threes forced its way into my mind, but I was unable to recall any of its nuances. For instance, what's the statute of limitations on that superstition? Is six months too long, or does it run for a year and should I be warning my remaining family and friends to watch their step? How bad does the bad news have to be to complete the trinity? I mean, does taking a bath on the market rate with losing your life as a tragedy? And why are the people who go around saying things like "Bad news comes in threes" never able to answer specific questions about what they say?

Of course I was stalling by considering such things. What I really had to do was let Sean's death wash over my emotions. I'd been resisting that because I knew it was going to push me back psychologically, maybe as far back as July, or even June. I didn't want to think about falling back to May. April was unimaginable. Sitting in that car staring blankly ahead, I could literally feel the shock of Sean Denby's death hitting me in waves; my body rocked gently, the way a stationary boat does when waves come up on a calm lake. Conscious thought drained from my mind; a deep black pool of self-pity spread out in front of me, and I got ready to dive into it. It'd be warm, I knew from experience.

An angry horn blasted nearby. In my rearview mirror I saw a face to go with the sound. The light was green and I hadn't noticed.

I let my reflexes deal with it. The turbocharged motor in the Nissan 300ZX roared into action, hitting about five thousand rpms before I popped its clutch. Car tires squealing in delight, I crossed the intersection as the light turned amber. The honker behind me sat gaping as the light went red.

What could it have been—twenty, maybe twenty-five seconds I'd sat at that light? Not much time by most standards, but if you're going to sit around in the middle of a busy street with your grief hanging out it's quite a lot. In truth, it's an extraordinary amount of time for the world to wait for you.

At that time of night, the very early editions of the next day's newspapers are available around parts of Toronto. Not, however, around the parts of Toronto I was passing through. I resorted to the radio, but got music on all the stations I dialed in. No mention of Sean Denby. If he'd been a rock star I'd have been swamped with memorial music shows.

If I'd listened to the radio instead of those tapes while driving back from Detroit I'd have known more about what had happened to Sean. Then again, my knowing earlier wouldn't have helped him, but would have given me five more hours of feeling shitty.

I was approaching Eglinton Avenue when it came to me: for information about a crime where better to go than a police station? I made a quick illegal left onto Eglinton and sped east.

As I approached Yonge Street I came face-to-face with something I'd been avoiding for months. Going south on Yonge, or going further east to Mount Pleasant and then south were the best ways to get to the main police station. But either of those roads would take me past Mount Pleasant Cemetery, which I had not laid eyes on in six months. Intentionally, I had to admit to myself. I thought about what I'd been doing as I turned south onto Yonge. It couldn't go on forever.

No, but it could go on for at least one more night. When I got to Chaplain Crescent I made a right and headed west again. Back at Avenue Road I made a left and headed south. Out of sight, never quite out of mind.

My detour took me only about a mile out of my way, so I was at the police station in less than ten minutes. I grabbed the first parking spot I could find and hiked the final fifty yards.

I slowed at the front door of the soon-to-be-replaced headquarters building on Jarvis Street and took out my billfold. In a few seconds I found what I was looking for in the slew of stuff that proved I was Richard Cane, thirty-three years old, six-one, 205 pounds, hazel eyes, dark brown hair, of Toronto.

As always when I go into a police station, I felt guilt by proximity. I hoped none of the cops inside would notice my unease. What I wanted them to notice were my press card and my bootlicker's grin. Only the grin was phony.

The sergeant at the front desk ignored the grin but not the press card. He took it away for examination. The hand with my card in it dropped out of sight behind the desk.

*"Toronto, Toronto?"* he asked unbelievingly. "You here to review our cafeteria cuisine?"

I had to smile. *Toronto Squared,* as the magazine was nicknamed, was relentlessly thorough and infamously cruel in its restaurant reviewing; imagine a three-page story on the hot dogs served out of pushcarts. I would be lucky if his brother didn't own a place we'd recently panned. "No cafeteria review," I said amiably, "I review cars."

"You want to borrow a squad car?"

"It's the Denby thing. Is there anyone I can talk to about it tonight?"

"The last show goes on at midnight. Unless of course we break the case in the middle of the night. Take those stairs . . ."

"I've been here before, for the *Star.* Has the drill changed in the last couple of years?" It sounded like I'd seen it all in the cop shop, but my visits had been few and far between, usually filling in for a regular guy.

"Nothing ever changes around here," the desk man said in a slightly lowered voice. There was a subtle but unmistakable edge of bitterness. No one ever says "Things never change" in a complimentary way. Probably because keeping up with the times is the accepted thing to do.

But the sergeant was right, no matter what you do to a police station it will always be what it is—a place where society's hired guns take their bad guys. Its purpose rebuffed the best efforts of reformers, architects, criminologists, renovators, police commissions, whatever. You can paint a rock any color you like, but it's still a rock.

Then I walked into a meeting room and realized that next to the permanence of some relationships the ambience of a police station is an ephemeral affair. Charles "Chuck" Blyth and I had a dislike for each other that was Sphinxlike in its size and immutability. He did not have to do anything to generate this feeling in me; a reminder of his continued existence was enough. And when he looked across the room as I entered I could tell I had the same effect on him.

I can't say for sure why this is. I'd never thought about our mutual hatred until my wife Elizabeth called me on it one night. We'd run into Blyth and some bimbo at a social gathering. After three seconds Elizabeth and the bimbo were moving away from Blyth and me as they would from two rabid dogs who were about to fight. Elizabeth was shocked by the way Blyth and I were with each other. Flippantly, I'd explained that "He's an asshole and deserves to be loathed. It's an easy job and I love to do it." I don't know why he hates me, but I suspect his motives aren't dissimilar.

Blyth was holding court for a half-dozen young TV and radio reporters, who were likely in awe of the status, money and visibility he earned as the news commentator for a very parochial local TV station. In my view his commentaries matched his personality: pompous, shallow and melodramatic. Worse even was a TV commercial for Blyth's reports; imagine John Belushi in the role of a foreign correspondent.

Blyth stopped talking to watch me take a seat as far away from him as I could. His admirers turned to see what sort of hapless prey had just stumbled into their lion's den. They exuded hostile conceit straight out of *Front Page*.

In a stage whisper Blyth brayed, "We must be in the wrong room, guys. If *Toronto Squared*'s here they must be announcing a new shade of wallpaper."

"Ha, ha, ha. Ha, ha, ha."

The high road, I said to myself, take the high road. I turned Blyth's way and said around a tired smile, "How are you, Chuck?"

He ignored my peace offering, so I turned away and tried to look vacant.

"Maybe you're not with *Toronto Squared* any more, Cane. Maybe you're with the *Rosedale Reporter* now."

Blyth touched a soft spot with his crack about Rosedale and its nonexistent newspaper. Either he sensed I was uncomfortable living in one of the best parts of town or he was a good guesser. Either way, he had me squirming; I still wasn't at home owning a house there. But if I let that jerk Blyth see that, I'd never hear the end of it.

I tried to be funny. "No, Chuck, we have no paper in Rosedale; we have servants who tell us the news." I did say I tried to be funny.

The hostility in Chuck Blyth's group went up a couple of degrees. Who likes a rich smartass anyway? I turned away from them to concentrate on the business of not biting my foot just because I had it in there.

There was some confusion from Blyth's group: They knew I deserved to be hated, but not exactly why. Ever-willing to explain anything to anyone, Blyth proceeded to serve me up for his audience in bite-size bits. "Cane was a jock," Blyth began in a slightly lowered voice I pretended not to hear, "who played football and all that shit. Couldn't make pro ball. So he weaseled himself a job with the *Star* after university. He did general reporting and then lucked into their automotive writer's column. A couple of years back he moved to *Toronto Squared*, doing automotive and general features. But his biggest break was marrying money. A few months ago she was killed. I don't know where he was at the time." The last sentence was delivered as an accusation of criminal neglect.

Blyth was wrong—I hadn't married money, I'd married Elizabeth in spite of her money. Aside from that, everything he said was true, if slanted. It was a view of myself I hadn't been able to shake since Elizabeth's death, though it had been fuzzy until Blyth's talents had put it in focus. Hearing it in Blyth's unsympathetic terms, I could at last see that it was a wild distortion of reality.

I felt a kind of gratitude to Blyth; thanks to him I realized I'd been much too hard on myself. By way of appreciation, and as a legacy for future generations of TV viewers, I decided to do a summary emasculation of him right there in the police station.

My intentions must have been telegraphed because Blyth and his friends fell into silence: He to wonder if he'd at last gone too far with the wrong person, and they to consider what excuse they'd give for not helping him out when I attacked.

I was almost standing when a hand gently touched my shoulder. In a matching voice someone said, "A police station is a very bad place to commit a homicide, even a justifiable homicide. It takes the fun out of the chase for the police and greatly reduces the number of stories I'd get out of it."

Dropping back into my chair I looked up and smiled into the face of Anthony Wright. "I'm sorry, Tony, it was selfish of me to consider doing it here."

Wright's Boston Blackie mustache levitated at one end. "When you do it, and after you go into hiding, prepare a series of clues and send them to me at the *Globe and Mail*. Make them cryptic, with at least two arcane literary allusions, so I have to explain them to my readers and the police."

"Either official language?"

"*Mais oui*. Maybe even Latin, though that might be a trifle arch."

"A trifle."

This exchange cooled me off considerably. Blyth was suitably cowed, as he always had been by Tony Wright's imperious intellect and dismissive attitude toward him. The group around Blyth had distanced themselves from him in the face of the disapproval of one of Canada's most respected and feared reporters.

Tony carefully lowered himself into the straight-backed chair next to me. Seated, he undid the buttons at the neck of his cape and let it drop onto the back of his chair. Its lower regions he folded on his lap, spreading it flat with his manicured fingers. He lifted his hands to adjust a bow tie that was already straight, and then smoothed down a head of hair that was perfectly in order. His notebook with attached pen he took from his small leather shoulder bag. When all this was done, he assumed an air of total self-satisfaction.

Tony Wright, at about forty years of age, was the most celebrated and recognized print journalist in Canada. There were two reasons for that: He was a spectacular collection of affectations, and he was—bar none—the best in the business. Even he admitted it.

The affectations were designed to link Wright's deepest personal eccentricities with his need to be recognized on sight. That way his reputation as a journalist would precede his appearance at an interview. The clothes, the mustache, the attitude, the dandified speech, the blanket suspicion of everyone—everything about him perfectly complemented his feelings as a person and his skills as a reporter.

Wright crossed his legs and rested his notebook on the top one. "I can't think of anything less trite to say than I'm sorry about Elizabeth. She was a wonderful and beautiful woman. You must miss her terribly."

Tony was the first person to mention how much I must be missing Elizabeth. The truth and novelty of his comment stung. Coming on the heels of the feelings Blyth had stirred up in me, Tony's reminder that I missed her made my lips draw tight and my eyes blink. I was on the verge of tears for the first time in six months, and it was in the middle of a police station with a scumbag like Chuck Blyth watching. My timing was always masterful.

I had to change the subject. And I would as soon as I could speak.

But Tony Wright did not get to be as good as he was by being inobservant. He showed me he understood my situation by completely ignoring it. "I'm thinking about doing a piece on the automotive business in Canada," he said. "More specifically on the colonialization of this country's automotive industry by the U.S.; how we're nothing more up here than hewers of plastic and carriers of chrome." He stopped to enjoy his own remark before going on in the same vein, clearly aiming to talk for as long as I needed him to. It wasn't that long before I could speak. I said it was a great idea, which he took as being a redundant observation. We batted his idea around for about ten minutes, with me agreeing to steer him to some contacts of mine in the automotive industry.

Our discussion was just trailing off when some booted feet marched into the room behind us, killing conversation as they passed by. I was surprised to see the room had filled up while Tony and I had been talking. Nothing like the death of a star to bring them out, even at midnight.

The uniformed police superintendent put some papers on the desk at the front of the room and waited until he had total silence. He looked like a man who'd been ordered to teach touch-typing to a cage of unruly chimpanzees. With great effort, he pried his thin lips apart and started to speak.

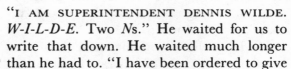 "I AM SUPERINTENDENT DENNIS WILDE. *W-I-L-D-E*. Two *N*s." He waited for us to write that down. He waited much longer than he had to. "I have been ordered to give you this briefing. When I have given you all the information you're entitled to I will entertain a few questions. And only then." He looked around the room to ensure that this sunk in. Wilde was obviously one of those Toronto cops who had never overcome his military background.

Before Wilde could continue, Tony Wright asked, "Are you entertaining questions now about the questions you'll entertain later, or must I save my question on what questions you'll entertain later until you're entertaining questions later?" Everyone in the room except Tony and Wilde grinned. Tony seemed totally sincere, and Wilde totally confused.

"What?" Wilde said.

"Are you restricting questions to subjects you raise, and are you only going to answer questions in front of this group?"

Wilde looked really confused at the second bit.

"Are you going to talk to us one-to-one?" Tony said patiently.

The policeman was relieved that at last he understood what he was going to refuse in any case. "The questions will be restricted to matters I raise, and there will be no personal interviews later."

Sean Denby, aged thirty-three, had been dead since sometime the evening before. He had been bound and badly beaten before being killed. He was found the next day by his cleaning lady, who phoned the police. The police had investigated the scene thoroughly and a team of investigators led by Inspector Ian Hurst was following up several good leads. End of statement.

Wilde then issued about seventeen "That's classified"'s to as many questions before the assembled reporters all got the message. When five seconds had gone by without another question being asked, Wilde picked up his notes and marched out of the room.

He left behind him the most dangerous thing in public relations: a roomful of frustrated journalists. If it hadn't been so late, they would have stuck around interviewing each other and coming up with ideas the police would then have to waste time checking out.

But the media people were tired and cranky, so limited themselves to bitching and whining. "That's even less than they told us the last time," one angry voice observed from the crowd around Chuck Blyth. "And we still don't even know the cause of death for sure."

Blyth stood up looking like he knew something none of the rest of us did, and he might have, since he had a lot of contacts on the force. "They've got their reasons for keeping their mouths shut," Blyth said in a conspiratorial tone. He was a diligent apologist for the cops, which explained his contacts; they scratched his back, he kissed their asses.

Aside from Blyth, Tony Wright was the only one in the room who didn't look distressed over what had happened. He knew he'd get what he wanted someplace else, and extra work never put him off a story. He got his information by not kissing anyone's ass. Tony reasoned—correctly—that if you're kissing someone's ass it's impossible to kick them in the balls when you have to, as you do from time to time.

For a few moments I sat staring at the wall behind where Wilde had just stood. I was probably more disappointed than anyone in the room; since it was personal, rather than professional, my need to know about Sean's murder was greater.

Beside me Tony Wright was doing up his cape. "When was the last time you saw Sean?" he asked me.

"I saw him all the time, because he was famous. The last time we saw each other was about twelve years ago, when we were in university together."

"The University of Toronto?"

"Yeah."

"Were you close?"

"Yeah."

"What happened? Why didn't you try to see him in all that time?"

I shrugged my entire body. Tony waited patiently for me to figure it out and then tell him about it. That was his talent as a journalist I envied most—his complete conviction that he had every right in the world to know someone else's business.

11

"Let's go for a coffee somewhere," I said. He agreed and we walked out into the cool air of an October night.

Maybe telling Tony would make me understand it—and myself—better. As we walked along I felt the need to talk grow in me until it was almost overwhelming. I had lost my best audience when Elizabeth had been killed. Six months without talking had made me more than a little ready to start again.

"Christ, it's pushing twenty years that I've known Sean," I said to Tony as we walked west on Charles Street toward Church. "We were fourteen, maybe fifteen, in the second year of high school. We both went out for the football team. For the next eight years we were teammates, friends. Especially in university when we moved to Toronto. First year here we roomed together on campus, then it was three years of various apartments around town. Yeah, we were friends. I've thought about it since and I guess I was Sean's best friend in those days, because I can't think of anyone who was closer to him. Not that I knew about, anyway."

We reached Church Street and I stopped my awkward narrative to work out with Tony where we were going exactly. I readily agreed to a little place Tony knew about up by Bloor Street. I kept quiet until we were inside and had ordered coffee and two pieces of the house cheesecake Tony called "pedestrian, but adequate under the circumstances."

Tony picked up my thread. "Sean didn't have many friends in school?"

"He was popular enough," I said testily, feeling the need to defend my friend's name even in death. I also felt the need to be honest. "But he didn't have many friends in the sense that I'd use the word. What I mean is—" I didn't know what I meant for sure, but I said, "he didn't have many friends if I was his best friend."

I couldn't blame Tony for looking puzzled. "You didn't get along?"

"Sure, he did with everyone." The waitress arrived with the coffee and cheesecake, giving me a chance to work out what was

12

in my mind. When she was gone I said, "It's just that I never felt real close to him. I don't know that he ever was real close to anyone. That might have changed in the decade we've been away from each other. He must have gotten close to someone, though, 'cause he did get married a few years back."

Tony imparted a disdainful look using only his right eyebrow and the corners of his mustache. "Don't project your own experience onto everyone else," he said. "I, for instance, have been married three times. Each divorce was the consequence of my wife and I not being close enough to each other. It's my opinion that insufficient propinquity should be a legal ground for divorce, just like mental cruelty, marriage breakdown, and good old infidelity." Tony thought about what he'd said as he chewed daintily on some cheesecake. He swallowed, then added a clarification. "I mean spiritual nearness, of course, not physical; my wives and I propinqued like rabbits." He again smiled at his own joke.

I shot back my "Damn straight, fuckin' A Bubba" look. Studs united. Not for the first time the familiar bonding patterns of heterosexual men made me uneasy. I wondered why Tony was more concerned with his reputation as a sexual athlete than with his burgeoning name as an emotional cripple.

It occurred to Tony that we'd gone from my past into his bedroom. He sat up straight and asked me, "Did you ever meet Denby's wife? They're divorced now, of course."

Of course. "No, I never met her. I haven't seen him in person since the summer after university," I reminded him.

"Yeah, what about that? How come so long? Any special reason?"

"I can only speak for myself, but there was a special reason: stupid pride."

"That's a very fashionable reason these days," Tony said lightly. He was trying to put me back on the stand while making me feel better.

I appreciated his concern for my feelings, though it did little good. "After university, Sean took a vacation. I think it was Colombia—Bogotá. I went home. After his holiday,

13

Sean went to British Columbia to play pro ball. That fall I came back to Toronto to work at the *Star*."

"That'll be the job you weaseled for yourself," Tony deadpanned.

I was now able to smile a little at Blyth's rendering of my life, so I did. "That's the job. Anyway, Sean was in Vancouver and I was in Toronto. When you're that age you aren't smart enough to keep in touch with your friends when you're apart. I was so busy enjoying myself at the paper and around town that I just didn't see Sean for a few years. He didn't contact me, either," I said, sounding and feeling overly defensive.

Tony Wright listened attentively, but his attitude was totally noncommittal. Most people are uncomfortable with this attitude and will play right at it, hoping to force the listener into displaying an opinion of any kind, pro or con. To this end they will do many things, including saying more than they should. Which is of course another reason Tony Wright's such a good reporter.

I used the coffee and cheesecake as a cover for collecting my thoughts. "Sean was in Vancouver for five years before the trade that brought him here," I said slowly. This is where it got tricky as far as my actions were concerned. "When he got here there was a big media blowout put on by the Metros to introduce him to the press. I was still working cityside at the *Star* then but I went along with some sports guys. I figured it was a good way to see Sean again after so long. The meeting would be casual, unplanned, so it could go whatever way it had to go."

"I gather it didn't work out," Tony said.

I shook my head at the still vivid memory. "The place was chaos—media guys stocking up on scotch for the winter, ballplayers getting a free meal and a good laugh, and about four hundred other people with no reason to be there that I could see. And all of them wanted to be near him—Sean, I mean. It was unbelievable."

"He was just hitting his stride then," Tony said.

I nodded. "I guess I'd been expecting a quiet, private re-union. When I saw all those people clutching at him I couldn't bring myself to go near him, like just another sup-plicant hoping to touch his raiment."

"People calling out 'Hi, do you remember me?' is one of life's most self-demeaning sights," Tony said with a shudder of distaste. "You were afraid Sean would give you the brush?"

I looked into my coffee. "People change. Especially people with a lot of demands, fame, adulation and money pressed on them."

"You don't sound like you had a lot of faith in Sean's character."

"It's not that. I guess I was just never sure about where we stood. Maybe there was less to our friendship than I thought at the time."

"Maybe you just made a mistake." Tony said it with no malice, so I returned none in the look I gave him. "Surely in the five or six years since there've been chances for you to find out," he said.

"For a long time I waited for an accidental meeting." I thought about that for a moment and then let out a shallow laugh. "I was still waiting for an accidental meeting up until about two hours ago, I guess. But as time passed it seemed less appropriate for me to call Sean up and reintroduce my-self. He would have thought I was after something."

Tony gave me a look that said that sounded reasonable. "And of course he never called you." Tony meant it to ease my sense of guilt, but it didn't.

"He never would; it wasn't his style to approach other people. Early in life he got used to being the one who was asked, not the one who does the asking. I knew that and should have acted accordingly."

At my description of Sean's way of living Tony looked off to one side. I'd touched one of his personal nerves. His brow knitted as he tried the idea onto someone in his own life, maybe even himself.

"Anyway," I said a little too heartily, to bring Tony back,

"that's all psychic masturbation now. What matters is that Sean's dead and it's too late to get in touch with him now. Unless you know a good medium."

"The only good medium I know costs me fourteen dollars at a steak house in the west end," Tony said. "Besides, there are other ways to find out about the past, which is what you're going to do, isn't it? That's why you were at the cop shop scrum tonight."

He wasn't really asking so I didn't really answer. I turned the tables on him. "What were you doing there? The last thing I heard about you, you were trying to sniff out a story on Ontario Hydro's consistently bad planning."

"If I told everyone what I was working on, there'd be no reason for them to read my stories in the newspaper." He was serious, but I smiled at him anyway.

"What do you know about Sean's death that I don't?" I asked Tony.

"Not much. Only that it certainly was not pleasant."

 FROM TORONTO'S MAIN POLICE STATION it is less than a five-minute drive to where I live. When I pulled the 300 ZX into the drive-way about 1:15 A.M. the only light on was the dim second-floor hallway lamp my housekeeper leaves on.

Ten yards in from the road I stopped the car long enough to push a sequence of numbers on the six buttons embedded in a fold of an oak tree—one of my father-in-law's more original and ostentatious toys. He'd had it installed when he and

Elizabeth lived in the house, before he'd given it to her as a wedding present and built himself a place further north. Usually it embarrassed me, but that night I was grateful that it turned on lights in the driveway and in the garage, and opened the garage door.

The automatic door had completely closed behind me before I was at the back of the ZX getting my luggage, a flight bag and the briefcase I'd filled with papers at the housing conference in Detroit. I hauled them and my weary ass up the stairway to the house. In a couple of seconds I'd unlocked both deadbolts and was in the kitchen. From there I moved through the house, always in light. My father-in-law had had the house wired so there was a switch at every door to a room. He had a deep fear of walking into a dark room. I'd scoffed at that. Then Elizabeth died and suddenly I didn't like to enter a dark room either.

From the moment I'd first seen the house I'd thought it overgadgeted, but there were times when I wished Wilfred had extended himself as far as an elevator—like whenever I was whipped and had to drag myself and my luggage all the way to my rooms on the third floor. That night I considered putting one in myself. Sometimes I have trouble dealing with the fact that I've inherited a lot of money, and sometimes I don't.

I have only limited experience in having lots of money, but I have to say that it's much better than having just enough. People with money usually seem sober and unhappy around people without money. I could never figure it out. Now I know it's an act. Rich people act that way because they're gracious and unwilling to make poor people jealous, or because they're embarrassed by their privileges, or becuase they're afraid poor people will realize they have money and try to take some of it away. I've ranked them in inverse order of occurrence. But for whatever their reason, it's all a front; rich is much better.

It's better mostly because it means you don't have to wait for things: like the next paycheck to buy something you want; like for a bank teller since you rarely carry money; like to pay for your groceries because someone else does your shopping; like for a check in a restaurant because you run a tab in a few of the better places; like for times to get better.

It was my own fault that I had to walk to the third floor at all. I hated having someone living above me, the way servants had done when Elizabeth and her father had lived in the house. As a wedding present to me, she'd had the place renovated, turning the entire third floor into an apartment for us. The servants moved out to be with Elizabeth's father, and we replaced them with a cook-housekeeper and a cleaning woman, who both came in days. A couple of months after Elizabeth died, they both were tired of my pervasive glumness and quit. I tried living alone and hated it. That's when I hired Melinda Holt as a live-in housekeeper. Her husband had run off leaving her busted and unskilled with a seven-year-old son. All she could do was look after a house and cook, so I'd invited her to do that for me. Her son, Gene, was a good kid and I enjoyed his enjoying the big house.

I dropped the flight bag on the couch in the big bedroom on the third floor and went through the connecting door to my study-office with the briefcase. The desk had been clean when I'd gone to Detroit. It wasn't any more because I am a print junkie; I read anything, everything. I have subscriptions to about fifty magazines and buy others as they strike my fancy. Add to that various newspapers from around the world and the junk mail and I am not a very popular fellow with my mailman, except at Christmas, of course.

I flipped through my mail, hoping to find something interesting enough to keep me up another thirty seconds. Fat chance. At some point in my lifetime mail became an advertising medium, worse than any other in the ads-to-content ratio. It's our own fault—hardly anyone writes any more.

My mail went back onto the desk unopened, and I went to bed. Because I did not like the alternatives, I thought about the present woeful state of the mail I was getting. The last conscious thought I had was that there would be more of the same waiting for me the next morning at *Toronto, Toronto*'s office.

Thursday morning I set off for the magazine with a fuzzy head. It was still fuzzy two blocks from the office, and I could not face the people there with a fuzzy brain. So I headed toward Nissan's head office. I wasn't supposed to return the 300ZX until the next day, but I had a good enough impression of it after six days' use to write a review of it.

The westbound Gardiner Expressway, Highway 427, and the 401 from there to Mississauga Road are not without their challenges at any time, so I kept my mind on my driving, worrying only about not pranging Nissan's expensive equipment on the way back to its hangar.

I drank some tea with a PR staffer who told me how much she liked working with the media. It didn't sound like a lie, so I figured she must be new at the game. By that time it was far enough past nine A.M. to risk driving back into Toronto. So I picked up the leather jacket, gauntlets and helmet I'd left in the 300ZX, took them down to where my motorcycle was parked, put them on, mounted up, and rode out into the bright October morning. After a quarter-mile in the tail of the highway's rush-hour traffic my brain was as clear as the December air in Vermont.

It's good to have a clear brain when you're riding a 750 cc motorcycle at seventy or eighty miles an hour in heavy traffic, because it has a way of demanding your attention. It's the best motorized thrill you can get on a public road. Every sense you've got gets cranked up so that life feels like an LP played at forty-five rpm, with a few moments of seventy-eight rpm thrown in to keep you honest.

Without question the best way to approach Toronto is the way I did that morning, along the north shore of Lake Ontario. Most of the way it's big-city highway—small industry, homes so close to the road their windows are never open, scuzzy little shopping malls. But when the Gardiner Expressway begins so does the postcard view of Toronto. On the right the rocky, gritty beaches of the cool, deep lake are serviced by private clubs and public bathhouses. On the left are the train lines that provide the Toronto area with its superior mass transit and make the city the rail hub of the country; beyond the tracks are parks, hospitals and private homes. Ahead the tourist view of Toronto unfolds: Ontario Place with its futuristic mélange of entertainment buildings and facilities; the dowdy and aging Canadian National Exhibition, which is basically a Victorian version of a state fair; Exhibition Stadium, where the pro baseball and football teams do battle; the office towers huddled downtown for warmth; and, finally, the CN tower, the world's tallest free-standing structure, looking like nothing more than a giant hypodermic. The southern route through town is the one to take for a crash course in Toronto.

I rode past all that to the *Toronto, Toronto* office on the southeast edge of the part of "Tonyronto" that tourists with money find interesting.

Before I went in, I grabbed a couple of coffees from the small takeout place next door. One I dropped on the desk of the magazine's receptionist, a brassy twenty-two-year-old who should be dead in a year if there's any truth to the notion that caffeine is a carcinogen. Unless nicotine is its antidote. Between grunts into the phone at her ear she drained the coffee she had going and cracked the top of the one I'd just given her.

"Is Sam in?" I asked.

"Meeting," she mouthed silently without breaking the rhythm of her grunts into the phone.

I went beyond the receptionist into the magazine's general office space, where three people I did not recognize were working. Out of the slot under my name in the mail caddy I pulled a fistful of mail. It was the usual rundown of stuff: most of it was of absolutely no interest to me, but came my way in someone's general media mailout; there were a couple of invitations to social events; several "How could you say that?" letters; and notices for two new-car previews, one in Detroit and one in Arizona.

The Detroit one was a Ford production I'd said earlier I'd attend. General Motors wanted me to go to Phoenix, where they have a test track. I called up the guy at GM who'd sent me the invitation and told his secretary I'd like to go, especially if they could provide me with a car to drive there in. The way she reacted to the notion of my driving you'd think she worked for an airline's PR department, not a car company's. But she'd forward my request and they'd do what they could, which was what I wanted, since all the car firms love media coverage.

After a few more phone calls declining the social invitations, I walked back toward Sam Rideout's office. He was the magazine's executive editor, and the man I wanted to see. Through the glass partition in his door I could see he was meeting with two full-time staffers and three free-lance writers.

The five visitors were talking all over each other. Sam looked like the only line judge at a five-player tennis game. He sat quietly, stroking his tie with his left hand and making continuous notes with his right. The tie-stroking was a dead giveaway that Sam was being thorough about a very serious subject. When he used the length of his left index finger to heft the shock of black hair that fell across his forehead I knew the subject at hand must be practically life and death. I turned so as not to disturb him but he'd seen me through the glass. His left hand came up to his shoulder and he flashed me five fingers and then two more.

I nodded and turned away, smiling. Seven minutes. Not five. Not ten. Seven. It must have been 10:23 A.M. When Sam Rideout scheduled a meeting to end at 10:30 it ended at 10:30. That was one of his strengths: He knew what he had to do and how much effort it would take to do it.

Waiting for the meeting to break up, I fleshed out on a typewriter the notes I'd made while test-driving the 300ZX. I was waist-deep in that when I heard and smelled the people come out of Sam's office.

Sam was at the window he'd just opened, taking deep

breaths of air. The office was getting cool, but at least the ashtray smell was on the run.

Inclining his head only a little away from the fresh air, Sam said to me in his soft voice, "I wish I was pushy enough to ask them not to smoke in here."

"The serious smokers you have to let smoke if you want to get any work out of them," I said as I sat down. "Sometimes, when the pressure was really on at the *Star,* I used to wish I smoked."

Sam shot me a look of real surprise. He and I often gloated with each other because we'd been lucky enough not to start smoking. "You wished you smoked?" he said, disbelieving.

"It looked comforting, or inspirational, or something. At the desk next to me there'd be a writer whose stuff I admired, and he'd be smoking. For a couple of minutes he'd sit hunched over that keyboard, staring intently at the blank page. He'd suck on that cigarette like it was . . . like it was rolled up leaves from the tree of knowledge—"

"Rolled up leaves from the tree of knowledge?"

"Give me a break, I'm making this up as I go along. Anyway, after a couple of minutes he'd take a deep drag on the cigarette, perch it on his ashtray and, Bam, attack the story. He'd pound away like a madman and not touch the cigarette the whole time. When the story was done he'd rip it out and read it over the last two drags on the cigarette. Then he'd butt it out and hand the story in. Usually it'd be a piece I wished I'd written."

Sam considered this in silence for a time, obviously intrigued by the idea that there might be a good reason for anyone to smoke. He shook his head resolutely and said, "Yeah, but if you took their cigarettes away from them their work would be used dogshit, if you got any work out of them."

I laughed. "Only for the first year, until they got over their addiction."

"Someone was just telling me heroin addicts say it's harder to give up cigarettes than to give up heroin."

"It was a smoker, I'll bet."

"Vern Goodleigh, the worst of the bunch. He keeps the Virginia plantations on overtime all by himself." Sam moved from the window to his desk. "We were just talking about a series of features on Toronto's drug scene, and I suggested we include the huge addiction to nicotine."

"It didn't go over?"

"The consensus was our readers would find it a little sensationalistic of us to lump tobacco in with things like heroin, coke, speed, angel dust, and what have you. I had to agree." Sam sounded disappointed in his own judgment. "And if we ran an anticigarette story too close to a cigarette ad we'd risk violating our contract with its sponsor."

"Not to mention violating all the standards of journalistic hypocrisy."

Sam looked very glum now. He got around most of the pressures to compromise that came an editor's way, but once in a while he came face-to-face with one he could not dodge. This was one of those times.

I tried to cheer him up by saying, "If all those guys are working on it, it'll be a damn fine series of stories." I was mocking Sam gently by using his ultimate compliment to something—"damn fine."

The glum went right out of him. "Do you want in on it?" Sam was of the opinion that work, not love, is good for anything that ails you. Since shortly after Elizabeth's death he'd been trying to administer his personal cure to me. Gently, but relentlessly, he'd offered me the chance to write just about every story he'd ordered since Elizabeth's funeral. For the first time I didn't reject his offer out of hand. At least I didn't reject the idea of work. I wasn't crazy, however, about diving into a series on dope.

"I'd like to do something besides the car reviews, Sam, but I'm not sure the series on dope is the right thing just now."

Sam nodded understandingly. Not for the first time did I feel a rush of appreciation for him as an editor—hell, as a human being.

"What, then?" he asked, picking up quickly on what he saw was a change in my attitude to work.

"Sean Denby."

Sam's left hand went from his desk to his tie. He gave it some slow, cautious strokes. When he saw that I wasn't going to elaborate, he said, "Were you thinking of a personal recollection?"

I wondered how he knew I could do a personal recollection, since I was sure I hadn't told him I'd known Sean Denby. I told hardly anyone that.

He correctly read my look of befuddlement and said, "He told me you two went to school together, played ball together."

"He did?"

"A couple of years back. I met him somewhere. When he found out where I worked he told me he knew you in school. He didn't ask to be remembered to you. I got the impression that you hadn't seen each other in years, that there'd been a falling out."

"No falling out, I was just stupid."

Sam nodded his easy acceptance of that idea.

But I wasn't feeling stupid at that moment, I was feeling very sad and a little pleased. Sad that I hadn't reestablished contact with Sean, pleased that he hadn't forgotten me, indeed that he knew what I was doing.

Sam stroked his tie a little faster as he watched me reviewing my thoughts and emotions. As usual, he saw where I was going before I did. "You were thinking of a lost-friendship piece." It wasn't a question. He was already considering it as a story possibility.

If he was adept at knowing my questions before I asked them, I was adept at knowing his answers before he gave them. "Not exactly," I said, knowing that would derail the refusal I could see him framing in his mind. "Just let me poke around in it for a while, and see what I come up with."

On principle Sam was opposed to free-lancers doing that,

because he was usually expected to finance the poking. Such was not the case with me, however, and we both knew it.

I wasn't even sure I wanted to write anything about Sean Denby. What I wanted was Sam's backing if anyone official checked up on my poking around. Also, I wanted a defensible professional interest to hide my vague personal reasons behind.

"So poke," Sam said. He took his story book into his hands and flipped through it. "You have a piece due soon on . . ."

"The new turbocharged Nisson 300ZX."

"Is it expensive enough to interest our readers?"

"Something to give the kid graduating from high school." I was exaggerating—a little.

"The next issue is tightening. Better keep it to four hundred and seventy-five words." In his to-hell-with-the-rules voice he added, "Plus a photo. When can I have it?"

I thought about having to wait seven minutes to see him and his wanting a story 475 words long. "One oh-six today," I said.

Sam looked disappointed. "I was hoping for twelve fifty-eight."

 **4** WHEN I'D MADE SOME CALLS, WRITTEN the 300ZX story, and had lunch with Sam Rideout, I left *Toronto, Toronto*'s offices and grabbed a cab for the short trip over to the financial district. My destination was a vertigo-inducing tower that housed the corporate offices of the Toronto Metros football team and several Norris Harlan enterprises.

All around me buildings proclaimed their owners' importance by stretching out of sight. "Look at me," they boasted, "mine's bigger than yours." And when you realize that most of those reinforced phallic symbols belong to Canada's banks, you have to wonder about the virility of Canada's male bankers.

I paid the cabby, went into the building that was home to Norris Harlan's companies, and passed up an elevator set to go up the outside wall. When you are really and truly afraid of flying, the way I am, you pass up anything that reminds you of the experience—like a glass-walled elevator. The lobby clock blinked off forty-two seconds before an enclosed elevator arrived. The timing was going well: I had about three minutes before my appointment with Norris Harlan, Sean's employer and a man whose help I needed.

In my book, showing up late for appointments is just plain rude, while showing up early is a mistake. It looks like you have nothing else to do. In big-time business, this creates a view of you you'd be better off without. And with a guy like Norris Harlan, who was famous for his punctuality, it mattered that you looked like your time was important to you. Otherwise, why should it be important to him?

Everything you did mattered to Norris Harlan; he was the complete manipulator. He could read a person, a situation, a changing circumstance one second and be using it to his advantage the next. I'd seen him operate up close a couple of times and had followed his career with interest, so I knew what he was like. This is not to say I disliked him for his talent with people. No, he was as adept at making people feel better with his analysis as he was at using it to his own advantage. In fact, he was so good the two things often overlapped.

All really talented manipulators make me nervous, however, so I got on guard before the elevator doors sighed open and I stepped into the hush of the fifty-second floor.

Entranceway to a flock of firms Harlan owned, the reception area looked like one of the better visiting rooms in a very

26

classy funeral home. Not surprising, since Harlan owned a chain of such places. One was looking after Sean Denby's "final arrangements." When I'd read that, I'd remembered Sean's request to me concerning his funeral arrangements. He'd just finished reading *The American Way of Death*, Jessica Mitford's comical exposé on the funeral business. After more than a few beers I'd promised to have him buried by someone named either Jessica or Mitford. It had been funny at the time, but I hadn't really paid much attention since we were both very young and obviously never going to die.

Seating was provided for about a dozen people on the fifty-second floor, but only four of the leather chairs were holding up visitors. An attractive woman in a brown suit put a cloth marker in the hardcover book she was reading. She stole a glance at a datebook open by her elbow and smiled a greeting at me from beneath her stylish glasses and loose blond bun. She said, "Good afternoon, Mr. Cane." We hadn't met and there was no reason why she'd know me. She was just good at her job.

"Good afternoon," I said pleasantly before sitting down in a chair next to her desk.

She pushed an intercom button and announced me. To me, she said, "Mr. Harlan will be right with you." She did not reopen her book right away, waiting instead to take her lead from me. If I wanted to talk she'd match my banalities for hours. If I wanted silence she'd be a stone. So when I didn't talk she discreetly reopened her book.

Out of habit, I read what was available to read: Norris Harlan's corporate menu. Making out the sole owner's business past was easy enough—auto parts, new and used cars, package tours, funerals, sports teams and real estate development. The business future was there too, though the specifics were uncertain, since "Nor-Harl Investments Incorporated" does not yield the same information as does "Toronto Metros Football Club."

I was counting corporations when their owner burst through a door on my right. Harlan's entrance made the room's voltage rise at once, and for a moment I thought the people were going to as well. I kept counting.

Dynamic entrances I usually ignore on principle. This time I couldn't because Harlan was coming right for me with his hand out and his famous lopsided grin in place. It seemed to me an overly familiar greeting. We'd met professionally a few times at media shows, and personally at a couple of society affairs Elizabeth had dragged me to. It was the slight personal relationship I'd used to secure our meeting. I'd reminded him on the phone that I was still Wilfred Teller's son-in-law, and then asked him to meet me right away on a serious personal matter. I figured he wouldn't say no because I was an unknown quantity, with some potential. The little information he had about me wasn't enough to nail me down tight. I might be in thick with my father-in-law, who was a national business wheel of some size. Or I might have some scheme of my own to pitch. He'd want to know what I was up to, and a meeting would give him a chance to find out.

Norris Harlan demonstrated the strength of his moral fiber by the way he shook hands. I'm a big guy and have done in a few beer cans in my day, but Harlan nearly turned me into a southpaw. And if his handshake weren't enough, he put his left vice on my upper right arm and gave it a squeeze. His baby-blues misted over as he looked me in the eye from about eighteen inches away. He said, "I'm real sorry about what happened to Elizabeth."

I still didn't have a reply to that, even after six months, so I just nodded.

"Come on in," he said. "You read the part about the car accident yet?"

I opened my eyes and my mouth wide and stared at Harlan. I thought he might be making some bizarre allusion to Elizabeth's death, and I was missing the connection. But he wasn't looking at or talking to me. He was spreading the charm around to the receptionist.

"No," she said excitedly, "but I love the book already."

"Well, then keep it when you're done and let the lucky man in your life read it." I was surprised to see someone as apparently sophisticated as the receptionist blush with pleasure at such a line. Blush? She was glowing. Harlan was really good. He had to be to reheat that chestnut.

Before going to Harlan's office I'd considered a plan of attack to get the man to open up to me. It was very important to get him on my side; he was clearly the key domino, and without him precious few of the others would fall. He could open doors to information no one else could open. And I still didn't know what tack to take. I might even have to resort to honesty. Well, I'd be semi-honest—which is like being semi-pregnant.

From the cathedral hush of the lobby we went into the money-market babble of the general office. This, after all, was where business was done. And business was good for Norris Harlan, very, very good. He was a millionaire many times over. He'd tell you that if you asked him. Hell, he'd tell you that even if you didn't ask him.

Harlan went through the desks in the large, open-concept office like a halfback doing some broken-field running. The path we were on took no particular line, and he spoke to or looked at no one, but everyone he went near picked up their pace or talked business a little louder as he passed.

The only person who took no notice of his proximity was the only one he spoke to. She typed diligently away outside two unmarked oak doors and made no visible sign when he told her to hold his calls.

If Norris Harlan's secretary wasn't impressed with this order, I certainly was. He was famous for taking and making his own calls. Having him hold his calls for me was quite an honor, customarily granted to God knew what poobahs.

Naturally Harlan's office was huge, with a desk as big as the tables most people go to billiard halls to use. But there was nothing on it. The rest of the place was full of standard-issue Self-made Man furnishings—expensive bric-a-brac bought with new money shouldered up against the pieces of memory-rich junk from the poorer beginnings. One entire wall of the office was glass, providing a breathtaking view of Lake Ontario as it lay sparkling less than a mile south and a quarter-mile straight down. I turned my back to that panorama.

Now that I was in the lion's den, I decided on my course of attack: honesty would just have to do.

 NORRIS HARLAN DROPPED HEAVILY INTO one of the four armchairs grouped around a large glass coffee table in his office. He reached into a rolling mahogany cabinet and fished out one of six cut-glass containers and a matching glass. About four ounces of scotch went into one glass before he raised his trimmed eyebrows at me.

"Rye and water, rocks," I said from the chair I'd settled into across the table from him.

He exchanged decanters and made me my drink. When he handed it to me he raised his own in a silent toast. I did the same.

"How's Wilf?" Harlan asked.

"Fine, I guess." It was me who should have been asking. "You'd probably know better. I'm sure I don't see him as much as you do." That was a gross understatement. Harlan and my father-in-law moved in the same business and social circles. I'd seen Wilfred Teller once—no, twice—since his daughter's funeral. And it had been that—his daughter's funeral, not my wife's funeral.

"You never really did get to know him before Elizabeth died, did you?" The way Harlan said it, it was a rhetorical accusation. "You should. Wilf Teller is one of the finest men I know. He's also a hell of a businessman. But that's not as important as the fact that he's an admirable man and a part of your family now. It's important not to underestimate the power of the family. And by family I do not just mean the fabled nuclear family; I mean those people with whom one has common concerns."

Harlan took a drink at that point and I took a quick look around the room for the possible locations of the microphones. It's my experience that people talk differently when they know they're being recorded, and I couldn't believe Harlan talked that way regularly. He hadn't in our previous personal meetings, so he had to be talking for the record.

Under Canadian law it's okay to tape a conversation as long as one of the participants knows about it. On a personal level I didn't much care if my words were being recorded. It wasn't likely that anything I said would turn up in his memoirs. If they did I could live with it, since I had a personal rule that I never said anything to anyone anywhere at any time that I'd be embarrassed to see later in print. That sometimes meant I kept my mouth shut.

Harlan calmly waited for me to speak, to get to the point.

So I did. "Norris, I appreciate your seeing me on such short notice. I'd like to talk to you about Sean Denby. His murder's really got me rattled. With Elizabeth's death and all . . . Anyway, we were friends once."

"You went to school and played ball together," Harlan said.

My past, at least how it related to Sean, seemed to be an open book. Out of curiosity, I asked Harlan how he'd come to know, adding, "Did Sean tell you?" The rider seemed very important to me as I threw it in.

It seemed very important to Harlan as well. He looked away and sipped at his scotch, supposedly to search his memory. Something else was really going on—he was con-

31

sidering his reply. "I don't think so," he said fuzzily, to protect himself if he had to reverse his stand. If he ever went into politics he'd soon be adding, "Within the parameters of my best recollections at this point in time, so I'll have to caveat my response."

"It's unimportant," I lied, trying to sound just as fuzzy as he had. "What is important is that Sean's dead, horribly murdered." Harlan uncrossed and then recrossed his legs at this. "I want your help so I can find out what I can about Sean's death. I'm also considering doing a piece on Sean for *Toronto, Toronto*. But, really, I only told them I'd do it as a smoke screen, for myself and for everyone else. Hell, I may not even write it when the time comes. I don't know." I sounded confused and distressed. I was confused and distressed.

Harlan's silence this time was openly designed for consideration of my remarks. His face told me he wasn't yet convinced either way.

I continued. "Look, Norris, I know I'm taking advantage of our personal relationship—bending it out of shape is more like it—but I really have to do this. I need to know more about a man who used to be a very good friend. We were close in university and then we just drifted apart. I don't know why. I regret it now, though." I was surprised at the solid ring of truth in my words; I hadn't realized how badly I did want to do this and how bad I felt. First Elizabeth, then Sean. People I cared about were getting knocked out of my life at a frightening rate. And there weren't many left, if the truth were told. That made me feel worse. I needed some answers. I needed some rationalizations. I needed something.

Norris Harlan, master reader of human beings, heard the ring of truth and desperation in my voice and was apparently moved by it. But first, a homily: "You should always cherish friends. My close friends are in my family, my family in the way I explained to you before. Keep yours close by for when you need them . . . or for when they need you, of course. Now, what can I tell you?"

I cut to the chase: "Who do you think might have killed Sean?"

Harlan pretended to look overwhelmed by the question. "Jeez, Richard, we've only got about twenty minutes here." It was a stab at black humor, which I rewarded with a black laugh. "All I know," Harlan went on, "is that if all the suspects turned up at the next Metros' home game we'd have one of the year's best crowds."

Harlan did not know enough to quit while he was ahead. "You're taking this pretty lightly," I said, sounding both hurt and pompous.

He seemed genuinely offended by the charge. "You just have to keep a sense of humor about life, that's all. My sense of humor's gotten me through some bad times, I can tell you. You'd be well advised to keep yours about you during these trying days."

"Don't you ever stop lecturing?" I thought. Out loud I asked evenly, "Could you be more specific on who you think might have done it?"

"Actually, there aren't as many people as you might think. The chief and I were kicking it around last night, and he—"

"The chief? Lawrence R. Herkimer? That chief?"

"Yes, that chief. He ran down a list of suspect types that was so long it surprised me. I guess I see the natural goodness in people too much." Neither the tone of Harlan's voice nor his facial expression suggested that this trait was a weakness; on the contrary. The list of suspect types Harlan relayed from the chief was a couple longer than mine, and I was not surprised. I never had the problem of seeing too much natural goodness in people; on the contrary.

"I'll be frank with you, Richard," Harlan said, using the expression that always made me wonder what the speaker was being the rest of the time. "I've given this a lot of thought, and I'm convinced it couldn't have been someone associated with the game." He meant it as a checkmate move.

"The game? Football?"

"Of course football. What the hell other game is there?" He smiled.

I didn't. "Well, if you take out all of the people in the game that might have had something to do with Sean's murder you certainly cut down on the crowd for the Metros' next home game."

There must have been something in my voice when I said that because Harlan looked at me sharply. He dragged out his real big gun: "The chief puts more faith in the idea than you seem to."

I struggled to keep the incredulity out of my voice. "Our chief of police agrees with you that Sean couldn't have been murdered by someone associated with football?"

"I think he's coming to share my opinion on this matter," Harlan said archly. "He's quite an open-minded man." Which meant I better pretend to be open-minded in the same way if I wanted to get anywhere with Harlan.

My estimation of Harlan rose dramatically at the notion that he could convince a veteran cop of such an idea. That it couldn't have been anyone associated with football just because they were associated with football was horseshit strong enough to choke flies. I knew Lawrence Herkimer was a jock-sniffer of some accomplishment, but I couldn't believe he'd go that far to get in good with the team. I'd have been less shocked to see him on his knees after a game running his Rudolph nose along the bench.

The human in me wanted to snort derisively and tell Harlan how ridiculous his theory sounded. The reporter in me told me to keep it to myself and milk him on this. It didn't take much milking, just, "I'm not sure I understand. Can you explain it to me?"

Harlan gave me one of those looks that assumed we shared certain givens before he spoke. "You used to be in the game, Rich." He used a nickname I hated and said "the game" as if it were capitalized. But he didn't say anything more. Obviously, he hoped that if I thought back on what it was like to butt heads with bigger and tougher guys the answer would get knocked loose. When he could see it wouldn't come loose he continued—a touch testily. "Well, maybe you weren't in it long enough, or didn't go far enough." This riled me because he hadn't gone even as far as I had. I sat on that thought, however.

"It's the greatest game in the world, you know that, Rich. It embodies in a highly competitive arena all the things that make men great: talent, individual effort, dedication, commitment, sacrifice, altruism, team spirit, courage, everything." He stopped long enough to get a little dewy-eyed before closing with, "I like to think of a football stadium as a crucible of human effort, in which only the toughest men survive."

I searched his voice and face for clues that he was pulling my leg about football being a crucible. I could find none.

Harlan reflected on this pronouncement for a moment, before adding, "To get into pro football, either in this country or in the U.S., you've got to be one of the best." He smiled expansively. "Cream rises to the top."

"So does shit," I wanted to say, but sat on that comment too.

Harlan looked at me with a smile. There was a meaningful silence.

Whoops. It was quiz time, when I got to show I'd been paying attention in class. I knew the answer he wanted, but I consulted the notes I'd made to give me time to take the sarcasm out of my mind, lest it creep into my voice. "Because football is such a wonderful game," I stammered, as if the force of Harlan's theory was so great it stunned me, "and has such a marvelous effect on the people who play it, by the time they make pro they're incapable of murdering one of their own. Is that it?"

"I hope you work on it some more before you write it, but you've more or less got the gist of it." Harlan smiled when he spoke, pleased with his ability to explain a complicated idea to a media dunderhead. With a motion of finality he threw back the remainder of his scotch.

I could have pretented to swallow the junk whole, but if I skimmed over it Harlan might get suspicious; he had had vast experience with cynical journalists.

It was a waste of time to try to iron out the huge wrinkles in the fabric of Harlan's theory, since I was sure he'd had it done in permanent press. But certain pro forma steps have to be taken, so I picked out the biggest wrinkle. "How about the growing drug problem among pro football players? In recent years we've been hearing a lot about ballplayers spending their big salaries on cocaine. All the leagues have admitted they have a problem there. Players have been suspended, jailed even. And we both know other drugs, prescription drugs, have been abused in pro ball and college ball for years. The game's full of addicts. There are guys in the NFL who can't blow their nose without the right pill."

Harlan squeezed a small smile out at my exaggeration because it was only a small exaggeration. "Richard, no one—certainly not I—denies that too many of the fine young men who play the game overindulge in certain medications, and that for many of them it's a problem. But what you have to remember is that it's a problem for them. They take the drugs; they don't take them down to the schoolyard to sell."

My chair was getting lumpy, since I was now also sitting on the observation that those doped-up stars were heroes to those kids in the schoolyard. Kids now assumed their heroes were probably on drugs. That was much worse than dope-peddling, it was dope promotion.

"You have to remember that there is enormous stress in football," Harlan went on, "and some of our young men have to have an outlet for that. Unfortunately, they turn to drugs as an outlet." He poured himself some more Scotch before continuing. "But I have to reiterate that drugs in the game are a minor problem, and a problem that's expressed inwardly. Murder is an outward expression of a problem."

36

My mind had been wandering during his monologue, but it snapped to attention when it noticed Harlan's final remark. On the strength of it, I re-revised my opinion of Norris Harlan. If he could say "murder is an outward expression of a problem" without laughing or blushing, he was much more talented than I'd thought.

I took a moment to exaggerate writing down what Harlan said, which seemed to please him. In truth, I didn't dare speak in case some of the contempt for his idea escaped me and ruined what I had done so far, which was keep my mouth shut way over my limit.

A perpetual-motion clock on a wall shelf behind Harlan was ticking away my time with him. You can't make a name for yourself as a punctual perfectionist if you let meetings run overtime. So five minutes remained, and that wasn't nearly enough time to ask Harlan what I wanted to. I comforted myself with the thought that with five hours I wasn't likely to get much out of Harlan; to him, information was like money—it was better to take it in than to pay it out. Besides, I had what I wanted most—his name to drop. Now I had to exploit the rest of my time with him.

"Norris, could you do me a real big favor and grease my way with your people, so I can really get to the heart of this thing as quickly as possible? I know it's a special privilege, but I'd really appreciate it." It was like asking the Godfather for a favor. I wondered if Harlan ever felt that way himself during such exchanges. Did he ever want to imitate Brando?

His eyes registered a large debit to my account and his hands used the phone. He punched a button and tapped out a three-digit number.

"Could you spare me a minute?" Harlan said amiably into the phone. Perversely, I hoped whoever it was would say no, but he didn't and I knew it'd been a hopeless wish when I heard Harlan say, "Thanks, Max."

Max would be Max York, the company's public relations man and the only person I knew who could smile and eat shit at the same time. In public relations a touch of servility is an asset. Max was full of servility.

"Max'll give you everything you need," Harlan said as he stood up.

He would if he thought Harlan really wanted him to. I got to my feet in a rush and went toward Harlan. There was a little tableau I wanted to set for good old Max. I moved quickly to head Harlan off before he got behind his desk. He was surprised to see me blocking his way. I put my head down and tried to look solemn. Outside the office door someone was turning the handle. Servility kept Max quick. I put my hand on Harlan's shoulder and said softly, so he'd have to lean forward to hear, "You don't know how much this means to me. I'm very grateful." Harlan looked a little confused, but York, who came into the room at just the right moment, couldn't see that. All York could see was the man who signed his paychecks in intimate conversation with me, an old and trusted enemy. York's eyes flashed dismay. Perfect. It was probably overdone for my professional needs, but personally it was just right; every now and then I enjoy giving certain people a little shot up the emotional wazoo.

Max swallowed his dismay and moved to set the tone for our greeting. I don't imagine a brother I owed half an inheritance to could have looked more delighted to see me. You'd never have guessed that the last time we'd seen each other Max was chasing me with a full glass of beer so he'd have something to throw in my laughing face if he caught me.

"Richard, you old . . . rascal, how are you?" Max was pumping my hand like he thought water would soon gush from my nose.

"Max," I said evenly.

None of this was lost on Harlan. "You know each other?" he said, sounding displeased that there was something he didn't know.

"Yes, sir. Richard and I go way back. Don't we, Richard?"

I nodded. Way back to the first time I'd asked York something and he'd blatantly lied to me. That kind of relationship endures.

"Good, that'll make it easier." If Harlan was picking up any strange vibes from Max or me he wasn't letting on. "Richard's doing a story on Sean Denby for *Toronto Squared*. I want you to see that he talks to anyone he wants, gets whatever he wants. He isn't just another media type, understand. Nothing that low. Ha. Ha. Ha."

Max York's smile bobbed in acquiescence.

Harlan was steering us toward the office door. "You tell anyone who asks that I said Richard Cane is to have whatever help he wants from my organization. I'll phone Coach Baird myself."

York's relief was palpable. Metros coach Bob Baird was an ogre of mythical proportions. He had left his lip prints on no behinds in his rise to the top; sheer ability had gotten him there. It would take a well-phrased request from the guy who hired him to get Baird to cooperate. So it was easy to understand Max's relief, since there are few jobs as unpleasant as being a PR man for someone who thinks public relations is something you scrape off the bottom of your boots.

We were at the door to Harlan's office when he said, "When they catch Sean's killer, I bet it'll turn out to be someone connected with his outside activities. I'm taking calls again." With that statement to me and the order to his secretary Harlan closed the door in our faces.

Before I went into Max's office I looked back and saw a tall, thin man carrying a black doctor's bag go into Harlan's.

**6** ASIDE FROM A LOOSE-LEAF MEDIA GUIDE and an invitation to join some of the players for a drink after that night's practice, I got nothing of value from my chat with Max York.

Mostly I put up with thirty minutes of unalloyed and unrelenting hype just so I could watch him squirm over finding an old foe in thick with his boss. Such a situation is undeniable proof that life is indeed a big wheel; it had just come crashing back and rolled right over Max York's toes.

According to the lobby clock, I'd spent exactly an hour on the fifty-second floor talking to Norris Harlan and Max York. When I stepped into the outside it felt like I'd been away from real air for much longer. I gave my lungs a treat by tossing back a couple of big lungfuls before starting my walk. I tried to imagine what it would feel like to spend eight hours a day breathing what passed for air in that office tower. But I couldn't, and not for the first time in my life I was grateful to have my imagination come up short.

I considered walking to the police station from downtown, but that would mean doubling back later to pick up my motorcycle, so I settled for the walk to the magazine's office in the noisy air of pre-rush-hour Toronto. I picked up my bike and rode up Jarvis Street toward Bloor. Taking advantage of the motorcycle's size, I did some creative parking on a square of cemented boulevard thirty yards from the police station. In less than a minute I was getting another wary look from the desk sergeant I'd seen the night before. If he recognized me he gave no sign of it.

"Who's running the Denby investigation?" I asked.

"Media people are restricted to regular briefings," the desk man replied. He obviously recognized me, but that didn't mean a thing to him.

"I'm here as a witness."

"A witness?" He used the nail of his right index finger to scratch the left side of his nose. "Last night you were here as a reporter, and today you're here as a witness. What am I to make of that, Mr. Cane?"

"That I'm trying to put a fast one over on you. But I'm not. I knew Sean Denby since high school and I just wanted to let the detectives know that, in case it can be of any use to them."

He considered this for a moment while he made out a form on his desk. "Okay," he said finally, and slid a visitor's badge across the desk at me. "Sign here. Fifth floor. Inspector Ian Hurst's in charge. And it's your ass if you're trying to be cute."

I nodded and headed for the elevators.

The fifth floor opened onto chaos. Phones demanded attention everywhere. People spoke loudly because they had trouble hearing above the din. Charts, graphs, lists and pictures littered the walls. But despite all the commotion, there was an eerie sense of calm pervading it all. It was the studied cop calm, the calm of having little else to see that was new or shocking. "Go ahead," the room said, "surprise me if you can."

A passing detective saw me looking lost. "Help ya?" He fixed me with the inscrutable stare cops are assigned with their badges and their guns.

"Ian Hurst?"

The young detective gave me a very human smile. "Are you sure you have to see him today?" He looked across the room to where a big man with no neck was bludgeoning the composure of six cops with his stubby index finger. His shirt collar seemed in danger of catching on fire.

"As a matter of fact I don't have to see him today," I said to the cop as we looked at Hurst, "but I have a feeling today's just as bad a day as any."

"Probably. Remember though that his bite's worse than his bark." With this the young cop moved quickly away, to disassociate himself from me should his boss want someone to blame for my existence.

I timed it so that I got to Hurst's desk just after the last detective had slinked away to the comparative safety of an alley full of knife-wielding junkies.

"Inspector Hurst, I'm Richard Cane." I'd have to do a lot better than that if I wanted to impress him. Hurst said nothing, he just fixed the best cop stare on me I've ever seen. "I'd like to talk to you about Sean Denby's murder."

Hurst tilted his head to one side and looked at me through mostly closed eyes. "You kill him?"

"No, of course not."

"The last eight guys who wanted to talk to me about Sean Denby said they killed him." As well as being angry with their incursion on his time, Hurst sounded dismayed that there were that many crazies running around loose in the city he was supposed to keep from harm. His head went to the other side of his neck and he blinked once, very deliberately, waiting for me to say something that interested him.

If I didn't interest him soon our meeting would be very brief. And dropping Norris Harlan's name would do me little good. He didn't look like a man with a taste for horseshit, so I moved to establish a common bond on that. "I'm sure none of the guys who tried to confess to killing Sean had anything to do with football," I said with a touch of irony. If Hurst knew what I was talking about, and shared my opinion of it, I'd be alright. If.

Hurst moved his head back to level and read my expression for a moment. His hands looked like gloves full of unshelled peanuts. He moved them up toward his head, passing them along his scalp through his short, combed-back hair. He laced them together at the crown of his head and smiled at me. "You're right there, Mr. Cane. No one who could survive that crucible would ever resort to murder." His smile widened, exposing a very small gap in the middle of his upper teeth. His eyes were heavily hooded now, almost closed. He was smiling at our exchange, but his anger at the stupidity of the idea was palpable.

"Did you know, Inspector, that murder is an outward expression of someone's problem?"

A pause to consider this in mock interest. "An outward expression? You don't say."

"As opposed to an inward expression, such as taking drugs."

"This certainly helps to bring some problems into focus for me."

"Football players—being fresh from the crucible and looking for somewhere to vent the pressure they live under—sometimes turn, sadly, to drugs. But they would never turn to murder."

Ian Hurst unlaced his hands and laid them on his desk. "That's an interesting wrinkle on the crucible theory you've got there, Mr. Cane. Where'd you pick it up?"

"Norris Harlan."

"Hmmm. I don't think it makes more sense coming from the horse's mouth than it would have coming from the horse's ass." Hurst said this with total disregard for who might hear him, despite the fact that almost certainly he was referring to his chief. "You certainly get your horseshit from a higher part of the pasture than I do, Mr. Cane. How is that?"

"I was a friend and teammate of Sean's in high school and university. We drifted apart. Him to gridiron glory, me to journalistic anonymity."

"You're in the media?" Hurst went cold, suspecting a scam to get an inside story.

"I'm with *Toronto, Toronto,* but this a personal visit, to see if I can help you in any way, or give you some background on Sean."

Hurst looked at me for a moment, obviously trying to sort out a memory. "You're Richard Cane. You're the lucky bastard who married Elizabeth Teller." His face went dark, presumably when he traced the memory a little further. "I feel for you, Mr. Cane. I can't imagine they come much harder to lose than Elizabeth Teller."

I was a little amazed. People seemed to know a lot about my past and the people in it. "You knew Elizabeth?"

He nodded sadly. "And her father. I was part of a detachment that guarded her for a while when she was a kid. When there was that unsuccessful try to grab her. She was quite a kid—spunky, intelligent, nice, pretty—the kind any father would be proud to have as a daughter." There was genuine admiration in Hurst's voice. "And she married you?" He seemed to be reevaluating me. Elizabeth continued to help me with my life, even though she was these six months dead.

But at the moment I was more concerned with something else. "Someone tried to kidnap her? I don't remember reading about that. And she never mentioned it."

"She wouldn't. And it was kept out of the papers."

I was wallowing in the surprise of my dead wife's past and losing control of my present. I didn't know what more to say to Hurst.

But he wanted something from me, and fast. "So what can I do for you, Mr. Cane?"

 IT HAD BEEN MY INTENTION TO BE COOL with Inspector Hurst, but when the big moment came I blew it and resorted to honesty again. "You ever lose anyone real close to you, Inspector?"

The policeman went away inside Hurst's head for a moment, and when someone came back to Hurst's eyes it was just a human being. He looked down for the first time in our meeting. "My brother. To leukemia, when he was fourteen and I was twelve."

"Did you know he was going to die?"

"My parents didn't tell us," Hurst said, wrestling with the memory.

"So it was a shock?"

"Look, where are you—"

"Bear with me. It was a shock that you never got over." He didn't deny it so I charged on ahead. "You know how my wife, how Elizabeth, died. It was a shock to me. So was Sean's death. Nowhere near what hers was, but a shock. Inspector, I need to be involved in this thing with Sean, to help me deal with losing Elizabeth. Do you understand?"

Hurst shook his head.

"Neither do I," I admitted. "But if you help me out on this I'll explain it to you if I figure it out."

The human being went away inside Hurst's head, and when someone came back to Hurst's eyes it was the policeman again.

Hurst blinked slowly a couple of times and then motioned to a cop sitting a few desks away, who came right over.

"This is Staff Sergeant Harry Varina, Mr. Cane. Harry, this is Richard Cane. Mr. Cane knew Sean Denby well when they were younger."

Harry Varina looked as Mediterranean as his name implies. He was minimum cop height, but sturdy. Hair seemed to spurt everywhere from his dark skin, spilling out of the open neck and rolled-up sleeves of his shirt. His nose was nothing to write home about, but it balanced his black mustache, which looked to be on the wrong side of Toronto's regulated length for cops. He sat down in a chair on the other side of the desk and flipped open a notebook. He spoke very quietly at first, forcing me to lean forward to hear him above the clamor of the squad room.

"Maybe you could be of some assistance to us, Mr. Cane. From our preliminary investigations we're finding out that Sean Denby pretty well kept to himself. Considering how much was written about him, very little is known of his personal life. So far everyone we've talked to only knew him in a business relationship. They speak well of him, but he doesn't seem to have had a personal life. Tell us what you can about him, please."

I thought about his request and realized I would not exactly make a natural biographer for my old friend. I offered up what I knew, however. "He was orphaned, at an early age. An aunt raised him. I didn't know her name or where she lived exactly. She died while we were in university but I didn't find out until Sean asked me if he could borrow a dark suit I had. If he had any family beyond that he kept it to himself. He had a lot of people around him in school, but he never initiated it. What I mean is, people would always go to him. He'd never call you to make arrangements for going somewhere or doing something. He didn't have to, since people were always anxious to have him around. As well as being a star athlete and reasonably good-looking he was good company—an excellent listener. When he did talk he was funny, kind, insightful, understanding, whatever the occasion demanded. I always thought he was the most self-reliant person I ever knew, that he needed no one."

"Even women?" Hurst asked.

"What?" I replied dumbly. I really did need to work on my repartee.

"Did he date many women?"

"I don't think so, but then he didn't really have to."

"How's that?"

In a sing-song voice I said, "You gotta be a football hero . . ." Varina stared at me like I was an unsubtitled foreign movie. Hurst let a smile loose. "He didn't date much because there were always lots of women around," I said. "Taking a date along would have been a coals-to-Newcastle thing. Women hit on him all the time."

Varina asked, "He had a lot of women, is that it?"

"Had? He was with women a lot. I can't say how many he had. He always treated them well, very gentlemanly. I admired that in him." I realized with a start that I was beginning to sound like Max York, the man with the kindest word for everyone.

46

Harry Varina waited patiently for me to finish. When he saw that I had he said, "That's not quite what I wanted to know, but thanks anyway."

"He did get married," I said. Unconsciously I felt Sean somehow needed defending.

"Yes, to . . ." Varina consulted his notebook ". . . to one Alison Denby. We haven't been able to find her. Would you know where we might look?"

"Vancouver. She remarried, a hockey star this time. I can't think of his name, but the last team I remember him playing for was Vancouver. I can't be sure though, I don't follow the game that much." Varina raised a disbelieving eyebrow and made a note.

"Mr. Cane, when you knew Sean Denby, what was his involvement with drugs?" Hurst asked.

Pause, two, three, four. "You're assuming an involvement, aren't you, Inspector?"

"Considering that you went to school together in the late sixties and early seventies, and considering that you were on the same football teams together for much of that time, and good friends, I don't think making that assumption is out of line."

He was right, of course. Being in school in those days meant being in the "drug culture," if only as a silent witness; noninvolvement with drugs was the next thing to impossible. I decided to own up. "Everybody did dope in those days, Inspector, even me. Marijuana mostly, and painkillers during the season. Some others went further."

Varina made a triumphant note, probably of my confession, as Hurst asked, "Did Denby?"

"I can't tell you for sure, but I don't think so. He never seemed that crazy about smoking grass even. As for painkillers, well, he didn't ever get hurt; he was tough, and talented, so he avoided a lot of injuries."

"But as you say, you can't tell us for sure," Varina said.

"As I say."

47

"Did Denby like to gamble?" Hurst sure liked to keep you off balance.

I had to think. When I had, I could honestly say, "Not that I know of. Penny-ante card games on the bus to an out-of-town game, of course. I don't recall his ever starting up a game."

"That would be in character," Hurst said, with just a dab of sarcasm.

"I always thought he played to be sociable, to keep up those bridges with teammates, to be one of the boys. It never came across that way; he was very considerate of the way he treated people."

Varina nodded impatiently at my reckless praise. "You've mentioned that," he said with a sharp edge, "but he obviously offended someone enough so that he killed him."

"More than one, I'd bet."

This caught Hurst's attention in a marked way. He sat forward an inch or two. "Why's that, Mr. Cane?"

"Because he was tough, and strong and a fighter. He never gave an inch when it mattered to him. I can't believe one person could do that to him." I shifted in my chair, aware that I was laying it on a little thick. Now I was making Sean out to be heaven's heavyweight champ.

"Maybe you don't want to believe one person could kill your friend," Varina said. Hurst gave him a look but he missed it.

I was defensive again. "You didn't know him."

Varina made an act of looking through his notebook before answering. "Apparently no one did." He put a superior smile on his face before he added, "Except for whoever gave him the dose he died with."

"Thanks, Harry. I'll talk to you later." Hurst was on the comment in a flash but it was too late, because it was out. Varina rose slowly, aware that he'd screwed up and would soon pay for it. He did not say good-bye before he walked away.

When Varina was out of hearing, Hurst said to me, "So what if Denby had VD when he died?"

Considering how long it'd been since I'd slept with anyone it certainly didn't matter to me personally. Professionally I couldn't whip up much enthusiasm for it either. "I wouldn't mention athlete's foot, so why should I mention that?"

Hurst nodded at my wisdom, but said nothing. I liked the way he didn't criticize Varina in front of me.

"What do you think, Inspector, did one person kill Sean Denby?"

"That's speculation. For the time being I'm sticking to facts." He made a sour face. "Though if more facts don't start turning up I'll be at speculation soon enough. Then I'll call in some psychics and get the guys in the squad room to switch to tea so I can read the leaves in the bottom of their cups."

"You don't have much?" I was acute as well as witty. "Can I see it anyway?"

"You're really not asking as a reporter, are you? This is personal."

I nodded.

"In that case, okay. But if any of this gets out—rich father-in-law or not, dead wife or not, high-placed friends or not, expensive lawyers or not—your ass is a star."

I didn't doubt it for a second, although I had no idea what he meant exactly. It was a threat, however, no doubt about that.

Hurst rolled his chair back to a table that ran along about ten feet of wall behind his desk. His back was to me as he flipped through various piles of material. After finding what he wanted, Hurst put one foot against the wall under the table, pushed off, and came rolling backward toward me. At just the right moment he turned and glided into his desk. In one of his huge hands he held a stack of photographs. He put them gently on the desk between us, with his hand on top of the pile. "Do you want to see the pics we took at the murder scene?" He sounded like he thought I wouldn't want to.

And he was right. "No, I don't want to, but I will."

He gave me an "I warned you" shrug and took his hand off the photos.

I picked them up and was instantly sorry. The first photo

was taken from just outside the bathroom door. The brilliant light of the flash lit my old friend's mangled body all too well. Handcuffs were the only thing Sean had been wearing when he died. A couple of fingers on his left hand stood out at an impossible angle, as did the lower part of his right arm—all broken. Blood had run from about a dozen cuts on his back and haunches. Elsewhere there were black and blue marks from a beating. I couldn't see his face, because his head was jammed in the toilet.

"He was drowned like that," Hurst said quietly, which explained why the cops hadn't announced the cause of death.

I looked away, closed my eyes and took some deep breaths.

"They don't get any worse."

Speaking seemed inappropriate, so I nodded. The next photo was a rear view of Sean's body and the toilet. I had to look away again. They didn't get any better, either.

"Awful thing to drown a man in your piss—at least we're hoping it's the killer's piss. You'd be surprised at what you can learn when you analyze a man's piss."

I feigned interest. How many corpses do you have to look at before you consider drowning someone in urine a clue rather than something to lie awake nights trying not to think about? I should have asked Hurst that but settled for something more mundane. "That may be something in the future. What have you got right now?"

"Not much else. There was no sign of forced entry, so it was probably someone Denby knew."

"Not necessarily. Sean Denby wasn't the kind of guy to look out a peephole before he opened a door."

"True, but there were no signs of a struggle in the front room of the house. Action was restricted to the living room, the hall leading to the bathroom, and the bathroom."

"Meaning you figure that whoever it was, was invited into the house before they turned on Sean."

"That's the theory we're working on."

"Any physical evidence worth mentioning?"

"Not yet," Hurst said, not hopefully.

While we talked I kept looking at the photos. They wouldn't stop being awful. I used my left thumb and forefinger to rub my eyes till they hurt.

"Want some coffee?" Hurst asked.

"Black."

While Hurst was gone I tried to summon up images of Sean's past to help me cope with the images of his forever. I wasn't at all successful.

"Nobody heard anything," Hurst said as he put a mug of coffee down in front of me. "Houses are far apart where Denby lived and the neighbors on both sides were out when we figure he was murdered. Preliminary medical evidence says Denby took a good shot on the side of the head. Coldcocked, we figure. He was cuffed and then he—they—went about their business. Best we can figure, Denby was probably only partly conscious for the—"

"Punishment? Torture? What do you figure?"

"I'm going with beating," Hurst said, "at least for now."

"It might help if we knew what the killers had in mind when they were doing it. Seems to me it might narrow things for you if you knew they were trying to get information out of him. Or if they were just punishing him because they're major-league sickos."

"I'm not sure if there are two types of beatings," Hurst said as he made a note on a slip of paper, "but I'll look into it."

"Anything else?"

The big man put his pen down delicately. "Remember my warning of a few minutes ago about you keeping your mouth shut about all this?"

"Clearly."

"Okay then." Hurst took a sip of coffee. "In a way it helps that Denby's famous, that people recognize him. Joe Nobody turns up on your street walking a dog and it goes unnoticed. Joe Famous and his dog show up and people are fighting each other to get the dogshit autographed."

"Sean's dog been crapping somewhere it shouldn't have been?"

"Sort of. A guy over on Duke Street called when the case broke to say he'd been watching Denby sneak in and out of a house there at odd hours. We went looking and found two other people who confirmed it."

I made the jump easily to the most obvious conclusion. "Why would he take women there? Wasn't there a bed in his house?"

Hurst took a long pull on his coffee before he spoke again. "We wondered about this, too. When we found the house's owner he told us who it had been leased to." He drank some more coffee, drawing it out like he did the suspense. "A lawyer arranged it over the phone in the name of Leslie Watson."

"Leslie Watson?"

I was spoiling Hurst's fun by being so ignorant. There was an edge to his voice when he replied, "Near as we can make out, Leslie Watson is this woman's maiden name. She is more commonly known by her married name—Leslie Harlan."

I sat up straight in my chair. "Norris Harlan's wife?"

Hurst nodded grimly.

"I think I hear the plot thickening."

Hurst laughed grimly.

 FROM THE PRESS BOX, A FOOTBALL TEAM practicing looks like a gang of uniformed mice learning strange tricks. So I passed up the chance to watch the Metros work out and went home after I'd left the police station. I had dinner and a shower before setting out on foot for Yonge Street.

The cab I caught there going south dropped me off twenty

minutes later where The Athletic Supporter was supposed to be. I could see no sign of the place from the curb, even though the street numbers the cabby'd seen indicated I should be right in front of it. What I was in front of was an old, freshly sandblasted brick wall with a big, unmarked door at one end. In the faint glow of the streetlights I noticed a small plaque next to it. In about eighteen-point letters were the street address I'd been told to go to and ILLINGWORTH ENTERPRISES. There was also something attached to the door. I couldn't quite make out what it was with my eyes so I put my fingers to work. When I realized what it was I pulled my fingers away quickly—it was an art blecho rendering of a jock cup. The Athletic Supporter.

You certainly wouldn't have walked into the place on spec, which was probably what its owner and regular patrons wanted. That kind of entrance usually fronts gay bars, which may have been what the owner and regular patrons wanted strangers to think. The only riffraff who would have entered the place by accident would have been brave riffraff.

The heavy outside door swung into an almost black entranceway, the last line of defense against unwanted visitors. I stepped carefully across toward a shaft of light at the bottom of another door. After fumbling a second for the handle, I pulled the door open.

Some bars have to be seen to be believed. The Athletic Supporter had to be seen and smelled to be believed. It was done in Early Locker Room. No, it *was* Early Locker Room. In the first place, there were no chairs. There were benches, benches such as you'd find in a locker room or across the sides of a football field. Along a couple of walls were oversized open-faced change cubicles. For seats they also had benches, with room enough for six normal people or four linemen. Each booth had the name and number of a Metro great across the top, and on the back wall pictures of the particular star in action. On the other, open walls were those hot-air blowing machines mounted high enough to dry hair as well as hands. Underneath were long mirrors. The pile of metal lurking in one corner turned out to be one of those machines designed to strain the muscles of your choice. Two guys in suit pants, shirts and loosened ties were using it while they talked. The serving bars for waiters were old training tables, the kind athletes lie down on in towels so someone can knead their sweaty limbs. The waiters wore sneakers, white sweat socks, navy warmup pants, bright blue Metros T-shirts, and towels around their necks. If there were bouncers they probably wore referee shirts.

Without the smell it would just have been awful. But there was the smell, like something you'd find at the bottom of your locker after four years of gym class. That set The Athletic Supporter apart.

There was room for about a hundred in the place, though only about thirty were there when I entered. Most of them eyeballed me and dismissed me as a nobody, just a brave member of the riffraff that the liquor-licensing regulations said they had to let in. I would have taken a hike under any other circumstances, and made us all feel better. But I stayed put and soon Max York was bouncing his way across the room toward me. He watched me taking the place in for a second time.

"Quite a joint, huh?" Max said when he was close enough for me to hear him. "First time here?"

"First time," I said to him. "And last," I said to myself.

He led the way toward a booth in the back. Just before we got there we went past an empty one with Sean Denby's name over it. The front of it was blocked by a black crepe-paper cross. More black crepe paper outlined the action pictures of him on the rear wall. Inside hung a Metros shirt that said DENBY and 27 on the back. Underneath, on the booth's only bench, was a horseshoe of flowers with a ruddy brown floral football as a centerpiece.

I stopped to examine this memorial to my friend, and Max came back to stand with me. "Nice tribute, isn't it, Richard? Hank Illingworth, the owner of this place, is a dear, dear friend of mine and a big, big supporter of the team. He asked me what he could do in Sean's honor . . ." Max's voice trailed away modestly; he preferred to let the tribute speak for him.

"You suggested this, Max?" I asked, hoping he hadn't.

He nodded gravely.

"It's understated, but effective," I said.

Max smiled his thanks for the comment.

We turned to go to our locker-cubicle-whatever just as a great crowd noise swelled up around us. People in the bar looked to the door, then several of them joined in the cheering and clapping that was coming from speakers around the room. The faces were unfamiliar, but the body types weren't. Football players. The taped crowd noise subsided as the young studs nodded and waved slightly in appreciation of their reception.

I flashed a stunned look at Max York, who had of course joined in the applause.

"They play that every time one of the ballplayers comes through the door. It's great for their morale."

"If not their sense of modesty. Is that your idea, too, Max?"

"No," he said, regretfully.

We started on our way again. "Will I have to ask for something cute when I order my drink," I asked York, "like maybe a Full Scale Blitz, or a Down and Out, or a Quarterback Sneak?"

Max said "No" but there was "not yet" in his eyes.

A sardonic grunt arose from the booth at this exchange. Sardonic grunts are hard to get right, and nobody does it better than Anthony Wright.

"Tony," I said with obvious surprise. "Seeing you twice in twenty-four hours is more than any mortal should hope for."

"Yes," he said simply.

I couldn't have been more surprised; if you'd asked me to draw up a list of reporters I wouldn't expect to find in a place like The Athletic Supporter, Tony Wright's name would have been definitely second, maybe first. The other contender for top spot would have been me. I mentioned my surprise at seeing him there.

"Richard, my son, I have followed the scents of many a story to many a disreputable place, but this is just about as low as I've gone. I was just thinking about how embarrassed I'd be if someone I knew saw me here. Then I realized that no one I knew—and whose opinion I respected—would be caught dead"— he stopped cold and bowed his head in the direction of Sean Denby's memorial booth—"in a place like this."

I laughed. Max York didn't, but then he didn't seem to take offense either. Every job effects a person's normal responses in some special way. Inspector Hurst seemed unperturbed by mayhem. Max York had a duck's back for insults. After almost a decade as a journalist, I was almost impossible to impress.

For a few moments Tony, Max and I traded stories about the awful places we'd been in in the line of duty. There was a surprising number, but we easily settled on the Oshawa Holiday Inn's Auto Pub as the worst, what with the hubcaps on the walls and the exhaust systems on the ceiling.

Twice during our chat the cheering had been turned on to announce the arrival of Metros. I hadn't bothered to look up again, but the next time it started it had just caught its breath when it suddenly faded away. Other people in the room were quickly turning their eyes away from the door, so I just had to look. As did Tony.

At the door was a living example of my major reason for giving up football. In the first place, the doorway could barely hold him. You could say that about a lot of other guys who'd gone through it, though I doubted that many of them made the doorway cringe. He was about six-six and carried maybe 250 pounds quite easily in the chest, shoulders, arms and neck. But it was his face that made me turn back to my beer. Eight inches shorter and 70 pounds lighter, a guy with that look on his face would still have made me turn away.

Experience made me turn away. For Tony Wright it was

just instinct. "He's wearing his game face," I said quietly to Tony.

"I beg your pardon?"

"A lot of guys when they play ball have an attitude they like to get into to make them play tougher. It's a frame of mind that lets them kill and maim with abandon. It manifests itself in a certain look. Game face."

"Do you think he always wears it?" Tony asked.

"No, but that's assuming he enjoys normal sexual relations with women. Or gorillas. Or whatever he wants."

"Who is he?" Tony addressed Max directly for the first time.

"Paul Lacosta," Max said flatly, before looking back into his beer.

"The Paul Lacosta?" I asked. Max just nodded.

"Paul Lacosta." Tony tried to sound reflective, but he was obviously irritated because he didn't know what Max and I knew. He tried to cover by saying, "The name's familiar . . ."

"The name should be familiar, Tony, it got around some a few years back. He started out playing for the Metros. He wasn't great or anything, but he was as tough as petrified cleats. Too tough for pro ball, some said, probably the guys who lined up across from him. About five years back he quit when he got hurt."

"Hurt?" Tony risked a look at Lacosta's lumbering bulk. "How?"

"I think he dropped a car on himself. Anyway, he was around doing nothing for a couple of years, and doing very well at it indeed." I looked at Max for some sign of confirmation but he was trying to pretend he'd lost his ability to hear. Taking Max's silence as a non-denial of my version of Lacosta's story, I concluded, "Lately, I don't know what he's been doing."

"I do," Tony said, glad to be back in the know. "A few months back Norris Harlan had a press conference for one of his firms and that guy turned up casting a huge shadow on him. I think he's Harlan's bodyguard."

Max's deafness had gone into remission. "Chief of security," he said sharply. "Paul Lacosta has been the Harlan family of companies' chief of security for over a year now." I'd never heard Max display less enthusiasm for someone he shilled for. "You'll need to meet him, both of you."

Max got up and made his way toward Lacosta. Watching him, Tony said to me, "You get the impression Max's not looking forward to this?"

"I can't imagine him less enthusiastic if he were doing PR for his own executioner."

Max's famous bouncy step was gone; he sidled toward Lacosta. From a good ten feet away he said very heartily, "Paul, you got a minute?"

Paul slowed to see who Max was and who was sitting behind him and then kept on moving. When Max spoke again the heartiness was gone. "Mr. Harlan told me to introduce them to you." The big man stopped with his back to us and I saw his huge shoulders tighten a little in frustration. He turned and fixed me with a cold stare, the kind the Godfather's hoods flashed on a guy just before they took him for a ride. The Godfather analogy didn't seem as funny as it had that afternoon with Harlan dispensing favors in his office.

Lacosta was giving me the once-over as he neared the table. It was the second time in six hours that a big, tough, self-confident guy had examined me for defects and made it clear he found plenty. Lacosta's gaze was much more unsettling than Inspector Ian Hurst's, since the policeman at least had his sense of duty to keep him in check. I knew no such nicety would concern the arrogant and accomplished bully standing in front of me.

I looked up at Lacosta's muscular bulk and thought about how he'd do against Hurst for keeps. I would part with big bucks to watch, but not as a wager on either man; it seemed impossible that either could lose.

"Paul Lacosta, this is—"

"I know who they are, York, and what they are—reporters." He said it the way I say "child molesters."

Turning his eyes on Tony and me in turn, Lacosta finally said, "If Harlan wants to let you stick your nose in that's his business. But if you're thinking about writing something about me, just be goddam sure you get it right." The consequent threat was unspoken, and unnecessary.

"Does your melodramatic warning apply to itself?" In the silence that followed that remark I realized I'd made it. I wondered what I could hit Lacosta with when he started in on me. But Lacosta's stony look crumbled into a near-smile as he nodded with the slightest move of his head. He turned and headed deeper into the room.

Tony said, "You carrying something lethal?"

"Just my wit and a strong sense of mission."

"Great. If he comes back you hit him with those and I'll pummel him with my righteous indignation. What chance will he have?"

 ONCE THE SHOCK OF RUNNING UP against a world-class bully had worn off, Tony and I spent a while trading memories and jokes. It should have been more fun; it wasn't because I was spinning my wheels. The story for my magazine and the answers to my personal questions would not turn up if I spent too much time skipping down memory lane with an old friend.

I was wondering what to do next when a nice round of

applause arose from the growing assembly of fans and players. It was for Eric VanKaspal, the new starting quarterback for the Toronto Metros. All of a sudden I knew what to do next: talk to Eric VanKaspal. When you're looking for motive, after all, it's always a good idea to consider who comes out ahead when a crime is committed. Clearly, Eric VanKaspal came out way ahead. First off, he was out of someone's shadow, a big plus for any athlete fit to play in the Bigs. VanKaspal had lived with not being the star quarterback for three or four years because of Sean. Lately he'd been saying "Play me or trade me," the traditional demand of the second-stringer who figured he deserved better. Maybe he did deserve better. We'd know soon enough. The Metros wouldn't have traded him, since they were saving him for a Denby-less future. That future was here, a lot faster than anyone had expected, or hoped for, except maybe VanKaspal.

And the payoff for VanKaspal was also here faster than he'd hoped for; he walked through the bar obviously enjoying the clamor of people trying to become old fans of his. There would be more of that, and more money, and more chances to be a star, and more chances to play, and more money, and more and more and more. All because Sean Denby was dead. Looked at that way, I couldn't see how anyone else could hold a candle to VanKaspal as a suspect with something to gain. Of course, I was new at this.

"Max, can you get Eric VanKaspal to join us?" The PR man said sure and swallowed the last of his beer before going over to stand diffidently by while he waited for the right moment to speak to his new, improved client. That moment came and York and VanKaspal were soon heading our way at a leisurely pace, with VanKaspal acting like a dog who knows it's time to come in for a bath. I could almost see the gold-plated Norris Harlan autographed leash between York and VanKaspal. Max gave it one last, serious tug and the Metros new starting quarterback eased his lithe, lanky frame onto the bench across from me.

60

Introductions were brief and unencumbered by emotion. Tony had a notebook out before I even thought about going for mine. He uncapped his fountain pen and used it to go for VanKaspal's jugular. "Mr. VanKaspal, my information is that you aren't wasting much time cashing in on your new prominence. Don't you feel this is a little unseemly, considering the cause of your elevation?"

This was all news to me, and a perfect example of why good reporters prefer private chats with their subjects. I didn't know if Tony was doing me a favor by passing on this information, or if he was just too distasteful of such avarice to keep it quiet.

For a minute I thought the young Texan wasn't going to answer. Considering that sportswriters are usually demanding details of how the ballplayer got to be so wonderful and talented, Tony's opening sally must have come as a shock to VanKaspal. He turned to Max York for help, but Max was busy looking into his empty beer glass for a place to hide.

Left to fend for himself, Vankaspal quickly got over Tony's opening shot. He crossed his legs and his arms, assumed a tutorial look, and said to Tony, "Mr. Cane, do you know how long the average football career lasts?" It was a deft passing move, aided by what I figured was the nice touch of purposely calling Tony by the wrong name—just to show him where he stood in Eric VanKaspal's scheme of things.

But Tony was no bumbler. "Considering the brutality of your . . . sport, I would imagine not very long. I assume you are using this abbreviated career expectation as an excuse for your agent scuttling all over town to get you whatever product endorsements he can since Sean Denby's murder. Aren't you embarrassed by that?"

VanKaspal replied in a voice as archly calm as Tony's. "Aren't you embarrassed by the fact that you often make your living by writing about the personal tragedies of people whose only crime was having bad luck, such as people with a child dying of cancer? For that matter, do you have stock in the newspaper you work for, or are you the beneficiary of a profit-sharing plan there? If so, aren't you embarrassed that you're making money—indirectly, I'll grant you—from Sean's murder?"

I'm as big a fan of high-toned character bashing as the next guy, but I was feeling left out, so I jumped in before Tony could reply. "When you put it that way," I said, "you make Tony sound like a suspect in Sean's murder."

"Like me," VanKaspal said.

I smiled pleasantly and nodded.

"When you call him Sean, are you just being familiar or did you know him?"

"I knew him, Mr. VanKaspal. We played ball together in school. We'd drifted apart."

This information struck VanKaspal with more than passing interest. He looked at me hard for a second, apparently considering the chances of something. He couldn't seem to make his mind up on the matter, so he turned back to Tony Wright.

"Mr. Wright, football's a bitch of a tough sport. When I'm your age I'll probably be well out of it. But it's what I do best, and the only way I can make my living right now. I need to make money at it now, and in big bites. I could get injured tomorrow and be finished for life. I'm a pragmatist, and tender feelings on this will cost me money. But it won't cost me anything to be honest and tell you that, yes, I am embarrassed to be cashing in on Sean's death. That won't stop me from doing it, however." He stood up. "Now, if you'll excuse me, gentlemen, I have to go and see if I can turn up a few bucks here in this room."

As VanKaspal walked away I looked to see Tony's reaction to his comments. The complete pro, he was showing none, concentrating instead on getting down on paper what VanKaspal had just said.

VanKaspal didn't seem to have a particular spot in mind to go to, so I set out after him. I caught him just as he entered the gloom of a booth named after a Metros star gone from the team for many years. The guy had gone on to sell aluminum siding, and most likely would be embarrassed by The Athletic Supporter.

Before VanKaspal could get his back up, I said quickly, "You must be great at calling audibles; you changed the play back there quickly enough."

"Some teams have limited defenses. Look, I'm really not in the mood to play ethical handball."

"Nor am I, and certainly not with someone as good at it as you are. Are you just a natural, or did you get training?"

VanKaspal's edge softened. "One of the best things about football as a professional sport is that the only way into it is through college."

"Unlike, say, hockey."

"I made the most of the free college education I was offered. I never lost the taste for it; shit, I'm still there, working slowly toward my Ph.D. in philosophy. Ethics, to be precise. If there's no other benefit it makes you a terror in certain barroom arguments." The thought made VanKaspal smile. "But, please, don't make a big deal out of the fact that I'm not a mouth-breathing idiot; it's bad for the image."

"Sean and I skipped a lot of philosophy classes together," I said, hoping to build a bridge to VanKaspal.

He had a nice smile when he wanted. "Lots of them are worth skipping," he said. "You knew Sean reasonably well, then?"

"High school. University. On football teams and between football teams. I guess I knew him well, but after a little chat with a couple of cops this afternoon maybe not as well as I thought."

"He was a strangely private man," VanKaspal said quietly.

"Strangely private?"

"He was always having a good time with people, but I never saw him let anybody in. Not me, certainly." Van-Kaspal seemed sad about that.

"I found out today he was the same with me," I said. "When we were young I never noticed, and when I was older I never gave it much thought. Now that I know, I don't know what I think."

VanKaspal and I were silent for a few moments, probably thinking very similar thoughts about Sean Denby.

I broke the silence. "What do you think happened, Mr. VanKaspal, to Sean I mean?"

"I don't have to think, Mr. Cane, I know."

"Oh yes?"

"He did something he shouldn't have done."

"He might not have done something he should have done."

There was a glint in VanKaspal's eye. "You didn't skip all your philosophy classes, Mr. Cane."

"I just see the other side. It's a result of my natural perverseness and a journalism background. You, on the other hand, seem sure about what you say, Mr. VanKaspal. You know why he was killed. Or think you do." It was an instinctive remark VanKaspal could have easily taken offense at. He nervously pushed his hands into his pockets instead.

"Being in the newspaper business so long may have made you see things from a different perspective, Mr. Cane, but it has also sadly diminished your view of privacy." His voice had become more cultured, a sign I was coming to know signaled his displeasure.

"For reasons not worth mentioning, my view of privacy is probably more restrictive than yours. But that's beside the point. The point is that you know something—or think you know something. It's your duty to tell that to the proper authorities." God, I sounded pompous. While I looked for a way to get down off my high horse, the cultured Ph.D. candidate in ethics stood up and explained his position very succinctly: "Go fuck yourself."

Never having been able to come up with a witty comeback for that one, I watched in silence as VanKaspal walked away again. He was really good at making exits; maybe he minored in theater arts. This time he walked straight into a group of guys who looked like they were offensive linemen.

64

They closed around VanKaspal as he entered and a couple of them gave me a look that dared me to follow. I brushed off the bootlicker's grin I'd used the night before at the police station and flashed it at them. It must not have come out right because they looked a little disconcerted as they turned away. Probably gave them my madman's grin by mistake.

I decided to pass up their kind offer to beat me senseless if I went after VanKaspal. Even if I got to him he wouldn't talk to me. I needed some leverage, and I knew a way I might come up with some.

When I was about twenty-five yards from the door a fashion advertisement from *Gentleman's Quarterly* came through it. I stopped in my tracks to think about why he looked familiar. Maybe I'd just seen too many faces, so now they were all familiar. But this guy I knew . . .

His clothes, his hair, his features, his attitude—everything about this guy was well cut. He seemed to be about forty, maybe six feet tall, and thin. No, not thin, gaunt.

Whatever else he was, he wasn't a player or a fan; too slight and too old to be a player, and too detached to be a fan. He gave the room the critical, dismissive look he might give a rack of ready-made jackets.

The detachment was not returned; the noise level plummeted when he was spotted, and now an awkward silence was being directed at him. It was the kind of entrance many people dream about making, but he was unimpressed with the attention as he scanned the room.

When his gaze crossed me it stopped cold. I thought I saw a flash of surprised recognition. It lasted only a second, because the stranger and the rest of us were soon concerned with the figure of Paul Lacosta angling toward the door, walking right at anyone in his way, confident that they'd step aside for him. Which, of course, they did. By the look in his eye, I fancied that the well-dressed stranger might not move. He did stand still—rock-still, like a basketball guard waiting to draw a foul from a charging opponent. Lacosta stopped right in front of him, looking down on him from just a few inches away. It was more a position of intimidation than one to fight from. Whatever, it didn't seem to bother the stranger. I couldn't hear him but I saw his lips say, "Paul," in casual greeting.

Above the subdued chatter in the bar Lacosta talked and the gaunt stranger listened without watching. Taking his eyes off that big brute seemed to me an act of sublime bravery, or sheer recklessness. Take your pick. When Lacosta finished, the other man gave him a smile and a condescending nod before slowly making his way to the door.

I made for Tony Wright. "Who the hell was that?" I demanded. The room was buzzing a little louder now and getting out of Lacosta's way as he went back to his beer.

"You must recognize him," Tony said, more in despair than anything.

"He looked familiar." I was echoing Tony's tone when he'd pretended to recognize Lacosta, but if he picked up on my kidding he ignored it.

"Familiar? Hah. He should look familiar, considering how often his picture has been in the papers. Think of him in jodhpurs going over a jump. Think of him keelhauling the mizzenmast in the middle of a race. Think of him in a safari suit bwanaing his own expedition up the Nile. Think . . ."

Tony's healthy disdain for adventurous people would make him go on like that indefintely, so I blurted out "Julian Amory."

"It was my clues."

"Sure. Keelhauling the mizzenmast. So why did Frankenstein bounce him? Did Amory ask him to be his anchor?"

"It has nothing to do with sailing, or horse jumping, or any other sport—directly."

"Do I have to guess it exactly, or will you settle for close?"

"It has to do with sports indirectly, and is something you will never read about because it's illegal in this province, because it's too profitable and therefore run as a government monopoly. Julian Amory is the biggest gambler in Toronto, probably in

66

Ontario, maybe in Canada. Actually, saying that he gambles is wrong. What he does is take other people's money."

"I didn't think he needed money; someone in his family left him a pile, didn't they?" The way I said it implied criticism, which was ridiculous considering my personal situation.

Tony either missed my gaffe or was kind. "No, he doesn't need the money. Maybe that's why he's such a good gambler—he never lets fear play a part in his bets."

"Lacosta bounced him because the league doesn't like its players to be seen passing time with a man who bets money on what they do."

"Sounds good to me," Tony said.

I stood up quickly, said good-bye to Tony and remembered Max York's presence just in time to nod a farewell at him. Before the bar's inside door closed behind me, I looked to see what Eric VanKaspal was doing. Another beer was being handed to him by a waiter, and he was deep in conversation with two other players.

That was good. I needed to have him stay right where he was until I got back.

 **10** A CAB WAS CRUISING BY THE FRONT OF The Athletic Supporter as I hit the brisk night air. I flagged him, he pulled over and I climbed in.

"I need to go someplace where I can rent a car," I told the middle-aged, balding driver.

He nodded and pulled the car away from the curb. We made a right, a left, went about fifty feet and stopped. "That'll be a buck fifty."

"I could have walked, if you'd told me it was here."

"I don't sell directions, buddy."

I gave him a two and kept my wallet out as I went through the door of the car rental firm. I made it clear to the young woman behind the counter that I was pressed. She responded with the speed of the young and eager, so a pimply youth had a Ford Tempo at the door before I'd finished filling out the rental forms.

In less time than I'd thought it would take, I was back at The Athletic Supporter.

If luck was with me, my quarry would still be inside. I thought he would be, but I had to know for sure. I could have gone back in, looked around and left again. That would look suspicious, however, and I needed VanKaspal unsuspecting.

So I got out of the car and waited for a cab to come by. When one did it was the same cab I'd just ridden in to the car-rental firm.

"You again," the cabby said with a smile, "you want me to lead you somewhere else?"

"Do you know Eric VanKaspal?"

He held up a copy of that day's *Toronto Sun*, opened it to the sports section, and showed me a picture of VanKaspal. "This one?"

"That one. I'll give you five bucks to go in this place and see if he's still there. Either way, come back out and tell me."

"Five bucks to do that? You're a little gold mine, buddy. You ever think about taking on a private cabbie?" He laughed and got out of the car. He held out his hand. "Now." I gave him the money and he walked quickly to and through the door.

I moved away in case someone came out. No one did until the cabbie came hustling out a minute later. He looked around for me. I stepped out of a nearby doorway onto the sidewalk.

"He's there."

"Are you sure?"

"Course. I went in and said there was a cab outside for Eric VanKaspal. He personally told me he hadn't called me. Then he tipped me five for my trouble." The cabby showed me the five and what was left of his smile. "I think I'll hang around with you some more."

I crossed the street and got back in the rented Tempo. In a few minutes two guys came out of the bar and got into the waiting cab. As the car went by the driver waved to me.

Almost no one expects to be followed. I learned that years ago when I was a reporter working general assignment. One Friday afternoon I was in a store and noticed a fairly big-time politician at a cash register buying some perfume. I didn't care that he was playing hookey from work. What caught my eye was that the backside he kept fondling was not the backside I'd seen jeopardizing chairs with him at various political meetings. I wouldn't even have cared that much about his philandering were it not for the fact that he'd been obnoxious in promoting his status as a God-fearing family man whenever it was politically convenient. So I followed them for a while, just for the heck of it. They went into a bar for a drink, picked up some food at a deli and walked to a small apartment house, where he used his key to let them in. All the while he was being, uh, openly affectionate.

I was amazed at how careless he was despite his middling fame. I never made anything of the event, but it put me onto a new technique in reporting—following your subject around. A lot of time was wasted, but now and then it turned up information I couldn't have bought at any price, or gotten any other way.

Following had so far turned out to be surprisingly easy, requiring only patience, an aggressive driving style, the ability to not make yourself too obvious, and a feel for what people were going to do next.

That's what I was doing outside The Athletic Supporter: wondering which way VanKaspal would go when he came out of the bar, and in which car, if indeed he had one. It'd likely be sporty, but with a brace of ballplayers nearby there'd be a lot of sporty cars in the area. A quick look around bore that out. For instance, there was a Corvette in front of where I was parked and a BMW behind me.

It occurred to me that if either car was VanKaspal's, he'd see me when he came out, be suspicious, and notice me when I started to follow him. So I started the Tempo and did a U-turn to head away from the bar. About a hundred feet away were a couple of parking spots at the end of the block. I did another U-turn into the spot nearest the intersection and left the motor running. It looked good: far enough away so Van-Kaspal wasn't likely to walk right up to where I was, and not so far away that I couldn't see him when he came out. Now all I had to do was wait.

About an hour later I was startled out of my deepening boredom by the sight of Eric VanKaspal coming out of the bar. He put his right hand in his trouser pocket and did not look up and down the street, searching for his car keys and not a cab. I smiled at my foresight when he walked up to the BMW I'd been parked in front of and opened the driver's door.

VanKaspal blew the smile right off my face when he yanked the BMW out into traffic and roared off down the street away from me. "Shit," I said out loud to myself, "I should have rented a Porsche." By the time I was out on the street the BMW was already disappearing in front of me. I put my foot in it and the Tempo's four-cylinders began to howl in response. It was no contest, though; VanKaspal clearly had the superior car and intended to use it. He didn't even have to be as good a driver as I was to get away. My only hope was luck. He had to hit traffic patterns and lights that slowed him down if I was going to keep up.

VanKaspal drove the BMW through one intersection just as the light turned yellow. Three or four seconds behind him I had no hope of keeping up if I stopped for this light, so I ran it, hitting the intesection after the light had gone red but before any traffic had started through the other way. An angry horn went off to my right. I risked a sideways look and saw a cabbie giving me the finger and a stream of verbal abuse. It probably wasn't, but I hoped it was the guy who'd taken me to the car rental firm.

I eased up on the gas pedal a little. I didn't like the idea of being stopped by a cop for going twice the posted limit and, more importantly, VanKaspal was closing on a line of traffic that would slow him up as well.

Parking was heavy on the street, which meant it was restricted to one lane of traffic the way we were going. That lane was plugged by a glut of cars that seemed in no particular hurry at all. VanKaspal challenged it with the BMW a couple of times, but the row of cars just rolled sedately on. As for me, I was content just to stick to the BMW's rear. There was little chance VanKaspal would look back, and if he did I doubted that he'd be able to make me out in the dark.

We cruised on a couple of blocks. I could see VanKaspal getting frustrated. I primed myself to do something radical if I had to, to keep up with him. A block further on he made his move, nipping in and out of the right hand lane between two parked cars to pass the sedan in front of him. That put a car between us, which would be enough to make me lose him in the right circumstances. At the next red light VanKaspal stopped the BMW and flicked on its left turn signal. The newish Chevrolet sedan in front of me did the same thing.

VanKaspal watched the lights of the cross street. The driver of the Chevy watched his front-seat passenger. Van-Kaspal was going to go left quickly when the light went green, beating the cars going straight through the other way. There was usually time for one car with an alert driver to do that. There certainly wouldn't be time for the chatty guy in the Chevy and then me to do it.

A second before the light went green VanKaspal started to turn and was across the road before traffic going the other way got a chance to move. The guy in front of me was still gabbing, but moved up for his chance at turning. He went deep into the intersection to wait for a gap. One was coming, two cars along. I looked down the cross-street and saw the BMW's taillights fading in the distance. The gap in the on-coming traffic presented itself, but the chatty guy in the Chevy hesitated. I didn't. I pulled out from behind him and cut a sharper line through the intersection. The guy in the Chevy braked hard and looked startled as I blew by him on his left. I could imagine him saying, "Did you see that ass-hole?" to his friends. I hoped he could imagine my apology.

I set the Tempo's engine to howling again, at OPEC and catalytic converters and being asked to do what it really wasn't built to do. To these demands it responded by letting me fall farther behind the speeding BMW by the second. VanKaspal was going so fast I wondered if he might know I was following him. I couldn't think how he'd know that, so I put his driving down to his liking to go fast. He must have really liked it—I was doing sixty in a thirty zone and he was getting away. I began to think about giving up the chase. It was a wild fishing expedition anyway. VanKaspal might have been rushing home to catch the news and a good night's sleep. It just wasn't worth it, I decided, and let up on the gas. At almost the same second the BMW slowed up as well. It struck me that VanKaspal might be slowing up be-cause he'd seen me slowing up. I pulled the car up to the curb and stopped. Ahead of me a hundred yards VanKaspal did the same.

I was trying to figure out what had given me away when VanKaspal opened the BMW's door and got out. He went straight into a convenience store beside where he was parked.

I took the Tempo fifty feet past the BMW and pulled over to wait. Ahead about a half mile was the entrance ramp to the Gardiner Expressway. That was the route I hoped Van-Kaspal would take. Traffic on that road is always heavy, se-verely restricting your ability to go real fast in any kind of car. I'd learned long ago that driving a hot, fast car in Toronto was frustrating. There's just no place to give it its head. It's like owning a cheetah and keeping it in a small three-room apartment.

In my rearview mirror I saw VanKaspal come out of the store and climb back into his car. When I saw it start up I pulled out. By the time we were at the first corner he was right on my tail. In that position I could block him from getting ahead of me. He might be angry, but not suspicious, since it's common when you're driving a hot, expensive car to have guys in lesser cars work out their jealousy by inhibiting your fun. Of course, if VanKaspal made a turn from behind me I'd be left with a nice big pile of plans that had gone bad.

He did not, however, turn from behind me, so a block from the Gardiner I let him pass. As he whistled by on my right I looked away, and then pulled in behind him.

East. We were going east on the Gardiner. That meant turning north up the Don Valley Parkway in a few miles, or on into the southeastern part of the city. My bet was we'd pass up the parkway to go further east, into the beaches, whose residents mostly worshipped at Saint Henry Buildall, Church of the Wholly Renovation. And that's where we went, and—to my surprise—at something resembling a moderate pace. I had no trouble keeping up until we were past Greenwood racetrack and heading north up Woodbine Avenue away from Lake Ontario. He made a right onto Queen Street just as the light changed. Three cars back I waited for the light to go green again before I made my turn.

Moving along Queen I drifted in and out of the right-hand lane between parked cars, hoping to catch a glimpse of the BMW. Traffic was heavy, and a dozen cars were crawling along in front of me, none of them a BMW. He must have turned off Queen. I drove six blocks, looking up and down each side street as I passed.

At the next block I looked north and saw VanKaspal standing next to the BMW about thirty yards up the street. He crossed the street carrying the small bag of stuff he'd bought at the convenience store. Just as I was about to turn left he looked down the street and slowed his walk. I waited in the middle of Queen Street. He smiled and held up the bag. I waited some more. Then I noticed a guy walking up the street who was also holding up a small brown bag. Van-Kaspal smiled and angled back toward him. When an impatient horn sounded behind me VanKaspal and his friend looked my way. I turned left and went quickly up the street past the two men, who ignored me totally.

Five cars ahead of the BMW I pulled over and put out the Tempo's lights. I watched in the side mirror as VanKaspal and the other guy, a tall, thin, young black man, came closer. When they stepped off the sidewalk I turned to look directly at them. They went up the steps of a small house right across from where the BMW was parked. Even though the porch was dark, I could see them quite well. As Van-Kaspal searched for his keys the other guy leaned over toward him and kissed him quite firmly on the lips. The new starting quarterback for the Toronto Metros returned the kiss, put the convenience store bag under his arm, and used his free hand to fondle the other guy's crotch.

**11** WELL, I CERTAINLY HAD SOME NEW INformation about Eric VanKaspal, unless the person on the receiving end of that grope was an outstanding male impersonator.

I was irritated with myself for knowing. Eric VanKaspal's apparent homosexuality was not what I'd wanted to find out about. Evidence of his involvement in Sean Denby's murder is what I'd been after. Now I knew something about Van-Kaspal that could, if spilled in the wrong ear, ruin his pro football career. On the spot I swore I'd never mention what I'd just seen to anyone.

When I was sure the two weren't coming right back out of the house, I got out of the Tempo and walked cautiously down the street to the BMW. Something urgent in the way they'd embraced told me I could have taken a band playing Sousa marches down that street right then and they wouldn't have looked, but I've been wrong before.

Their porch light went on and I thought I was wrong again. I crouched behind the car, but an upstairs light went on and the porch light went out. Someone fumbling for the right switch, no doubt. I stood up and watched the house. The downstairs lights went out as another upstairs light went on. A minute later some lights went off upstairs, leaving just a low, pinkish glow coming through the curtains of a second-floor window.

I blushed and turned away, ashamed to be watching.

In my notebook I made a note of the house number and the BMW's license. The passenger door was unlocked so I popped it open and got in.

One sniff inside the car told me it was showroom new. Exactly 311 kilometers new, according to the odometer. So new its owner hadn't had time to personalize it with junk in the glove box, on the dash, under the seat, or anywhere else.

I got out of the BMW and went to its rear end, where for no good reason I could think of, I copied down the dealer's name.

A minute later I had the Tempo turned around and headed south. At the corner I made a note of the street name before I turned onto Queen. Two blocks along was a restaurant I knew, so I parked and went in. Inside I sat and waited for the pretty young man in the Hawaiian shirt and tight pegged jeans to follow up on his smile of welcome.

The waiter came to my table, took my order and walked away unaware that I was considering him very carefully. Up until fifteen minutes before, if anyone had asked me if I thought the waiter was gay I'd have said, "Of course." And, if asked the same question about Eric VanKaspal fifteen minutes ago, I would have said "Of course not." If my old friend Sean hadn't just turned up murdered, seeing Eric VanKaspal grab that guy's crotch would have been my big surprise for the month.

It had been a busy couple of days for me, but I didn't feel the least bit tired; in fact, I didn't want the day to stop. It was only 10:30, after all.

I called across the room to my waiter, "Is there a phone I can use?"

"Downstairs," he replied, cocking his head toward a door that said WASHROOMS.

I'd guessed that cops put in a lot of hours when they're on a fresh murder case, and I was right. Inspector Hurst was still in the building, and very shortly grumbling into the other end of the phone. He did not sound surprised to hear from me. He did not sound anything to hear from me.

"Inspector, have you got any information on where Alison Denby is?"

"As a matter of fact, she's in Room 1216 of the Royal York Hotel. I just had a chat with her."

"I'm impressed. This afternoon you didn't have any idea where she was and a few hours later you've interrogated her."

"Interrogated is a writer's word, Cane. We just had a little chat, and an unproductive one at that. As for finding her, I have to admit that was a stroke of genius on my part: when she called here to say she'd just flown in from Vancouver and could she be of any help I said yes and asked her where she was."

"No wonder you're in charge of this case. How is she? Is she coping?"

For the first time in my hearing Ian Hurst was vague. "I don't know. Who the hell can tell what women are feeling?" His inability to do so clearly bothered him.

"Do you think it'd be okay if I went over there to talk to her?"

"Now?"

"Soon."

"I can't speak for her, but it's okay with me. I don't think you'd be keeping her from sleep."

"Thanks, Inspector, I'll talk to you soon."

"Especially if you find out anything."

I thought about Eric VanKaspal. "You'll be the first to know anything." My stomach was tight; lying to a cop investigating a murder was a new experience for me.

About fifteen seconds later a weary woman's voice answered my next call and I realized I wasn't sure how I was going to go about this. As a reporter I hated cold-calling because I knew the failure rate that went with it.

"Hello"— hell, I didn't even know her new married name —"Alison."

"Who is this?"

"You don't know me, I used to be a friend of Sean Denby's."

"Are you a reporter?"

"No," I lied with ease. "My name's Richard Cane. Sean and I played football together in high school and college."

"Oh, yes." She sounded really impressed. "What do you want?"

"I just thought I'd ask you if there was anything I could do for you."

There was a pause. "What did you say your name was?"

"Cane. Richard Cane. Richard."

"Your name does sound familiar, sort of. Forgive me, but a lot of people say they used to be friends of Sean's and then get pushy, asking for things."

"That's one of the reasons I didn't see him after we left university. He got famous and I was always afraid if I made an approach he'd brush me. I should have known better; Sean wasn't like that."

There was another pause. "No, I guess he wasn't, Mr. Cane."

"Alison—forgive my informality, but I don't know your name since you remarried."

"I kept Denby when I remarried. It seems ridiculous to have three different last names in five years. If I had it to do over I wouldn't change it when I got married. One name should last a lifetime. So just call me Alison, okay . . . Richard?"

"Richard," I said, "by all means. Alison, I wondered if you'd like to have a drink with me. And a talk."

"When?"

"Now."

She thought about that. "Unless you're in the lobby, Richard, we better settle for soon."

"Soon then. It's ten forty-five now. How does eleven-thirty sound? Downstairs there in the Library Bar."

"Fine, but don't be late. A lady going into bars at that time of night gives conventioneers the wrong impression."

"Is there a convention there?"

"By the looks of some of the guys I've seen it's the annual meeting of the Royal Canadian Society for the Preservation of Ugly Suits."

I laughed. "I won't be late."

"How will I know you?"

"I'll be the one who's not in the ugly suit."

She laughed. "No, really."

"I'll know you. I've seen your picture in the papers often enough."

She sounded pleased. "All right then, eleven thirty in the Library Bar."

We said good-bye and hung up. I scurried up the stairs feeling very pleased with myself, a condition I had always been fond of but recently had been doing without.

My Budweiser was waiting for me on my table and when the waiter saw me sit down he brought over my turkey on whole wheat, side of fries.

It was ten minutes to eleven. If I ate reasonably quickly I could be on the road by ten after, which would give me lots of time to show up in the Library Bar before the ugly suits got presumptive.

As I ate and drank I looked out the window next to me onto Queen Street and the people using it. It was late, and the stores were closed, but there were still a few people out for an amble, or a nightcap, or something. Draining the last of my beer I took a final look out the window in time to see two people walk by and stop in front of the door. They exchanged a kiss before turning toward the restaurant. Eric VanKaspal was smiling when he looked in the window. Our eyes met and the smile disappeared.

I should have looked surprised, and maybe shocked. Instead I looked cornered, defensive. VanKaspal's look went from surprised to angry. He was through the door and leaning over my table in about two seconds.

"You son of a bitch. You followed me."

"Relax, Eric, I won't tell anyone."

"Tell anyone what?"

I didn't know how to answer that so I struggled to look trustworthy and sophisticated.

"Eric, is something the matter?" It was his friend. He held his hand up tentatively to VanKaspal's back. He looked around the room to see that the waiter and the two other patrons were all watching us.

Without taking his eyes off me VanKaspal addressed his friend: "Yes, this bastard's a reporter who followed me down here and found out I'm queer. Or are you more liberal than that, Cane? Am I gay?"

"Lighten up, VanKaspal, I don't care if you sleep with sheep." I shouldn't have said that, but I was getting pissed off myself.

The tall, thin black man said "Eric" in a strange voice and put his hand on VasKaspal's shoulder, as if to restrain him. VanKaspal shook him off. He reached across the table to grab me by my lapels. The force of his body knocked the small single-legged table over, sending the glass, the plate and the little flower vase onto the floor. With VanKaspal pulling on my jacket and with the table now across my feet I had to struggle to get up, but I managed it. VanKaspal's friend kept saying "Eric" very calmly. It was keeping Van-Kaspal from raising the stakes of our little encounter beyond some name-calling and tough looks. Only he wouldn't let go of me, so I brought my arms up from my hips. I put my arms through and then over VanKaspal's. This caused him to let go of me and fall forward. I wrapped my arms around him, pinning his to his sides.

He looked very surprised when I did that. But I was in no mood for trading punches like a couple of kids, and I figured going into a clinch was a good way to avoid it. It worked for boxers all the time. VanKaspal, however, apparently never watched the fights. He started to pummel my back with his fists. I lowered my arms, hoping to hold his arms low enough against his body so he'd stop trying to punch me. That didn't work.

I tried logic: "For Chrissake, you stupid bastard, knock it off." That didn't work.

From behind him VanKaspal's friend said the same thing in a kinder way. That didn't work.

VanKaspal kept throwing his harmless punches, and for no good reason backed up while doing it. Now we were doing the Gene Tunney two-step. I was getting embarrassed, so I put one of my legs between his and threw my weight onto him. That worked; he stopped punching.

I figured we'd go down to the floor with me on top, which would cool him off some. The plan was for us to fall straight to the floor. Because VanKaspal didn't know my plan, he tried to roll so I'd be the one on the bottom when we landed. Unfortunately for VanKaspal the table we were next to didn't know his plan so it couldn't get out of the way in time. His hip hit the table and that kept him in position to cushion my fall.

As we hit the floor a dinner plate gave me a sharp smack in the back of the head, just behind my ear. It was only a glancing blow, but it gave me a fleeting look into the inside of a fog bank.

VanKaspal was not so lucky. From bare inches away I watched his face register horror. His eyes slammed shut and he pulled his scrinched up face into mine. The move probably saved him the sight in one eye, as a knife from the table hit him just at the corner of the socket.

I closed my eyes and turned my own head to the floor, but the barrage was over by then.

"Eric!" his friend yelled from behind me.

I released my grip of VanKaspal and rolled onto my knees.

A stream of blood was running from the cut into Van-Kaspal's eye. A hand shot out of nowhere with something white in it and most of VanKaspal's face disappeared. It was the waiter pressing a cloth napkin onto the cut. With his other arm he was helping VanKaspal to sit up. For his part VanKaspal was just blinking rapidly with the good eye I could see and trying to take over the napkin from the waiter.

I was standing by the time VanKaspal managed to focus on me. He was still pissed off, but he stayed where he was.

"It missed the eye by about half an inch," I said. "You may need a stitch or two, but you'll be okay."

He said nothing.

I reached into my pocket and counted out four twenties as the waiter and the black guy helped VanKaspal to his feet. "Unless you want to play this some other way," I said to the injured quarterback, "I'll forget everything that happened after we left The Athletic Supporter."

No one replied. I put the money on a table. "Take the damages out of that and drink what's left," I said to the room in general and walked out.

I was in the rented Tempo before I realized my heart was going like a synthesized drum in a disco tune. I turned on the ignition and started to pull out into the street without lights or looking. Some kind motorist was glad to point these mistakes out to me with an angry horn blast. People seemed to be honking at me a lot in the last twenty-four hours. If I wasn't careful I might finish off the bad luck trilogy with a deadly car accident.

 TO HELP ME SETTLE DOWN AFTER MY little scuffle with Eric VanKaspal I rolled down the Tempo's window and sucked up some cool night air. After a few deep breaths I clicked on the headlights and pulled out—carefully—into the westbound Queen Street traffic.

I told myself to calm down, that there was no reason to hurry. Then I looked at the Tempo's LED clock saying 11:20 and I remembered I had to get to the Royal York in time to protect Alison Denby from all those ugly suits. So as soon as I felt calm enough, I started to drive like a minor-league maniac. For the second time that night I played hob with various traffic regulations and got away with it, so when I parked illegally outside the Royal York the clock in the car beamed out 11:35.

Inside the hotel I trotted past several people who regarded me oddly. I ignored them and hurried on.

At the entrance to the Library Bar I stopped to collect my wits and to take a deep breath. I got my breath before my wits, because when the smell hit my nose for the first time I wondered why such a ritzy place smelled like a hamburger joint in July. When I finally got my wits I knew it wasn't the bar that smelled, it was me. Of course. During my squabble with VanKaspal the condiments from the table must have fallen on me. I closed my eyes and tried to imagine what the upholstery in the rented Tempo looked like. I didn't want to think about what my jacket looked like.

I was heading to the men's room when I caught sight of Alison Denby at the bar. She had both eyes and both hands firmly on her glass as a flock of badly dressed vultures closed in on her.

"Hell," I said under my breath.

One of the ugly suits was about to take up a position next to her when I slid in between them—with my back to him, of course. He was about to comment on my manners when he caught a double-nostril load of my jacket. He retreated without a sound and headed back to his seat.

Alison did not look up until I said, "Alison? Hi, I'm Richard Cane."

A cool sideways look. "You're also late." She tried to sound stern but her wrinkling nose ruined it.

"I know about the smell," I said. "That's why I'm late."

"You're late because you wanted to put on a little extra cologne. What is that scent, Canal Number Five?"

"No, it's a new scent—Table Number Five."

"Oh, yes," she said again after sniffing, "the bouquet of relish is rather unique." She unleashed a smile that made me feel like a starving man sitting down to dinner. "What happened?"

"I'm going to have to tell the truth here because I can't think of a story that doesn't make me look as dumb as a six-foot condiment tray. I got into a little fight a few minutes ago, which ended when we fell into a table full of plates."

Alison let out an awe-filled whistle before saying, "True or not, for originality it beats hell out of any excuse I ever heard for being late."

"Unfortunately it's just true. Will you be okay here for a few minutes if I go to the men's room to see how much of it I can get off?"

"Are you mad? After seeing you these clowns will think I'm fair game for anything they've got to offer." She looked around the room in horror. "Do you drink scotch?"

"Only if there's nothing else to drink," I said, casting my eyes over the rows of bottles behind the bar.

"Where we're going there isn't." She drank up the last of her scotch, scribbled her name and room number on the tab in front of her, and stood up. "Scotch is all I've got in my room. If that doesn't suit you, why don't you order a dozen of what does suit you? You could pour them in your pockets and take them up that way. Certainly wouldn't ruin your jacket." Her laugh was low and lethal. "We'll get you what you want from room service," she added softly as she took me by the arm and steered me toward the elevators.

Alison was very businesslike when we got to her room, calling room service for rye and for someone to take my jacket away to be cleaned.

While she sat on the edge of the bed and talked on the phone I sat in a chair to enjoy my first real look at the woman I'd seen in Sean's company so often in the newspapers and on television. It is a curious thing about people you only see that way: if you ever meet them in real life they look like they're supposed to, yet significantly different. My guess is it's the extra dimension that alters them, and allows you to fit them into your personal perspective.

In Alison Denby's case the extra dimension was altering her in a very appealing way. Quite easily my look became a stare and then a gawk. I caught myself there and turned away, blushing slightly.

She hung up and we did one of those cautious conversational cha-chas two strangers do when they have someone special in common: When did you last see Sean? How long did you know him? Where are you living now? All the unimportant personal stuff was dealt with while we waited for the bellboy. That way, when he'd gone, if there was enough solid ground to move ahead on, we'd get into the important personal stuff.

84

Eventually the rye came and the jacket left.

I made myself a drink and waited for Alison to decide if our relationship could support a future. Apparently she thought it might. "Are you married?" she asked casually.

I took a drink. This was the first time I'd had to tell someone my wife had been killed; everyone I'd spoken to before had already known. I didn't know how to do it, so I didn't say anything for a few moments.

Alison mistook my discomfort. "I'm sorry. You're breaking up and you don't want to talk about it."

"No," I said, and drove right in, "she died. Six months back."

Now she was uncomfortable. Before she could speak, I said, "Please don't tell me you're sorry. I never know what to say to that."

She nodded and smiled weakly. For a time the only sound in the room was the ice tinkling in our glasses. Our friendship was in danger of being stillborn.

"I'm glad you're not taking Sean's death as hard as I took Elizabeth's," I said very evenly.

Alison took instinctive offense with my presumption, but it lasted only a second. Her face softened. "Me too," she said, and then stopped to consider her good fortune. I considered my jealousy at her good fortune. "How long did it take you to come to terms with it?" she added.

Brave smile. I leaned forward and poured us both another drink before saying, "I'll let you know as soon as it happens."

"What happened? How did she die?"

That was something else I'd never had to tell anyone. The idea of explaining was unappealing, since it meant thinking about it again. Of course, I thought about it all the time—I just never thought about it all the way through. Maybe there was something to that catharshis shit people were so fond of. Might as well give it a shot, I thought.

Where to start? How about the middle?

"We'd been married a couple of years. Never had a chance

for a honeymoon trip. Last winter we decided to go away for a couple of weeks, only we had a problem—I won't fly any more. That was what Elizabeth saw as the problem—my not flying. For me the problem was that she didn't like to travel by car. We hated each other's favorite method of transportation. A marriage made in heaven, right?" I laughed. It sounded odd, but no odder than my voice, so I pressed on. Actually there was no way I could have stopped.

"We settled on Atlanta, 'cause I could drive there easily enough in early April. I left Thursday afternoon and spent the night near Cincinnati. Friday I did Kentucky and Tennessee and down Georgia into Atlanta. It was a completely uneventful trip, even though Elizabeth was sure it'd be a disaster. I went to the Omni International, where she was supposed to have checked in earlier, after flying down from Toronto." I took a healthy pull at my rye and water. "Only she wasn't there. The only thing waiting for me was a message to phone her father. When I called him he told me Elizabeth was dead, and that I should come back right away. He offered to send his company plane for me. Naturally I refused."

Alison let out an understanding snort. "I don't blame you. I probably wouldn't fly again either if someone I loved was killed in a plane crash."

I took a few moments before I said, "You don't understand. She wasn't killed in a plane crash. It was a car crash. She was in a limo on her way to the airport when two drunks crashed into her. She died instantly, they tell me. I'm supposed to take comfort in that."

Alison was silent, unsure of what to say. I felt much the same way, but it was my story so I plowed ahead. "You wouldn't believe how many people tried to use her death as proof that flying is safer than driving."

"It is, isn't it? Statistically, I mean."

"Yes. But Elizabeth's death didn't show me I was wrong, it showed me I was right."

Alison considered that for a moment before literally throwing up her hands, saying, "I don't, uh . . ."

"Elizabeth said driving was dangerous. As it turned out, she was right. For her it was. Something in me knows that flying is dangerous for me. In light of what happened to her, I'm going to honor my fear by letting it have its way. So I don't fly."

"Hmm," Alison said. She wasn't convinced. But, then, neither was I. For the time being I could live with it, though.

We sat silently, reviewing our own thoughts. She was sitting opposite me in front of a window, her shoeless feet resting on the table between us. With the hand that wasn't holding her drink Alison yanked at the barrettes that were holding her brunette hair in a modified widow's bun. It fell out and she shook it down until it brushed against her shoulders. Something turned over deep inside me like a long unused motor.

From straight on her face was pretty, but when she turned to look out the window onto the city lights the profile she presented me with knocked the wind out of my soul. Generally, I do not notice things like eye color right away, so if I'd have been asked to describe her eyes at that moment I'd have said something like "soft, and mysterious." I found out later they were blue, but still soft and mysterious. When she blinked she seemed to do it in slow motion, so I enjoyed watching her eyelashes go up and down several times. The other thing I watched closely was her tongue. It darted out to lick at the remainder of her lipstick as she concentrated on what was outside the window of her room.

I tried to look out the window myself, but Alison Denby had my attention on a short tether. So I was looking at her when she—obviously forgetting my existence for a moment—reached inside the jacket of her tailored suit and scratched casually at the bottom of her left breast.

My self-conscious shift must have tipped her, because her attention snapped back to me at just that moment. She sat up straight and looked reflexively down to make sure her skirt hadn't pulled itself up around her waist while she hadn't been watching. When she was composed she said, "Earlier tonight, were you fighting over anything worthwhile, like a lady's honor?" Her delivery was pure Noel Coward.

I preferred Mickey Spillane. "Nah."

"Are you being insulting or coy?"

"I'm being careless. I promised I wouldn't say a word about it and here I am hinting at it with the first person I talk to. It's a habit of a reporter. You get hooked on telling everyone else the news."

"You're a reporter?" she said in her on-the-rocks voice, sharp and cool. "On the phone you said you weren't."

I tried not to look like I'd been caught in a lie. "I used to be a full-time newspaper reporter. Now I do some free-lance automotive writing for a city magazine. Mostly these days I try to do what I like to do. My wanting to see you had nothing to do with my being a journalist. I'm here as a friend of Sean's and, I hope, of yours."

For a minute Alison weighed the conviction in my voice against the fact that I had lied to her. She was good at keeping her emotions to herself, so I didn't know how I'd made out until she spoke. "Being the bearer of bad tidings is a perversely pleasant experience, isn't it?" It was turning out better than I could have hoped—it sounded like we had some job experiences in common. "For a couple of years I read the news on TV out West. A local show. I'd be reading the details of some disaster that horrified thousands of people and I felt proud of myself, and a little thrilled, for doing it. Perverse. It did strange things to my ego, like I was more a part of what was happening, and therefore more important. Very perverse. It was one of the reasons I quit. It bothered me that I felt that way, but I missed it when I quit." She sounded a little ashamed of herself for the feeling.

"I've felt the same," I said. "You should be glad that at least you realized what was going on. Think about all those talking hairdos that never had a conscious thought about that."

"Or anything else."

Terrific. We had lots of things in common. I considered asking her what she thought about Chuck Blyth, decided against it and poured myself more rye and water. Two more sips and I could put a serious question to Alison Denby. For insurance I kept up my end of the comfortable silence through four quick sips. Suitably prepared, I asked my question. "Tell me to mind my own business if you want," I began, then laughed. "I'm sure you don't need my permission to do that." She laughed too and shook her head. "Anyway, why did you and Sean break up?" I tried to sound frustratedly curious, like I couldn't figure out for the life of me why two nice people like them would break up.

Alison was silent for a time, before leading me down a path whose direction I could not at first make out. "When you were young, what kind of women did you go for?"

I knew the answer but had never given it voice before. When I heard myself say "Girls with big breasts, or big reputations, or both" I knew why. I sought the protection of the herd: "Like most guys, I guess."

"That's before you knew any better, is that it?" She waited for my nod before continuing. "When I was young, what kind of guys do you think I went for?"

A general direction to the conversation was becoming discernible. "The same kind."

"In my own way. Big bulges in pants and big reputations as athletes. Just like you guys, a lot of girls picked the most obvious things we could to focus on. And, like you guys, most of us got over it because we came to know better—or we ran out of guys with big bulges and big reputations. I wasn't as quick or as lucky as most other women—I never came to know any better or run out of guys like that."

"Meaning Sean, and what's-his-name the hockey player?"

"Meaning Sean and what's-his-name the hockey player. The thing we women do not learn until it's too late is that these guys are usually great to take to the beach but not to take home."

"Aren't you being unfair to some of them?" For some reason I felt the need to defend my gender.

"Not in my experience, and I've made an unofficial study of it from talks with other women, and I've met more than a few. Generally speaking, guys with bulges and athletic reputations do not cut it as mates."

"Sex and fame aren't everything, huh?"

"As a matter of fact, sex rarely enters into it." She stopped but I must have looked confused because I definitely was. "What I mean is sex is just another thing they don't bring very much of to a relationship. Sean included. And Derek Lewis, the hockey player. And a bunch of guys I could name but won't."

I felt strange knowing this about Sean. I shifted in my chair.

Alison picked up on my discomfort. "Don't feel bad, Sean was a very nice man in many ways." She leaned forward and lowered her voice to a more serious level. "I haven't told anyone else this because it used to be our business, Sean's and mine. Now that he's gone it's just mine. And you asked. The scotch made me tell about what's-his-name."

"Derek."

"Yeah, Derek. Just forget about that."

"I forgot already." I took a drink to wash the information away. "Was Sean seeing other women?" It was an assumption based on what she'd told me about Sean's attitude toward women and sex.

"Near as I could tell, no. 'Course, unless you're there in the room with them you never can be totally sure. But I'm pretty sure, for reasons I won't go into. No, Sean and I broke up because I started seeing other guys."

I nodded slowly. So much for my assumptions.

Alison responded by making a faulty assumption herself. "You're not one of those guys who think women have a lesser need for sex than men?" The way she said it I wouldn't have admitted it even if it were true, so I shook my head, obviously contemptuous of such an idea. "Good, because it's not true, especially in my case. I needed sex and I couldn't get it from Sean. I started to have affairs."

I was finding out lots of things I didn't want to know.

"Being unfaithful bothered the hell out of me," Alison said. "It's like someone on a diet eating banana splits; I hated myself but couldn't stop."

Her choice of imagery stirred mixed emotions in me. "Sean found out?" I asked to get my mind off my feelings.

"You're missing the point. I ended the marriage because of what was missing in it and because I couldn't stand the lying any more. It wasn't Sean's reactions to my affairs, it was my reactions." She lost herself in reverie for a moment before adding, "Maybe if he'd fooled around it would have been easier for me." She didn't sound like she believed that.

"Sean was never unfaithful to you?"

"I can't say for sure, but there were times when it was offered to him on a platter and he passed, even though I'd never have found out."

"There may have been times you don't know about, or he may have been that rarest of persons, the natural monogamist."

A knock at the door interrupted her laugh. It was the bellboy with my jacket. When he was gone I stood at the door holding the jacket. Its return had forced the issue. I waited for Alison to give me a sign.

She did better than that. She came over to where I was standing by the door, hung the Do Not Disturb sign on the outside handle, and put on the safety lock. I grabbed her the way a drowning man latches onto a safety line, and for the next two hours she pulled me to shore.

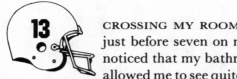**13** CROSSING MY ROOM THE NEXT MORNING just before seven on my way to some sleep I noticed that my bathroom light was on. That allowed me to see quite clearly a piece of paper folded over and perched on the toilet seat like a little tent. It gave me quite a start, as totally unexpected things always do. always do.

Feeling foolishly uneasy, I went into the washroom and picked the paper up.

I don't know what I was expecting, but I was greatly relieved to see that it was a note from my housekeeper. The only part that was written was the scribble that she claimed said "Melinda Holt." The rest of the note was typed, as all her notes had been since I'd innocently asked her to write more carefully. The note said: "Mr. Cane, Mr. Norris Harlan phoned six times last night, at (approx.) 7:25, 8:30, 9:15, 10:00, 10:45 and 11:15. He only stopped calling because I told him I was going to bed and planned to turn off the phone—which was a lie, I wouldn't do that. He made me promise to leave you a note you couldn't miss saying that you were to call him, NO MATTER WHAT TIME YOU GOT HOME, at 463-2658."

I dropped onto the closed toilet seat to consider whether I should call him now, and whether the capital letters were to express his insistence or my housekeeper's disapproval of my hours. Probably both. I reached for the phone on the wall next to the toilet. When he'd lived there, my father-in-law had had phones installed everywhere, on the theory that any time was a good time to talk business and make money. I wondered what business deals he'd made from that particular chair, and what the people on the other end of the line would have thought if they'd known where he was. With two digits of Harlan's number still to push I hung the phone up and went to use the one on my desk. Crossing the room I swore to myself that one day I'd change the things in the house I didn't like. That day would come when I stopped considering it Wilfred Teller's house.

Using the phone on the night table next to my pillow I put the call through. "Norris, it's Richard Cane. What can I do for you?"

Call me any day at 6:55 A.M. and you'd know you'd woken me up. Norris Harlan's one of those types that's instantly cognizant when roused—or else I hadn't woken him. Either way seemed unnatural. "Richard, I'm glad you called, but I can't talk to you about it right now. Can we meet somewhere soon?"

"We can meet, but I've got to get some sleep first. I've been up most of the night."

It was a poor choice of words, because Harlan laughed heartily before replying, "I bet you've been up most of the night," raising his voice on "up." Sometimes I hate male camaraderie. "I'll call you from the office at ten." Not a question, an order. I nodded into the phone and hung up.

I would have been willing to bet that ninety-eight percent of the clocks in my time zone were registering ten A.M. exactly when the first ring sounded. I grabbed the receiver and mumbled "Yes, Norris?"

"You heard something about my wife yesterday, and I want you to know it's absolutely off the record."

I thought I knew what he was talking about, but it couldn't hurt to hear him say it himself. "What do you mean?"

"You know what I mean. I mean about my wife and Sean Denby."

"What about your wife and Sean?"

"Richard, you're not very good at sounding innocent."

"You're right. You're telling me your wife was not having an affair with Sean Denby."

Harlan made a noise that was half anger and half disgust. "No, if you'd listen you'd know that's not what I'm telling you. They were having an affair. I just want you to know you can't use it."

I was confused. Without autographed and notarized pic-

tures of the two of them in bed, and maybe witnessed con-
fessions, no sane newspaper in Canada would even consider
using the information. Probably they wouldn't use it even
if they had undeniable proof, since it would have been an
outrageous case of unwarranted first-stone-casting. Norris
Harlan must have known that, but I put his lapse down to
overexcitement. When certain men are being fitted for
cuckold's horns they tend to act a little funny. "Norris, I
wouldn't think of writing that, even if I could prove it was
true. What your wife and Sean did in their private lives—
and I'm not saying they did anything, together or alone, or
you know what I mean—is nobody's business but theirs.
And yours, of course."

"Smart attitude. I'm glad you feel that way," Harlan said.
As he had been in his office the day before, Harlan was
pleased with himself for making a mentally suspect listener
understand something important.

That bothered me, so I said unnecessarily, "The only dif-
ference would be if it were somehow to turn up as an important aspect of Sean's murder. But if the cops haven't made
much of it yet I guess they're not going to."

Harlan did not sound worried by the idea. "Goddam right
they're not going to," he promised. "Just don't forget what I
told you," he said before hanging up.

I looked at the receiver in my hand, presumably hoping
that I'd see something in it that would help me better understand Harlan's call. There was nothing of signifance to be
seen, so I pushed the button on the phone that said "intercom"
and dialed the kitchen number. Melinda answered in about
half a ring and repeated my order for breakfast in a cool voice.
"In ten minutes?" I said. After I'd hung up I realized I was
feeling grateful because she'd agreed to do what I paid her
very well for doing. I needed to work on having money.

I wanted to make one more call before I had a shower and
breakfast.

Inspector Ian Hurst was back at his office, or still there.

He sounded like he hadn't been away, and never expected to be.

"A couple of things, Inspector. First, I forgot to tell you last night that Eric VanKaspal has a new car, an expensive new car."

There was a pause, then, "How is this important?" He said it in a voice that made me doubt my own feelings.

"Well, it may not be, but don't you think it's interesting that he buys something he couldn't afford, just a couple of days before, the big obstacle to his making more money is bumped off?"

"Bumped off?" I thought Hurst might laugh at that. Instead, he said in a resigned voice, "That assumes premeditation on a grand scale. Still, you may be on to something. What have you got?"

I read him the license number, the mileage, and the dealer's name from my notebook. He grunted as, I presume, he wrote all this down.

"What else?"

"Norris Harlan just called to tell me I better not use that information about his wife having an affair with Sean Denby."

Hurst was genuinely taken aback. "He knows you knew that?"

"He knew last night. His first call to me came at about seven thirty. I take it you didn't tell him, or anyone else." I tried to make it not sound like an insult in any way.

Apparently, I didn't succeed, because he was hot when he said, "I sure as hell did not tell anyone else."

"And I didn't tell anyone, so that leaves . . ."

"Varina." There was palpable anger in his voice when he said that. I thought about his warning that my ass would be a star if I crossed him. It's significance was taking on weight. "Is that all?" he demanded in a voice that was like a laxative for my conscience.

I fought it off, and lied by saying, "That's all." I promised to call him if I turned up anything else and he put the phone down in the middle of my good-bye. Called upon to list the people I wouldn't want to be at that moment, I would have put Sergeant Harry Varina's name near the top.

I ducked into the shower, put on a robe, and wolfed down the breakfast Melinda had prepared. Before I dressed, I called the public relations lady at Volkswagen and was reassured that the Golf GTI was indeed waiting for me at their Scarborough office. When I'd returned the rental car I caught a subway out toward the burbs. From there it was a short cab ride to Volkswagen, where the Golf was waiting, as promised. Twenty minutes later, just after noon, I was parking near the *Globe and Mail* building about a mile west of Yonge Street on Front.

Inside, for a modest fee I arranged to have the full and impressive resources of "Canada's National Newspaper" turned over to me on a computer terminal. Specifically those resources concerning Leslie Harlan (née Watson), wife of Norris Harlan. Most of what I had to wade through involved her businessman husband, but after forty-five minutes or so I had a fair amount of information about her, though none of it looked promising. She was an unenthusiastic society wife; all her offices in the organizations she belonged to were secondary ones. Her best claim to humanity was a series of regular afternoon appearances in a nearby hospital. There was a picture of her and another volunteer, Lucille Braverman, playing some silly game with the healthiest-looking hospital patients I'd ever seen.

I made a note of a few things, paid for the information and drove to the hospital, where the information lady offhandedly directed me to the office of the volunteer coordinator, who was still out to lunch at 1:15. A young Eurasian nurse told me there was no special staff cafeteria, only the general cafeteria a floor above where we were talking. It was about half full, split evenly between workers looking weary and visitors looking wary.

I have difficulty telling who's what in a hospital on the

medical side, but I think I know a volunteer when I see one. It helps when they wear smocks that say "Volunteer" over their name tags. At the far side of the cafeteria four of them were picking their way carefully across their luncheon trays.

"Excuse me, ladies, could you tell me if Leslie Harlan is on duty today?" Four pleasant middle-aged faces turned curious.

"Leslie Hammond? Is he a doctor?" one asked.

"No, Leslie Harlan. She's a volunteer, like you ladies."

That was greeted by much exchanging of puzzled looks, which grew more suspicious by the second.

A second volunteer offered, "I don't think so."

"Leslie Harlan?" a third said, savoring the name like a mouthful of wine. "Leslie Harlan?" She lifted the glasses that were dangling from a chain around her neck, put them on her nose, and looked me right in the eye. "The woman who was in the paper a few months ago? The rich volunteer lady?" Her tone was even more unflattering than her bejeweled bifocals. "You remember, girls, the one in the picture with Lucy."

"Her." "Sure, her." "Yes, I remember." "Leslie Harlan." There was something unflattering in the way they all spoke.

"No," the woman in the bifocals said, "she won't be here today."

"Or tomorrow," another said, laughing.

"Or the day after . . ."

"Or the day after . . ." another said.

They all joined in their not nice little roundelay until it collapsed under the weight of their collective hilarity.

"Is Lucy Braverman here, then?" I asked, confused by their bile.

Still laughing a little, the woman with the bifocals pointed out a woman about four tables away smoking a cigarette.

I thanked them and walked to where Lucille Braverman sat watching my approach with interest. I couldn't tell her age, but she struck me as someone who didn't have long to live no matter how old she was.

"Mrs. Braverman, my name's Richard Cane. May I talk to you for a minute about Leslie Harlan?"

"I was just going back for more coffee." Her voice was as lifeless as the skin on her face. The newspaper photo had more than done her justice.

"I'll be glad to get it," I said. "I could use some myself."

"All right, then, thanks." It was her first display of interest.

She was lighting up another cigarette when I returned, so I put the coffee in front of her and sat down in the chair away from the smoke's general drift. She caught this and moved the cigarette away from me.

"Thank you," I said.

She surprise me by opening up; I'd figured I was in for some teeth-pulling with her. "I learned to do that when my husband started to die. Lung cancer. Cigarettes killed him but he couldn't stay away from them at all. We kept them away from him, but then I figured—what the hell?—how many times can you die from something? Dead's dead. The last thing I heard him say that made any sense was ask for a smoke. If he knew what he was saying I bet he loved that. He was a big fan of irony. Loved irony. If something was really good, really ironic like, he'd get excited and call if 'delicious.'" She watched the smoke curl up from her cigarette.

"Leslie Harlan. Now that's some irony Leslie—that was my husband's name, too—would have liked. Your ever see *Bye Bye Braverman*, that comedy movie about some Jewish intellectuals who try to find a friend's funeral? Remember, the dead guy's name was Leslie Braverman. Like my husband's. My Leslie and I watched that on TV just before he died. Irony. Always with the irony. He would have liked the irony of your Leslie."

I had no idea what she was talking about, but I was afraid to ask in case I sent her reeling off on some bizarre tangent.

She didn't need any help for that to happen, however. "I started coming here four years ago July when they brought my husband here. At first I only came during visiting hours. But Leslie was so unhappy when I left I started staying later and later, and coming back sooner and sooner. Next thing I knew I was practically living here. The nurses didn't mind, they were happy 'cause with me here looking after Leslie there was less for them to do. And Leslie was a difficult man, you know?"

I nodded and sipped my coffee. There was a point to this somewhere that she was getting to in her own way. So I nodded and sipped.

"It was sort of tough, especially near the end when the drugs they were giving him for the pain . . ." she butted out her half-finished smoke ". . . made him sometimes not know who anyone was, or care. When he was like that, or unconscious, I took to wandering the hospital. You know, there are a lot of people here who never get any visitors." She seemed surprised and offended by this still. They way she said it, it offended me as well. "So I started visiting them when Leslie was, uh, you know, asleep. Then he died. Leslie." She drank some coffee and lit another cigarette.

My coffee tasted like it was made from what you'd scrap off a statue the pigeons were fond of, but I nodded and sipped, nodded and sipped.

"The day after the funeral, I went out for a walk," Lucille Braverman continued. "I live out in the West End, about six or seven miles from here. I was just walking. It was a nice day, like today. Same time of year. Leslie died October sixth. What's this, is it October yet? Yeah? Anyway, I just started walking, and before I knew it I was back here. I went up to Leslie's old room, up on Holly Six. There was another guy in there dying. He was alone, so I went in and started visiting." She smiled for the first time, and I could tell her husband's taste for irony had rubbed off on her. "One of Leslie's nurses came in. She was busy, I guess, sure as hell was distracted. She saw me and said, 'Hello, Mrs. Braverman.' Then to the poor bastard dying in the bed she says, 'How are you feeling, Mr. Braverman?'" She laughed at the memory. I joined in with a smile. "I think his name was Wolfgang Schmidt, or something like that. He was real SS material and that threw him, being called by a Jewish name. Imagine dying under someone else's name." All hint of laughter faded.

She lit another cigarette, even though she already had one going. When she saw what she'd done she butted the old one out. "The SS officer wasn't really a bad guy. I saw more of him than his wife and family during his final time. Lotta people are afraid to be near someone who's dying. And I think his family was sort of glad to see him go. You know what I mean? Still, his wife started to look at me funny when she'd show up and I'd be there. Maybe she figured he was being unfaithful to her one last time. Who knows. So I signed up, became a volunteer. Been doing it ever since. It's all I do now. I have no family and I don't need to make money. Notice how I didn't say I didn't need to work? Whatever else it is, the Death Patrol is work. That's what I do, I specialize in people that are dying. No one's ever said that to me, of course, but they're glad I do it, because if I didn't they might have to. I don't mind it. I figure you're alone when you're dead. So no one should be alone when they're dying." She looked over to watch her four fellow volunteers get up from the table. "When I go, I hope I go quick, so's I don't have time to be lonely."

I stayed silent, sensing we were almost where she was going.

"I think I'd seen Leslie Harlan maybe twice in the four years I've been here when Madge, the volunteer coordinator, arrives one day with her, a lady reporter, a photographer, and Mrs. Harlan's PR man, if you can believe it. And I mean four years, not four years of Tuesday and Thursday afternoons or when I couldn't find a fourth for bridge. I mean four years of mostly seven long days a week." There was no bitterness in her voice; she was just giving her bona fides. If anything she was just puzzled, maybe because she couldn't see the irony in all this, and wondering why her husband was around to point it out to her. "Madge is a good woman and she knows what's what. A picture and a write-up in the paper might do the hospital some good, so she was going along. If they were mostly interested in some society type, that was okay with her, but she was going to get one of us real volunteers in. We posed for pictures in three or four places, and the way they were treating Mrs. Harlan I felt like I was taking part in a royal visit. The PR guy was all over, making her look good. He was a little suspicious, because she didn't have any idea of what was going on. I even had to show her where the ladies' was—quietly, so he didn't hear. She was nice enough, and embarrassed because it was such a crock."

"And the irony your husband Leslie would have liked was that the amount of time Mrs. Harlan spent here was not mentioned in the story. And that she got publicity for something she wasn't really doing."

She smiled at me warmly for having actually paid attention to her, glad I hadn't just been humoring her as she'd rambled. Seven months ago I would have humored her at best. Most likely I'd have cut her cold. Losing Elizabeth had apparently mellowed me out some.

"Right," she said. "I know flower delivery guys who've spent more time here in the last month than Mrs. Harlan has in the last four years."

Pretending to be a hospital volunteer as a cover for an affair. Full marks for originality, if not morality.

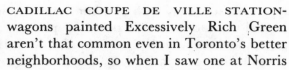

**14** CADILLAC COUPE DE VILLE STATION-wagons painted Excessively Rich Green aren't that common even in Toronto's better neighborhoods, so when I saw one at Norris and Leslie Harlan's back door I knew Simply Devine was making a delivery.

I have to take some responsibility for the car, since it was a comment of mine that prompted Elizabeth to have the customizing job done. The *Star* had seconded me to one of its soft sections and the editor there had sent me out to do a puff piece on a new store for rich women who were too busy getting their thighs waxed to shop for themselves. You can maybe tell my attitude to the story going in. The deal was Elizabeth and her people took on clients. Color and fashion consultants reviewed the woman's existing wardrobe, home decor, personality and husband's bank balance. Then the Simply Devine people shopped for the woman, picked out expensive clothes, tacked on a huge markup, and sent them to the customer. What they kept they were billed for, what they didn't want was returned. I listened to Elizabeth explain this to a gaggle of reporters and suggested sarcastically that maybe she should get a Cadillac delivery truck. Elizabeth said that was a wonderful idea. I shut my mouth. Silly questions were given witty answers for about twenty minutes and then she invited us to join her for a drink. I hung in to see if anyone asked the one question I wanted answered. No one did, so I cornered Elizabeth and asked her why she'd spelled Devine the way she had. She loosed a smile and a laugh on me whose memory makes me giddy to this day. It was all I could do to look when she pointed at a sketch on the wall I hadn't noticed before. I recognized him right away. Without giving myself away to the other reporters, I turned to Elizabeth and said in my best Andy Devine wheeze, "Hey, Wild Bill, wait for me."

Elizabeth laughed delightedly. "Not only are you the first person to ask about the spelling," she said, "but you're also the first person I haven't had to explain the reference to."

"I ate Sugar Pops for years because Wild Bill Hickok and his sidekick Jingles told me I should. Is Jingles your father, or what?" The smile faded and I regretted my smart mouth—not for the first time, but to a degree hitherto unknown.

"When I was starting the place up and ordered some letterhead over the phone, it came back 'Simply Devine.'"

"Must have been from Illiterate Brothers Printing."

"You know the firm?" Her smile was coming back.

"Sure. Some of the family work as editors at the *Star*."

The smile was back.

I looked away and swallowed the remainder of my drink. It was not like me to go to such lengths to make women smile.

"I kept the letterhead and the name, just for fun."

"Only no one noticed."

"Until now." She said it reflectively, as if she was having trouble believing it had been someone like me who'd picked up on it first.

Other media types came along at this point and I did not get a chance to say anything but "Thanks" and "Good-bye" before returning to the *Star*. When I read the story through I blushed at my own breathless praise of the place, and tried to laugh it off as a sop to the section editor. The day before it ran, Elizabeth called to ask me not to mention about the spelling of 'Devine.' I said I hadn't and she sounded pleased. She asked me to the official opening in a couple of days. Unwilling to be the designated hoi polloi, I demurred at first, but she convinced me with embarrassingly little effort. I went and surprised myself by asking her out. Two weeks later we were an item. Three months after that I was blushing through an interview with a reporter from the society section charged with writing our engagement notice. "Made for each other," Elizabeth would say whenever someone hinted at our disparate backgrounds.

I sat at the end of the Harlans' driveway thinking about all that and more as I looked at the rear of Simply Devine's customized delivery truck. It occurred to me that I had not given a moment's thought to the store's operation since Elizabeth's death. Not that it needed my help—on the contrary. And it wasn't even a source of income or loss for me. Elizabeth had set it up as a fund-raising method for a home for battered women. Helping those women and making a success of something on her own were the rewards she got out of starting the place. This she kept quiet even more religiously than the story of the store's name.

I now had titular ownership but no control beyond a voice on the board of directors I'd never raised. The idea of that felt uncomfortable, and I vaguely promised myself to do something about it someday soon.

First things first. I edged the Volkswagen Golf farther up the Harlans' alley and parked it beside the mammothly ugly Cadillac. There were no markings on the car except for the nameplates its manufacturer probably wished it could remove.

At the back of the Caddy I looked in the tinted window and saw a pile of boxes you could trade for a new mid-sized family car. It pleased me that the money would go to help battered women and not into someone's pocket, especially mine. It's pleasant to be rich, but there are limits.

"Quite a haul, huh?"

A friendly and familiar face was beaming down on me from the top of the Harlans' back stairs. Under the face was a traditional chauffeur's outfit, which reinforced the customers' image of themselves. There were departures from the traditional, however—the outfit was as Excessively Rich Green as the car and it had been designed to fit the woman who was now wearing it.

Woman and uniform came clomping down the steps toward me.

I made a mock face of distaste at the noise her boots made. "Do you still get your boots made at that kinky leather shop on Yonge Street?"

"Yes," the woman said as she put her elbow on the roof of the Caddy. "Do you still get your underwear there?"

I laughed and reached out my arms toward her. She came

104

into them and gave me a hug full of sadness. "Where the hell have you been?" she demanded. "How the hell have you been?" When she'd let go of me and stepped back to look me over I answered her questions with a shrug and a "you know" face. It was all I could get out. I put my hands in my pockets.

"What happened to Elizabeth was shitty."

"I can't argue with that," I said. "She'd be glad to see that rich women are still paying good bucks to be overdressed."

"Some things never change," the woman said with an edge in her voice. Gardenia Leggatt—Dena to everyone—had never been a big fan of people with money. Early on in life she had removed insignificant amounts of it from random people by rudimentary means. She went to jail for her trouble. When she got out she ended up with some jerk who beat her, almost for sport. Prime to resume her robbery career again, Dena crossed Elizabeth's path. Elizabeth never said how they met, but I've got the idea she was a target of Dena's. Following her own fashion, Elizabeth offered Dena a job delivering for Simply Devine and working in the house for battered women. Dena had become a pillar of both places. The delivery job especially pleased her because it made her feel instrumental in separating the rich from a lot of their money in a good cause. It says a lot about the shortsighted sensibilities of the customers that Dena Leggatt's blanket contempt for the wealthy was never noticed. The only exception she made was for Elizabeth, who was, in Dena's words, "Rich in class. The money just makes it easy for her to operate."

I got out of Dena's way as she opened the Caddy's trunk. "I'm glad you still like taking money from the rich and giving it to the poor," I said. I'd kidded her before about her Robin Hood Complex.

She looked at me over the stack of green boxes she had in her arms. There was a glint in her eye when she said, "I really like getting new ones on the line, ones whose husbands make a lot of noise about being rich."

"Leslie Harlan hasn't done business with Simply Devine before?"

Dena gave a definitive head shake that made a brown curl fall out from under her hat and bounce and swing madly on her forehead. She had made virtually every delivery for Simply Devine so was in a position to know. She looked to the door before saying conspiratorially, "The way this babe's been acting, I don't think she's been doing business with anybody."

I looked up at the large mansion. "How's that?"

"It's Christmas in October for her today."

"The women you deliver to usually don't get too excited?"

"The women I deliver to never get too excited," Dena said.

"A lifetime of getting whatever you want will do that to you."

Dena snorted her agreement and was about to say something when Leslie Harlan used an unsure voice to ask if there was anything wrong.

"No, ma'am, no problem," Dena said and started up the stairs.

"Good, I'm in a hurry and . . . I know you, but forgive me, I can't think of your name," Leslie Harlan said. The last bit was directed at me.

With a straight face Dena Leggatt said, "No, ma'am, I don't think you do. I certainly don't remember meeting you." The delivery was pure ingenuousness. "Dena Leggatt," she said with a vague nod of greeting as she went past Leslie Harlan into the house. Leslie watched her back for a moment before turning to face me. The wind blew her straw-blond hair across her pale skin. She had on jeans and a Toronto Metros T-shirt that were both too tight—but not for my liking. Sean had a name for women with figures like Leslie's—Schlitz, because they were full-bodied.

"You have met me, Leslie, I'm Richard Cane. We've met at various functions." I wasn't sure "functions" was the right password for her, but she smiled in faked recall anyway. To make it easier for both of us I added, "You might remember me as the guy who married Elizabeth Teller." True recognition dawned.

"Hello . . . Richard. How are you? How's Elizabeth?"

It was a mental slip, of course, nothing more; I couldn't

believe she didn't know about Elizabeth, or had really forgotten. She picked up the error in a flash and closed her eyes while she blushed rather winsomely. She lifted her hand to her cheek.

"Don't worry about it," I said, "I wish I could forget for a moment."

She seemed genuinely sorry for her comment, but before I could press my advantage Dena came hustling back out. "One more load," she said.

I waited for her to get to the back of the Caddy before saying, "I know you're in a hurry, Leslie. Are you going to Sean Denby's memorial service today?" It was a good bet she was.

"Why yes. Are you?" She didn't seem sure if that was the right question, so she posed it hesitantly.

I had noticed no cars around except for Simply Devine's Caddy and my borrowed Volkswagen Golf GTI. "Yes, I am. Can I give you a ride?"

"I was going to take a cab. But I'm not dressed yet."

"I was just on my way home to change. I only live a couple of blocks away, so I can be back before you know it. How much time do you need?" I'd learned long ago that if there was something you didn't want someone to say no to, you presumed a yes and bullied the conversation along. She looked a little swept away. Good salespeople are familiar with this look.

"Uh, I have to unpack these things," she said as Dena walked by with the last load of green boxes, "and get dressed." She was starting to sound suspicious. It was time to get moving.

"Tell you what," I said, sounding resignedly cheerful over the dressing habits of women, "I'll come back at three thirty and wait out front till you're ready." I headed down the stairs as I spoke, to forestall discussion. I threw a casual "See you later" over my shoulder and got into the Golf.

"Later" turned out to be 3:23 when I backed into Leslie Harlan's driveway. I rolled down the window and rested an arm on the sill. I sat facing ahead, apparently unmindful of the house if seen from inside. However, I had a clear view of the house's face in the passenger side mirror I'd worked into place with the remote control.

The view was not great in the mirror, but I did manage to make out someone move a curtain in a second-floor window a few minutes after I got there. For a few seconds the figure looked down on me, probably wondering what to do. When it disappeared I readjusted the mirror to its original position and stared straight ahead. At the sound of the front door I sprang out of the Golf and went to open the passenger door.

For all the personal contact I got I could have been a cabbie. Leslie Harlan looked straight ahead as she took businesslike strides that made her large breasts move very slightly behind the protection of her navy blue wool suit. Her full blond hair was tucked up in a wide-brimmed maroon hat, which meant her long pale neck was completely exposed except for a simple gold necklace. She put one hand on the hat and ducked her head to lower herself into the low-riding two-seater. The Golf's not designed to allow for graceful entrances or exits, but Leslie did a decent job of it nonetheless—except for one moment when the skirt yawned open to expose an eye-filling stretch of fine white thigh covered by dark nylon. It was firmly closed at the first chance.

I walked behind the car thinking about the long list of fine-looking women I had known Sean Denby to be involved with. Sadly, Leslie Harlan's name would be the last on the list. Out loud I said to myself, "Last, but certainly not least."

"That suit suits you Leslie," I said as we rolled onto the street. "Simply Devine has very nice things."

She jumped at the chance to get answers to some of her questions. "Is that what you were doing at my back door this afternoon? Do you work—are you involved with Simply Devine?" All things considered, it wasn't a bad guess, and she'd worked up an understandable amount of suspicion in the hour since we'd talked at her back door.

"I used to own it with Elizabeth," I said, leaving the present state of its ownership vague, to mirror my feelings about it. "It was just coincidence we arrived at the same time. I

108

went around the back to say hello to Dena, the driver." I concentrated on getting into the heavy traffic going north up Mount Pleasant Avenue. When I'd made the turn safely I added casually, "Actually, I dropped by to talk to you about Sean Denby."

Leslie gave me a quick look to see what clues my face was offering before responding just as casually, "Sean Denby? What about him?"

We only had about two miles to travel to the service, so I didn't have much time for word-mincing. At a red light I turned to Leslie and said, "I know about your affair with Sean, but you don't have to worry about me writing about it."

"Writing about it?"

"I may be doing a story about Sean for *Toronto, Toronto.*"

"You write for a magazine? I thought you had money from Elizabeth."

Incredibly, considering the topic of the conversation, it was I who was irritated and on the defensive. Leslie Harlan seemed mostly confused.

"I like to work," I said by way of keeping the record straight. "But as I say, you won't have to worry about my writing anything about, you know, your affair with Sean Denby."

"That's good, Richard, I'm glad you won't be writing anything about my affair with Sean Denby." The way she said that made the hairs stand up on the back of my curiosity. It was like she was parroting the name at first hearing, or like she was relieved it was her affair with Sean I wasn't going to mention, rather than her affair with someone else. I was confused into silence as we drove further up Mount Pleasant. She didn't care that I knew about her and Sean. At least she didn't sound like she cared.

She heightened my confusion by asking forthrightly, "Would you like to hear some details of my affair with Sean Denby?" "Sean Denby," she kept saying, like she wanted to identify which Sean we were talking about.

"If you like."

She seemed neither to like nor to dislike, she just did.

"We've been seeing each other for a couple of years, at a house in the West End."

"The one you rented in your maiden name on Duke Street."

She was disconcerted that I had some details. "How did you find out about that?"

"The cops told me. I'm sort of working on this with them."

The way she said "You are, eh?" confirmed my fear that my remark had indeed been pompous, and she had me feeling defensive again. She went on, "You must know, then, that they were entirely satisfied with my ali . . . with my account of my movements the night of the crime." Television has a lot to answer for, including much of the jargon it's infested society with.

There was a note of petulance I wanted to beat out of Leslie's voice. I thought I had just the weapon. "I hope you didn't tell them you were working a double shift as a hospital volunteer."

A sharp intake of breath told me I'd drawn blood. "What do you mean?"

I made the turn into the crescent-shaped driveway of the church where the memorial service was being held. A functionary was directing cars that had disgorged their passengers. "I'll let you off here and go and park the car," I said, as we pulled to a stop. A young man in a dark suit opened the passenger door for Leslie but she just reached over and pulled it shut. The motion caused the navy blue skirt to part again, exposing lots of nice thigh on both legs. This time she either didn't notice or didn't care.

Neither did I. I was more taken with the fact that she was frightened and angry. "How did you find out about me and the hospital?" she said.

"I'll tell you that if you tell me the address of the house you and Sean used to use."

She hesitated, then said, "I'll think about it. But you have to promise to keep this to yourself if I agree." Inspector Hurst's unhappy face flashed in my mind. Keeping it to myself meant not telling him, which would displease him if he

110

found out. "Richard?" Leslie Harlan demanded. There was genuine concern in her voice and in the way her hand held my forearm.

The guy in the suit opened the door again and begged, "Could you move your car, please, sir? There's a line forming behind you."

Leslie ignored him and kept the pressure up. "Okay, I won't tell anyone," I said, my tone making it obvious I wasn't happy about it.

Leslie Harlan smiled her relief and gave my arm a squeeze of thanks. With her left hand she closed the gap in her skirt by gripping both front seams. With the other she opened the car door. I watched her walk in front of the car, striding a lot less resolutely than when she'd approached it. I pulled ahead slowly, keeping an eye on her progress to the church.

Norris Harlan stood at the doors by the end of the canopied walkway. He wasn't talking to anyone, or watching his wife approach him, he was looking at me.

**15** LESLIE HARLAN RESOLUTELY IGNORED ME while we stood in the church's antechamber after the boring memorial service to my dead friend and her dead lover. She stood at her husband's left, a half-pace back, being his consort as he accepted the respects being paid him by almost everyone in the place. The only people who made a point of avoiding that duty were myself, head coach Bob Baird, and Hank Graff. There was no reason for me to pay my respects to

Norris Harlan, since he was not related to Sean Denby and my name was not on any of his payrolls. Baird was on Harlan's payroll, but he was a legendary loner. Graff, I learned from a pleasant blond Georgian halfback, was the Metros' way-over-the-hill offensive tackle. He stood a full pace back on Harlan's right, speaking with no one. Any eye contact was strictly accidental.

Aside from us three oddballs, everyone made a point of symbolically kissing Norris Harlan's ring. There was even something pontifical about the way he greeted people, something in the way he waved his hand and bowed his head. Pope Norris I. It saddened me to see those big, tough young guys making sure he saw them in attendance. If they didn't now have the wherewithal to thumb their noses at him, would they ever? Probably not. And what set him apart? To a man they could whip Norris Harlan in any test of physical prowess you'd care to mention—except carrying a payroll. One by one they filed past where he and Leslie and Hank Graff stood, lacking even the *cojones* to cast a leer at the luscious Leslie. "What's become of today's young people?" I asked a phalanx of backs near me, who responded by shuffling a little further away.

I lapsed into silence and leaned up against the plain white wall of the church's anteroom. Sean's memorial service had renewed the dreadful sense of finality I'd first experienced at my wife's funeral. I closed my eyes and stared at the nothingness that resulted, trying to imagine an eternity of that. Without sense, without warmth, without feeling, without anything. Forever.

I snapped my eyes back open and shook my head. Those kinds of thoughts serve no purpose beyond wasting what little time you've got.

The residue of those thoughts was in my mind when I felt a woman's body press up against mine. I clutched it gratefully but Leslie Harlan went stiff in my arms. I'd badly misjudged her action. She hadn't noticed my angst and tried to comfort me, she'd used the hug as a method of slyly putting her hand in my jacket pocket.

Each surprised by the other's reaction, we both pulled awkwardly back. Leslie looked at me for a moment, not unkindly; I'm sure I saw concern there. It passed quickly when she realized people must be looking. "Eighty-one Duke Street," she said very softly. "You might as well have that."

"Lucille Braverman told me." She nodded and walked away.

People weren't looking at me now, just her, so I headed for the door, putting my mind to wondering what "that" was she'd slipped in my pocket.

Outside, sitting in the Golf, I fished a key out of my pocket. The key to 81 Duke Street, I assumed. Being given the key crystallized some formless thoughts I'd had—I was going into 81 Duke to look around. It seemed like such a good idea, sitting in that church parking lot, that I decided to look around in Sean's house as well. I even had an idea of who could help me get in there.

At a phone booth in a nearby gas station I called the Royal York Hotel and asked for Alison Denby's room. Just before we'd fallen asleep the night before, she told me she was going to skip the public services for Sean and have a private one, something special to them as a couple. It sounded good to me, and I didn't press for details.

Her voice was dreamy when she answered, like she was lying down on that big double bed, stretching. The image of that was so powerful I couldn't respond right away. When she said hello again it was in a much sharper tone.

"Sorry," I said, "the sound of your voice sort of shorted my circuits."

"There's nothing short about your circuits, sailor."

"Give me a break, here, I'm trying to do some business."

"Business, is it? Is that why you left the twenty on the dresser?"

"Yeah, and I'm coming over to pick up the change."

"No change, fella, only extra merchandise."

I couldn't believe the conversation, or its affect on me. See where women's liberation has taken us. Isn't it great? "If I come over there and let you have your way with me," I said, "then can we talk seriously?"

"Sure, but make it snappy. I have to be outa here by seven fifteen, latest."

It was just after five. "That doesn't give us much time," I said.

"It's not my fault if you're slow."

She did say she loved sex.

At 7:20 Alison and I were walking down the hall away from her hotel room. I carried her purse under my arm while she used one hand to hold a small mirror and the other to brush her hair. I had my hands in my trouser pockets, fingering the key in each one.

Outside the elevators I dropped the keys in my pockets and pushed the down button. "You in a rush to get the key back?"

Alison finished brushing her hair. "I never want it back. There's no way I'll ever again use Sean's place when I visit Toronto."

"I can appreciate that," I said as the elevator doors glided open.

We stepped into the elevator and returned the stiff smiles of three couples already aboard. The men were with the ugly-suit convention, and the ladies were tricked out for a most-unnatural-hair-color competition.

Alison took her purse from under my arm and said quietly, "When will I see you again?" She was on her way to one of the hotel's restaurants to meet friends for dinner. I was headed for some discreet snooping.

"You're insatiable," I whispered out of the side of my mouth.

"You should be glad," Alison replied. Our fellow passengers were doing their best not to be seen listening.

The elevator stopped at my floor, one above where Alison and the six other passengers were going. I kissed her and

114

stepped off the elevator. Timing would be critical here, so as soon as the doors started sliding shut, I turned to her and said, "Call me any time you've got the five hundred, Mrs. Reagan." The last thing I saw as the doors closed was Alison's flaming face. I hoped I was not imagining the start of a laugh as well.

The only word to describe the way I crossed the lobby of Canada's most famous hotel is "strut." A very pleasant and successful hour with a sexy, healthy woman will do that to me. Add the high I felt from what I was planning to do that night, and you've got my version of Egos on Parade.

I pushed the Golf a little bit going home, and was taking off my watch as it changed to 7:45. When I came out of the shower I sneaked a few looks at the stuff I'd taken out of my pocket and piled on my desk. Maybe I thought the keys would've disappeared. They hadn't, of course. They just lay there next to some coins, gaining significance by the second.

It's one thing to feel invincible when you're striding through a hotel after an amorous encounter; it's something else when you're standing around in socks and jockey shorts blow-drying your hair.

"The other place first," I said out loud as I looked at the keys, "then Sean's house." I figured 81 Duke would be easier to take than the murder site. I further figured that by the time I got to Sean's house maybe some of the tension I was feeling would have worn off.

To get that off my mind I considered what I should wear, something I rarely do. It was easy not to pay much attention to what I should wear because my wardrobe was evenly divided into three sections: brown stuff, green stuff, and blue stuff. Almost always I took the appropriate number of items from one color choice. When I was daring I picked two items from one color choice and one from another. My fashion-conscious wife used to say I didn't dress, I covered myself up. That night I voted the straight dark blue ticket—jacket, slacks and turtleneck. I didn't worry about my socks matching because all I had were identical black socks lying singly in a drawer. Elizabeth used to go into the drawer behind my back and pair the socks off, just to keep her sense of order from going berserk.

I stood in front of the mirror and examined my dark blue reflection. The affect was melodramatic.

"Maybe you should burn a cork so you can blacken my face," my reflection said to me mockingly.

"No, but maybe gloves."

"A trifle overstated, unless it's a formal break and enter."

I agreed with myself. "You're right, I won't wear the gloves. And it's not a break and enter, just illegal entry. I think."

"Well then, gloves would certainly be overdoing it," my image said with finality.

Attempting repartee with myself is a habit I long ago realized was caused by excessive nerves. Though understandable in the circumstances, they were nonetheless irritating. They stuck with me during the thirty-minute drive west to Duke Street. Along the way I gave them a nice, sharp edge by bawling out any drivers I encountered who raised my ire.

With the Golf at the curb I had a final consultation with my street map, then made a right, a left, and presto, there was Duke Street—four short blocks of houses and a convenience store at its west end.

I cruised Duke slowly, watching for watchers and house numbers. By counting buildings from a well-lit 73 I figured that a dark two-story place set well back from the road was the one I wanted.

At the east end of Duke I made my way along some other quiet streets until I was in front of the house that sat back-to-back with 81 Duke. I walked the route I'd just driven, trying to look like a local walking to the neighborhood store. I bought a magazine there and retraced my steps back to the car. That gave me three good looks at the house I was about to enter. There didn't seem to be anyone in it or watching from the outside.

At the Golf I dropped off the magazine and picked up my

courage. The house behind 81 Duke was dark, so I just walked up its driveway. I took a chance there was nothing waiting to trip me up in the dark and ran across the yard. Using the momentum from the run I put my hands on the top of the five-foot steel mesh fence and vaulted it. It was pretty sturdy, so the distinctive clinking and clashing such fences make when assaulted was slight. When I thudded to the ground in 81 Duke's backyard I took a few minutes to enjoy the quiet that had returned.

I walked quietly up the length of the house to the front. Four long strides across the lawn, one leap up the three cement steps and I was pulling open the storm door. The keyhole on the main door was easy to spot even in the dark, but hard to operate. I worked the key back and forth for a while, feeling exposed, like I was doing it on national television. Finally, the tumblers moved with the quiet of a tank shifting gears.

One easy push and the door swung open into the house, letting me step into the deeper darkness beyond.

 **16** WITH THE DOOR CLOSED BEHIND ME, I looked into the house—for all the good it did me. The darkness of a house with its heavy drapes closed and its lights out can be overwhelming. I'd forgotten that.

My eyes and my heart went about the business of getting used to being in a strange, dark house. The wall of black in front of me was becoming familiar shapes of dark gray. My heart was doing about as well, choosing to hold at about the rate of a sprinter after eighty meters.

Shapes were turning into chairs, tables, a stove, lamps, a fireplace.

Across the hallway in front of me was a kitchen, but I wanted to go into the living room on my left because the fireplace mantelpiece held a strange array of small shapes I couldn't make out. I groped them for a while and discovered that they were soapstone carvings—a bird, a seal, a man with a spear, that kind of thing. The seal had just gone back into place when I noticed a smell I could not pin down. It was familiar, but irritatingly elusive. It wasn't something that had gone bad in the kitchen, and it wasn't something musty. I stood quiet and motionless.

In the house's silence the deep breath I took was surprisingly loud. The smell was surprisingly strong, and my mind ransacked its files to pin it down. The longer I couldn't place it the greater my sense of alarm grew. I didn't like the idea of there being something in that house I couldn't get a handle on, even an odor.

I was just about to give up on it and do . . . something, when it came to me. "Liniment," I said out loud in relief, a perfectly understandable smell in a place frequented by a football player. But the paranoid in me argued, "It's a little strong still, don't you think?"

Before I could answer myself, someone else did. He took a deep, sharp breath that was surprisingly loud and then let out a little grunt of effort.

My knees creaked in protest as I spun around and dropped into a crouch. They were uncomplaining, however, when I saw a large shape rushing at me and I asked them to get us the hell out of its way.

Getting the hell out of someone's way I'd done a thousand times on a football field, but the big guy charging at me was no rookie. When he saw he wasn't going to plow into me with his body, he lifted his arm and caught me a good one across the neck and shoulders. His hand felt like a lead baseball glove.

Pain shot down from my shoulder all the way to my fingers, so the dive I was making when he whomped me wasn't too graceful. The side of my head hit the floor, and instead of tumbling up onto my feet I ended up on my back with one leg through the doorway to the dining room and the other up against a wall.

Behind me there was a welcome grunt of pain, some curious rumbling, and a couple of heavy thuds. Without my body to slow him, he'd gone too far and crashed into the fireplace, scattering the soapstone figures, some of which had fallen to the floor.

There was a lull while he regrouped. I spun onto my hands and feet and pressed myself against the wall. Looking up at him like that my assailant seemed even bigger than he probably was, which was too damn big for me. I rejected the idea of springing at him and using my head to give him a pop in the chest. With a normal guy you can get away with that kind of shit, but normal guys don't go around jumping people in the dark.

When he didn't come at me right away, I thought, "He must be an offensive lineman." His instincts told him to sit tight until his man got back up. Until he overcame that instinct I was going to stay put and wait for the pain to stop streaking from my shoulder to my hand.

I strained to make out his face, but it was too dark.

Not too dark that I couldn't see when he was coming at me again. I sprang for the front door and got there just as he burst into the front hall. I gripped the door handle and opened my mouth to yell for help.

Nothing came out. His right arm had clamped around my neck, drawing me in, as helpless and as quiet as a baby. His body hardly moved when mine was jerked up against it. The arm tightened on my neck. I did my best to keep my chin down, exposing as little of my throat as I could. This resistance spurred him to tighten his arm. He grunted a weightlifter's grunt and raised me off the floor.

Above the sounds of his controlled breathing were the noises of my life being choked out of me.

His arm was covered in liniment so heavily my eyes teared. There was a second smell—his breath, which I could feel on my cheek.

Garlic, I thought, ridiculously. My life was seconds from ending and I was concerned with my killer's personal hygiene habits. I felt stupid, then angry. Angry with him and with myself. No way was I letting some guy take me out with a vacuous thought on my mind. What if the last thing you consider as you die is what they use to seat you in heaven?

By way of self-defense to this point my left hand had been pulling on the wrist that was choking me while my right clutched the doorknob. Both actions were futile, and if I didn't come up with something I was dead.

I let go of the handle and clamped onto the elbow at my ear. Using his arm and strength for support, I jackknifed my body and got my feet on the door. He leaned back and stepped away, figuring I was going to use my legs to shove off and send us to the floor. Or try to. Even if I pulled that off it would mean only that I'd die lying down rather than standing up. The floor was where I wanted us to go, all right, but only if I could get an edge on him before we got there. For that I needed my body out of the way.

While I still had my feet on the door I angled my hips and legs to the left as much as I could and let go of his elbow with my right hand.

My actions cracked his concentration, and he loosened his grip on my throat enough for me to squeeze in a desperate half-breath.

He took a solid step back and the door moved away from my twisting legs. One shot was all I'd get. Raising my right arm as high as I could, I made a fist of my hand and swung it down hard into his crotch. Bull's-eye.

He groaned and expelled a blast of bad breath across my face, which didn't bother me at all this time. His arm loosened as his body struggled to adjust to the pain and the shock of my blow. He wanted to double over and moan for a while but was too busy carrying both of us backward.

120

My legs were falling but still off the ground, so I found the doorway to the living room with my right foot and pushed off of it hard.

We were going to fall, and I needed to be free enough to turn the tumble into a full rear somersault when we landed.

We hit the floor with a thud, and the wind rushed out of the guy under me in another groan. His grip was loose enough for me to flip off away from him, so I did, as quickly as I could.

My roll carried me into the kitchen, where one of my legs smashed up hard against something. I paid no attention. I stood up and looked into the front hall, where he was curling up into the fetal position with his face turned away from me. I had a pretty good idea who he was.

Even though he sounded sufficiently hurt, I didn't want to step over him to get to the front door, so I went through the kitchen, intending to go out the back way. Only I couldn't find a back way. "Always know where the back door is," the warning goes. What a time to forget it.

I was going back into the kitchen for a weapon—a sharp one—when I heard him in there grunting and thumping to his feet. So much for the kitchen. Going upstairs was out, too. That left the living room.

With the soapstone carvings.

He was following me through the kitchen when he crashed into the table, making its rubber feet squeal on the tiled floor. Swearing and grunting, he heaved the table out of his way. Before he'd been coolly competent, now he was just pissed off. Maybe he'd be too angry to think about picking up a weapon—a sharp one.

The swearing and the grunting didn't sound right, which was crazy because I'd never heard the guy I suspected swear and grunt. Also, I was on my knees in the living room, searching for a suitable carving. I searched with my hands and kept my eyes on the door to the dining room. My fingers latched onto a carving that felt about right just as he lurched into view, blocking most of the doorway as he stood in it.

I got up slowly, keeping my hands tight to my sides. The soapstone piece felt cool and hard along about eight inches of my right thigh.

"Please don't hurt me," I whined. "Let's work this out."

He didn't answer, but I thought he stood more gingerly and less defensively. As he crossed the room I kept up the pleading while backing closer to the front door. About six feet from me he pulled himself erect with noticeable effort. I must have really caught him a good one.

He raised his arms. It was in his mind to strangle me face-to-face. Maybe he wanted to look into my eyes as he killed me. Maybe he wanted me to see his face before I died. Maybe he was just completely wacko.

I stood still, whimpering and pleading, which seemed to relax him.

With his hands just inches from my neck I made a big deal of drawing back my right knee. He flinched, dropped his arms, and sucked back his crotch. That's when I swung the soapstone carving up in a quick motion, aiming for the side of his head.

He was fast. Real fast. But not fast enough. He pulled his left arm up to deflect the blow, so I hit his hand and his head. There was a small thud as the carving hit his head. There was a big thud as his body hit the floor.

It was hard to tell in the dark, but he seemed to be motionless. I thought about rolling him over to see who he was, but that would have meant getting close, dangerously close, so I passed.

With the soapstone carving in my hand I backed away from the still figure toward the front door.

From the safety of the outside I looked into the house in time to see the big shape move on the living room floor.

I slammed the door shut and sprinted for the back yard.

**17** SPEED, NOT SILENCE, WAS MY OBJECTIVE as I left 81 Duke Street the way I'd come in. I pounded up the driveway and across the backyard. I clamored over the steel fence instead of jumping it. I didn't even slow down for a car coming into the driveway I was running through. When I sprinted into the glare of its headlights it squealed to a stop. Five jaws dropped and ten eyes popped as I raced between the house and the car. Behind me a male voice yelled out "Hey," more in surprise than in anger.

I ignored it and everything else. Getting away from there was what mattered now.

I'd left the Golf unlocked for just this kind of situation, so it was only a couple of seconds before I was behind its wheel and startling the rest of the neighborhood with a screech of tires.

The car lights were still off as I ignored the stop sign and slipped through the empty cross street. On the other side of the intersection I got a shock when I saw someone in the rearview mirror coming after me, but it was only the guy whose family I'd startled. The guy I'd popped on the head wasn't on my ass, and that's all that concerned me.

What a jerk I'd been. Not being suspicious when Leslie Harlan gave me that key was primo dumbo. I'd been so dim-wittedly happy. I made an angry face at myself and hit the Golf's steering wheel hard with both palms. "Stupid, stupid, stupid," I yelled angrily.

I was so worked up I almost missed another stop sign and stopped just short of running into a guy going through the other way. He eyed me suspiciously as he went slowly by, and turned his lights off and on. The Golf's lights still weren't on. I flicked them on-off-on in greeting.

There was no other traffic, so I sat tight and did some deep breathing.

I'd made some monstrous mistakes in judgment and had almost been killed for them. I'd completely forgotten that I was dealing with killers, vicious killers; think about being

123

drowned in a toilet. Instead of watching what I was doing I'd been bouncing around like a kid on a scavenger hunt.

Moments of severe reappraisal can be beneficial. I tried to think how this one could be turned that way. "The guy didn't honk at me," I said out loud after a minute's reflection. Other times when my brain was on hold I'd needed horn blasts to bring me to my senses. That could be a sign of improvement. And though I'm burdened with my share of stupidity, I don't have a history of doing things so extraordinarily dumb, so it was transient, a temporary aberration caused by the strain of my wife's death. Finally, now that I knew how magnificently wrong I could be under great stress, I could consciously do more to compensate for it. Even then I knew I'd hatched a world-class rationalization, but I needed it.

I pulled the Golf away from the stop sign and aimed it in the general direction of Sean Denby's home. The murder site.

Leslie Harlan had cold-cocked me, so to speak, because she was a woman. My social conditioning had conned me into thinking that women just do not set other people up for murder—especially young, attractive, rich and intelligent women. If Norris Harlan had given me the address and the key you'd have heard my alarms going off five miles away. But let his blond, guileless, Jell-O-breasted wife do it and I was Mr. Trusting of 1986. What really amazed me was that an hour before Leslie'd set me up we'd talked about the duplicity of her affair with Sean Denby. To miss all that I really must have been blind, or viewing her through my twenty-twenty libido.

Women do that kind of thing now, I thought. Women look you in the eye while they're stabbing you in the back. See where women's liberation has brought us? Isn't it awful?

Like most pro athletes who compete for Toronto teams, Sean Denby lived in the West End of the city, near its one major airport, which isn't in Toronto and isn't called the Toronto airport. It's named after a sixties prime minister,

Lester Pearson, and sits on the eastern side of Mississauga, a city given over mostly to light industry, tract houses and plazas. But I wouldn't have to go out of Toronto to get to Sean's. My street map told me that the house must be in a rather well-to-do neighborhood since the streets ran haphazardly in all directions, the popular local method of keeping through traffic in the poorer neighborhoods where it belonged.

The nimble Golf took me along a Boulevard past several Ways, a few Drives, a Place or two, and a clutch of Crescents. There was money around all right. It would be a great place to have a nighttime accident, what with all the people living nearby to offer medical and legal attention.

Sean's street, Marshlands, was precisely where my map said it should be, and only ran off the Boulevard to the right, so I didn't have to wonder which way to turn.

It was late evening and a night wind was blowing. It rustled the thousands of leaves that had recently fallen from one yard to another, oblivious to the hours of raking that had gone on that day. Nature's not as neat as most humans would like it to be. Nor as quiet. The wind whipped around with a hurried whoooosh, pushing a gentle rustle of leaves in front of it. The trees whistled in concert, thrashing their branches about to release more leaves. Those leaves that hadn't fallen waved in front of the streetlights, turning the lawns and the road into a kaleidoscope of shadows, and making the ground look unsteady.

I drove further along the street until I saw a number, which was too high. I'd gone beyond Sean's house, so I backed the Golf up, counting down as I drove. Around where Sean's should have been I saw a dark house with more leaves on the lawn than any of the others. I went past its driveway, stopped, and turned the car toward the house with the high-beam switch held on. The brights swept from left to right as I moved the Golf up the driveway, exposing the low, wide house. A two-car carport was empty, but the mailbox was full, stuffed enough to keep the lid from closing properly.

Beyond some metal lawn chairs a fern brushed along the house. There were some numbers under the door, but I couldn't read them until I was halfway up the drive: 158. I was at the right place.

I stopped, and then backed the Golf onto the road and down the street until it was across from the house next to Sean's. I got out of the car, took the key to Sean's house from my jacket pocket, and bent down to pick up several pieces of loose gravel to put in its place.

There was even less activity on this street than there had been on Duke, which had been quiet enough. Again there were no signs of police surveillance and, more importantly, no sign of my big belligerent friend. There was no doubt in my mind that he'd been up and mobile shortly after I'd left the Duke Street house—despite the crack I'd given him. But even using the thought processes of a clinical paranoid I couldn't come up with a method whereby he'd know where I'd gone. He hadn't followed me. I was sure of that.

I kept my eyes and ears open for movement as I crossed toward Sean's place. It was a waste of time. The wind would provide excellent sight and sound cover for anyone trying to keep himself hidden. If someone were watching they'd know I was there by now, so why hide it? I kept an eye on the shadows big enough for a man to hide in but I saw nothing, and nothing jumped out at me.

At the front door I had one more look around the yard, even though there was nothing to see. I turned to the door and put my finger on the bell. It rang and rang and rang through the darkness inside.

**18**   SEAN'S HOUSE HAD NO STORM DOOR, JUST
an unusually large oak one with a round win-
dow two-thirds of the way up. As I rang the
bell with my right hand I cupped my eyes with
my left and peered inside. Streetlight flooding through the
uncurtained windows let me see. Still, it wasn't exactly lit well
enough to photograph in; there were enough shadows so that a
careful person could not be seen from the outside.

I hadn't really expected to see anyone who might be waiting for me inside, but it was worth the effort. That effort
wasted, I moved to the next careful step. I stopped ringing
the bell long enough to get the key noiselessly into the lock.
That done, I took a deep breath, leaned on the bell like a
madman, turned the tumbler and eased the door open. I slid
inside but kept my finger solidly on the bell. From inside the
house the noise was much more demanding than from outside. I kept ringing the bell until there was no good reason to
keep it up any longer, then I realeased the bell button and
eased the door closed.

The house seemed to sigh in relief at the end of the inces-
sant ringing before it lapsed into a thick silence, which I was
going to add layers to.

I'd used the doorbell ringing as a cover for my entrance,
and to lead anyone who might be in there ahead of me to
think that it was just pranksters giving themselves a thrill by
sounding a knell for Sean Denby. With the return of the silence, someone in the house might relax enough to make a
noise and tip me off that he was in there. That was the plan,
anyway, and it seemed damn good to me. When it was still
holding up after fifteen minutes of silence on my part, I took
the next step.

I fished the pieces of gravel out of my pocket, feeling for a
small one as they came out. I threw it underhand across the
living room. Nothing. If a rock falls in the living room and
there's no one around to hear it, does it make a sound? The
next one was bigger. It hit something with an odd tinging
sound. A lampshade? The next one was even bigger. It
bounced off the wall before hitting something wooden. Any

one in the house had to know the sound came from inside. There was no follow-up noise that I could make out. Two more pieces of gravel would be required. In quick succession I tossed them in different directions. I hoped the confusion of noises would prompt anyone else in Sean's house to reveal themselves, if only to laugh out loud at my amateur-hour techniques. But when both bits of gravel had made their noises the house lapsed back into silence.

My bag of tricks was empty now. That meant overt action was all that was left for me. The soapstone carving I'd brought along from the battle of Duke Street had been reassuringly heavy in my coat pocket, and felt even better dangling from my right hand.

I took a determined step away from the front door just as the living room came to life with the lights from a car turning into the driveway. Light poured in through the deck of windows, sweeping left to right, giving definitive shape to things I'd been staring at in the dark for twenty minutes. To my relief the lights showed the room to be empty.

At just about the last second it occurred to me that if I was standing in front of the door the lights would expose me as well. I dropped to a crouch as the car headlights shone through the window of the door.

When the car lights went out I straightened up for a look, hoping and fearing that it would be a police car. It wasn't. My next guess was the person I least wanted to see, the guy I'd fought with at 81 Duke Street. "It can't be him," I whispered to myself angrily. He couldn't have followed me and I could think of no way for him to know I was coming here.

Whoever it was got out of the car; I heard the door slam.

If they were coming into Sean's house, it wouldn't take them long to get to the door. I scrambled across the hall and into the living room. I thought I could remember where everything was from the seconds of illumination the car lights had given the room, but I was wrong. I gave a small table holding up another soapstone statue a good rap with my left thigh and sent everything wobbling. I bear-hugged the table and the statue into immobility, then crawled the rest of the way to the front window.

I took a chance and looked out the front window.

"It can't be him," I said to myself again, still not believing me. A big man was standing at the back of a car in the driveway fiddling with some keys. He was real big.

Whoever it was looked down toward the street before turning the trunk lock. As it began to rise he turned his head to scan the house, so I dropped below the bottom of the window.

I heard the muffled, clattering noises people make going through a trunk looking for something. When the trunk lid slammed I risked another look. I wanted to know what he'd been looking for.

A tire iron. It was in his hand as he took long steps toward the front door despite his odd walk. He walked like he was limping, or favoring something sore.

I dropped below the bottom of the window again. My rational brain may have thought "It can't be him," but my right hand certainly didn't—it clutched the soapstone carving in a death grip.

About four seconds was all the time I had to get ready for him, if he was going to do what I thought he was. I spent half that time crossing the living room into the welcoming dark of the room behind it.

I just managed to burrow into the blackness of a corner before the glass window in the door exploded under the blow from the tire iron. He poked at some remaining glass shards with the tire iron, then simply reached in and unlocked the door. I heard and felt the wind blow through the open door. There was some crunching as he stepped on the glass and then he slammed the door shut. Whoever he was he wasn't subtle.

He didn't move right away, presumably while he got used to the dark. The way he'd come in showed he didn't know someone else was already there, or didn't care, so his silence wasn't precautionary.

He locked the door and crunched more glass as he moved away from it.

Consciously I tightened my grip on the soapstone carving, but it was too late, my subconscious had already seen to it.

He was in the living room now, moving across it. There were a few seconds of silence before the living room drapes whirred closed, plunging the house into total darkness.

I heard him padding carefully through the dark living room. My guess was he was going to pass through the archway about three feet from me on his way to the rear of the house. I blinked my eyes rapidly in the dark as I cocked the heavy figure. If I was going to bop him with the soapstone it'd be nice if I knew where he was.

I could just make out his huge frame and head as he came through the archway. He stopped, and I thought I saw him turn his head to his left, away from me. That was my cue, so I took a half-step forward to get some weight in my swing. He must have heard me or sensed me because he fell away. I'd been aiming for the back of his head, but I missed, and made contact with something softer, probably the back of his shoulders.

He grunted from the force of my blow and kept going down, less in control now than before. I thought about hanging around to pop him again, decided against it, and headed for the door.

The first two steps were fine. The third came down on the tile floor of the hallway, on some broken glass. My foot went forward and to the left. My body went backward and to the right. I let go of the statue and braced to take the fall on my right arm. With luck and skill I wouldn't go right down. My palm hit a shard of glass, making me cry out but not fall. I wasn't on my ass, but my recovery wasn't as deft as I wanted it to be.

I stood up and moved carefully toward the door. Falling again might prove fatal. I gripped the door handle with my right hand and let out another yelp of pain. The glass I'd fallen on had imbedded itself in my hand, which made cranking the door handle difficult. But not nearly as difficult as his locking the door did. I fumbled at the lock with my left hand, turned it quite easily, and swung the door open. I ignored Satchell Paige's advice and had a look back. Something was definitely gaining on me. I went through the door and pulled it shut behind me.

I did not look back again as I ran across the lawn to the Golf. When I opened its door, light spilled out all over me. That's when I looked back and saw the guy whose skull I'd just tried to break standing in the darkness of the house doorway, looking down at me.

I jumped into the car and closed and locked the door behind me. The darkness was welcome, but probably came too late; the guy must have seen my face as I got into the car. I kept my attention on getting the car started before I looked up to see how far away he was. He hadn't moved.

Luckily, since I had trouble getting the Golf in gear with the bit of glass in my hand. When I finally managed it and had the car moving he started toward me, but in a casual walk—quick, but nonthreatening. I slowed the Golf, hoping to find out who he was.

Halfway down the driveway he stopped and reached into his pocket. A warning bell went off in my head, but it didn't look like a threatening gesture so I didn't speed up too much. I was just about at the end of the driveway and still staring out the window. The way the guy was standing there so casually kept me from driving off. I stopped the car.

He lifted his hands to his face. There were a couple of sparks, then a steady flame. He held the lighter at chin height to illuminate his features, so I could see who he was. The small light dipped and waved in the wind, causing shadows to lick and crawl around his face. I knew who it was though. It was Paul Lacosta. And he was grinning.

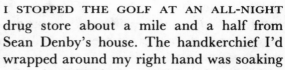

**19**   I STOPPED THE GOLF AT AN ALL-NIGHT drug store about a mile and a half from Sean Denby's house. The handkerchief I'd wrapped around my right hand was soaking up the blood, but the glass shard was painful and made gear-shifting awkward. In the store I picked up some tweezers, gauze, antiseptic ointment and a roll of adhesive tape.

When I got to the cash register the only other customer in the store was there ahead of me putting his money on the counter. The young woman in the trim store uniform and rose-tinted glasses gave him a real smile.

"Here money," the man said. He was in his mid-fifties and had on a good light-brown suit with a couple of dirt spots, tan shoes, a white shirt and a dark brown tie. His features were slightly Slavic, though I might have seen that through his accent more than anything else. He picked up the money he'd just put on the counter and restacked the bills, two ones, two twos and a five, in a different order. "Here money," he said again evenly.

The cashier looked to see what he was buying, and when she saw he wasn't carrying anything her smile faded some. It came back with her idea that maybe he wanted something from the displays behind the counter. She turned a quarter-step and held up her left arm to the display racks and her best smile to the customer, just like she'd seen the models do when they uncover the prizes on the game shows. "What would you like, sir?"

He was paying no attention to anything on the normal plane of existence. Again he restacked the five bills. "Here money," he said in the same even voice.

I moved closer to look at him. His eyes fluttered about like trapped birds. There was no threat in his look or in his voice; if anything his face showed a trace of fear. "Here money." He moved the bills around again.

The cashier was rapidly losing control of the situation. Her

132

arm fell and she took another step back before looking to me for help.

"Take the money," I said quietly, "put it in the cash register, and give it back to him." If the man heard this he gave no sign.

The woman did what I'd suggested and went with her biggest kilowatt smile when she handed him back his money. "Here you go, sir."

Without looking at the money, the man stuffed it in his jacket pocket. His eyes were much more settled when he turned and went straight to the door and out.

The cashier and I watched him get into a car and drive off into the darkness, which entitled us to share a gawk of disbelief. "Nothing like that happens where I come from," she said in awe.

"Where's that?" I asked strictly from manners.

"A small town in Alberta. You wouldn't know it."

I didn't argue, since I probably wouldn't. Instead, I pulled my right hand out of my jacket pocket, exaggerating the care I had to take so's not to hurt myself, and got the look of concern I was after. "I know something else that probably doesn't happen to you in small-town Alberta." She showed me her small-town delicacy by putting her hand to her mouth as I unwound the bloody handkerchief. "I bet strangers there never ask you to take a piece of glass out of their hand," I said.

She looked like she wanted to get out of it gracefully, so I said, "I'd do it myself, only I'm right-handed. I have to get across town and it's real hard to drive my car."

Silently, she bent over to look before taking my hand in hers and turning it to catch the best light. When she picked up the tweezers in her right hand I looked at the display behind her. There were a couple of small twinges in my palm and then she let go of my hand. She was all business now. "Take this stuff back and get some good stuff. The liquid kind." She held out the ointment.

When I'd done as I was told, she popped the top of the

disinfectant and sloshed some on a strip of gauze she'd cut off. The application of that hurt more than the removal of the glass. She wrapped some gauze around my hand to cover the cut, ripped the loose end longways, put half of that around my hand, and tied the ripped ends together. Neat and quick.

"I'll have to charge you for the gauze," she said, "but I can put the tweezers, the scissors and the antiseptic back on the shelves. After I wipe them off, of course."

"Of course. Listen, thanks a lot. You did a great job."

She tried to show me that it was nothing special, just what one human should do for another. I knew they maybe should but hardly ever would. It occurred to me that I might tip her, but that would have offended her sense of honor, and hurried her down the hill toward the more common reaction of never doing anything for anyone without payment. I didn't want to contribute to that.

I took out a five and put it on the counter. "Here money," I said, trying to duplicate the voice of the man who'd just left.

She took the five without comment. I thought my joke had fallen flat. But when she turned back with the change her eyes were fluttering in their sockets. "Here change."

We laughed together and I managed to get a smile as far as the door of the Golf. All traces of it left when a yellow police cruiser went howling along Bloor Street with its lights flashing and *whhooo-gaaa, whhoo-gaaa* siren sounding. The siren was a sure sign that whatever he was going to was major-league—like a break-in at a murder site? My paranoid side wondered over the objections of my rational side.

Bloor Street was the straightest but slowest way downtown; in spots it moved along okay, but a lot of the time it was creep and crawl. That didn't bother me so much becuase it was nice to be stuck in a crowd of people whose aim in life was, well, life, not death.

Eventually, I made it all the way downtown and came near the rock's office. The rock was Inspector Ian Hurst.

Paul Lacosta was the hard place. The rock and the hard place, indeed. Asked to list the two guys I knew that I would not want to have after my ass, Paul Lacosta and Ian Hurst would be one-two, or two-one. My quarrel with Lacosta was obvious enough—we'd tried to kill each other. The extent of my grief with the policeman was yet to be determined. I didn't know what he'd do, but I was sure he'd be mightily pissed at me for invading a murder scene, engaging in a couple of serious fandangos, and generally disregarding a number of major laws, including not telling him.

On balance, I figured it was best to leave Hurst alone until I'd settled my little problem with Lacosta. How I was going to do that was another matter. I couldn't count on luck or surprise to work so well for me again. An angle was what I needed, and the place to start looking for one was Leslie Harlan. She had to have been the one who put Lacosta on my ass. I had no idea why, but maybe when I found out I'd have my angle.

Home was dark and warm and safe when I got there just before midnight. It was tricky to shower using only my left hand, but I managed it. Mixing a large rye and water was easier, and sitting on the couch staring into a small fire was dead simple.

I stared at the fire until almost two A.M., but the thoughts I had swirling about in my brain wouldn't form recognizable shapes any more than the flames would. My patience ran out about the same time as my fourth drink. The only conclusion I took to bed with me was that I didn't have enough facts to reach any conclusions.

As I lay in bed fighting sleep, a wave of self-satisfaction washed over me. It surprised me, so I picked at it. Basically, I felt good about myself because I'd survived a couple of serious situations even though my psychic batteries had been low. Also, I had not gone and cried on the police's navy blue shoulders; I had taken the burden of dealing with Paul Lacosta on myself. Shaky reasons for self-satisfaction, but good enough to hold my ego up. So on that note I surrendered to sleep.

Sleep did not surrender me until nearly nine hours later. I used the intercom to weasel some breakfast in bed out of my housekeeper, who brought it up about ten minutes later with two days of mail as punishment. I pretended to welcome it all, including the newspapers.

"Any messages?" I'd switched my phone off the night before.

"Nope." Clearly Melinda was upset with me and I thought I knew why. Her impressionable son thought I was hot stuff, and lately his idol had been kicking himself with feet of clay. Staying out all night, coming back wounded, and sleeping in until all hours are not the kind of things healthy role models do. I had trouble with this hero business because I'd never had one, so I didn't know what kind of effect they could have. I knew what disappointment felt like, though. I promised myself to make it up to him later. When I solved the Denby case there'd be lots for Eugene and Melinda Holt to admire about me. My ego had wobbled to its feet again.

Some people say that looking at a newspaper is like going off the ten-meter board into reality's deep end. Not me. A newspaper is reality's sampler: all the shapes, patterns and colors are there, but in small doses you can skip over if you find them too unpleasant. Real unpleasant reality is intense and inescapable, like eating Air Canada's mystery meat as you fly into turbulence next to a guy who can't find his air-sickness bag. So I picked up the *Globe* and scanned the front page, confident I could handle whatever was there.

"Hospital Volunteer Murdered," a headline said near the bottom of the page. I had to turn away and take a deep breath. Reality had upped the ante when I wasn't looking. Above the headline was a section of the photograph I'd seen the day before in the *Globe*'s office, the one of Leslie Harlan and Lucille Braverman helping the patients. Under the photo it said, "Lucille Braverman, 57, widow, Metro's 48th murder victim of the year."

"I hope at least she died quickly," I said to myself, then forced the story down: Body discovered near hospital about 11:30 P.M. Badly beaten. No witnesses. Few details. Police on the job.

The *Globe* story was eight, nine, maybe ten hours old, and a lot can happen in ten hours. It was possible more details were now available. By that time of the morning the cops could have already caught the guy. I sat bolt upright in bed. Or be looking for the guy they think might have done it—the guy who talked to Lucille Braverman in the hospital the afternoon of her death. All my grief for that poor woman was gone in a flash, replaced by concern for myself. That may be the mechanism that ensures the survival of the human race, but it ain't pretty to watch, especially in yourself.

The phone call making me a strong suspect had probably already taken place, or soon would. I even knew how it would go:

"Sergeant Varina, Homicide."

"Sergeant, uh, Barino?"

"Varina. What can I do for you, ma'am?"

"Sergeant, it's about Lucy Braverman. About her awful murder. It's just awful that . . ."

"Yes, ma'am. What's your name please?"

"Me? Oh, I'm Mrs. Ozzie Nelson. Harriet Nelson. I live over on Swirling Leaves Crescent, 2662. But I work—well, I'm a volunteer actually—over at the hospital where Lucy Braverman worked. Well, she was a volunteer, too. That's how I knew her."

"What about Mrs. Braverman, Mrs. Nelson?"

"I'm not sure if it's important . . ."

"Let us be the judges of that."

"Yesterday, the day she was killed, this man came into the hospital looking for Lucy. He spent a long time talking to her."

"Do you know what they talked about?"

"I wouldn't eavesdrop, of course, but maybe about Leslie

Harlan, Norris Harlan's wife. It was her this man asked about first, you see."

"Do you know his name? Can you describe him?"

"Well, he wasn't very well dressed; no tie. And he had a shifty look. I said that to my friend Hazel, I said doesn't he look suspicious . . ."

The best thing I could do was call the cops and tell them I'd seen Lucille Braverman the day before, so they'd know my visit didn't have anything to do with her murder. The phone had rung once when it occurred to me that maybe my visit did have something to do with her murder. The coffee I'd just drank went sour in my stomach. I put the phone down.

If someone could set me up to be killed, why not Lucy Braverman? It was easy to believe they could, but impossible for me to explain why they would. Why kill Lucille Braverman? What could she know that was important enough to kill for? The only answer I could imagine was Leslie Harlan's pretend career as a hospital volunteer. Was that enough to kill over? Presumably, but why?

Maybe I was supposed to be half of a daily double for Lacosta. Kill me and then kill Lucille Braverman. I tried that on for size but it didn't feel right because of the timing. He couldn't have done it after our tussle at Sean's house. No time. He would have to have done it before that, which meant between our run-in at 81 Duke Street and our tussle at Sean's. No time, just no time. Perhaps the time of death the *Globe* had given was wrong, either because it was a snap guess at the site or because it suited the police to list the wrong time of death in the papers; times of death can be tricky, and so can cops looking for a killer.

That idea brought me back to the fact that the police were looking for me, or soon would be. I arranged the facts that I felt comfortable giving Hurst. It was heartening to find that limited truth would do, since I wanted to tell him as much truth as I could, so as not to leave any holes in my story big enough for him to drive his fist through.

138

At first he wasn't too thrilled to hear from me again. He brightened noticeably when I told him I was the guy the department was probably looking for in the Lucille Braverman murder, the guy who'd talked to her at the hospital. And they were looking for me, thanks to a citizen phoning in.

"I figured I'd let you know it was me, so you wouldn't have to waste any time searching." I wanted him to feel grateful, so I wasn't above pointing out the obvious. He was not overcome with gratitude, however. He wanted to know why I'd been talking to Lucille Braverman. I told him the truth, including the bit about Leslie Harlan hardly ever being there, and then I shut up.

"Is that it, Cane?"

"We also talked about how her husband died of cancer, and her work as a volunteer."

"The Harlan woman wasn't there because she was seeing Denby, is that what you're saying, Cane? The volunteer thing was a cover?"

"That's what it looks like."

"Lucy Braverman didn't know?"

"They weren't exactly friends; they only met once. Besides, the subject of her being Sean's lover didn't even come up."

"What did come up?"

"I told you, Inspector." I hoped he was too busy to keep talking to me. What he was was too much of a good cop. A good cop on a murder case.

"What did you say to Leslie Harlan when you drove her to the service for Denby?" Hurst asked. I wasn't surprised that he knew. The cops probably took pictures of everyone at the funeral of a murder victim.

"You know, things." It was a terrible equivocation. We both knew it.

"Cane." Hurst was testy now.

There seemed to be no way around telling him the truth. Or most of it. So I recapped what was said between Leslie

Harlan and myself, giving fair coverage to what I considered her queer reaction to it all. I even told him about the deal we'd made—the address of her meeting place with Sean Denby in exchange for my telling her how I'd found out she hadn't been at the hospital very often. I held my breath waiting for him to ask me why I wanted to know that.

He was more interested in the link between Leslie Harlan and Lucille Braverman. Only he wasn't sure why. "So Leslie Harlan knows Lucille Braverman told you about that," he said, puzzled, hoping I'd be kind enough to point out the significance of that. It was significant, I could feel that, but I didn't know why either.

So I said I had no idea. Neither of us spoke. The urge was building up inside of me to tell him I'd been given a key to 81 Duke Street, which would undoubtedly lead to a telling of the whole, sad story. A voice from Hurst's end spoke up and ended the tension for me. Hurst said, "Tell him I'll be right there. When can you come down and make a statement, Cane?"

"Statement?"

"Yeah, come down here and make one. Then sign it."

"Jeez, Inspector, I didn't know it was that important."

Hurst spoke away from the phone again before saying to me in a harried voice, "Well, I guess it's not crucial. And we're as busy as a toilet paper dispenser at a laxative testing plant. Come in Monday or Tuesday."

"Fine," I said and he hung up.

I put the phone down and crossed the room to my desk, taking my breakfast with me to eat in big bites as I looked for the Harlans' telephone number. It was unlisted, so I had to rummage through a box of Elizabeth's things in a closet looking for her personal phone book. I found it and tried the number. The Harlans' answering service told me Mr. Harlan was at the office and Mrs. Harlan was out until at least two P.M.

By this time my breakfast had lost its appeal. But I was still hungry, so I called Melinda on the intercom again and asked her to have lunch ready no later than 1:30. Because it was nearly noon by that time, it meant I had some time for a few chores before I had lunch and then walked over to have a little chat with Leslie at two. I was really looking forward to that.

 WALKING THE FEW BLOCKS TO THE Harlans' I wondered about what Sean Denby and Lucille Braverman might have in common. What link could there be between a pro football star and a middle-aged widow who spent all her time keeping dying people company?

Leslie Harlan.

And, of course, me. But I was out of the running as a suspect. Not Leslie. Was there a jury in the world that would think it coincidental that she was the only thing their lives, and deaths, had in common?

I rang the bell of the big three-story house. And waited. I rang it again. And waited some more.

Standing out there, I had the feeling that someone was in the house and just not answering the door. I did that all the time when I was home alone. When I did it, I sometimes thought the person at the door could tell I was inside ignoring them. And if they were persistent enough in ringing, I usually went to the door just to stop the noise. So I really leaned on the bell, the way I had at Sean Denby's house the night before. Repeating that action made me tingle with recollection. It was bright daylight as I worked the Harlans'

141

bell, but my mind's eye was focused on Paul Lacosta's taunting look from above his flickering lighter.

Without letting up on the bell, I leaned over and grabbed the door handle with my left hand. I was going to rattle it and the locked door to show whoever was inside how angry I was, but when I gave the handle its first turn it rolled over obediently and let the door open. Stillness spilled through the door to cool my anger. The door being open when the house was supposed to be empty was bad business—I could feel that all through me.

I pulled the door shut, made a disparaging face at my own caution and opened it again. Some instinct kept me from going through the door. Bad vibes is a dated sixties expression, I know, but I've yet to find a better one for certain feelings. And bad vibes were what I was getting from the Harlan house. I leaned carefully inside and pulled the door shut again.

An approaching car turned into the driveway behind me. Without looking back I started pushing the bell again. When it was no longer possible to ignore the noise of the car in the driveway, I turned my head and shoulders to see who it was.

I had been hoping for Leslie Harlan and fearing Paul Lacosta. It was the cops, two detectives in an unmarked, dirty green car. This was not really a surprise, since they were as capable as I of seeing Leslie Harlan as the only common factor in two recent murders. Unless they were there for me. They may not be as sure of my innocence as I was. I was very glad I hadn't gone into the house. I put my left hand in my pants pocket.

Sergeant Harry Varina got out of the passenger side. A male cop I did not recognize popped out from behind the wheel looking professionally guarded. They approached the door in such a way as to make my bolting unlikely—not that I'd planned to.

Except for their car, their regulation haircuts and mustaches, their clothes, their shoes and their attitude, you would never have known they were cops. I did not mention this, however.

142

I took a step down toward them, which made them slow up a bit and watch me more carefully. I could have bumped the tension here by taking my hand out of my pants pocket, but it is not a real bright idea to make men carrying guns uneasy, so I put my right hand in my other pants pocket. "Sergeant," I said evenly, trying to look and sound amiably innocent.

Varina did not return my greeting. He stopped about ten feet away from me. So did his partner.

"Just leaving, Mr. Cane?" Varina asked.

"It seems there's nobody home."

"Seems?"

"No one answers the doorbell. Maybe that's because they knew it was me." I said the last in a self-deprecating tone with a grin to match.

Varina either missed my comic intent or ignored it. "Why wouldn't they want to talk to you, Mr. Cane?"

"I don't know. I was just joking. Maybe you'll have more luck," I said as I walked toward them and the street beyond.

Varina blocked my way quite openly. "What's your business with the Harlans?" he asked. While he spoke his partner worked his way behind me, just out of arm's reach, I noticed. They were pros, all right.

"My business with the Harlans, Sergeant, is just that—my business."

I kept my manner unworried, superior. I was not sure, standing there between two cops investigating two murders, just what my rights were. It didn't really matter, of course, since most cops will act first and repair rights later. One way to stop this is to hint at a promise of trouble after the fact. If you look like sixty-four miles of bad road leading to a lawsuit and/or criminal charges, they'll be more inclined to grant you your rights. It does not hurt if they think you have the bucks as well as the inclination to give them grief. If the cop is out-and-out crazy, hope for mercy.

Varina didn't strike me as crazy, he struck me as ambitious, which would work in my favor. He took a moment to examine me up close before reacting to my remark. As I waited to see which way the little street drama would go, I realized that this was the first time I'd played my haughty little game with a cop when I had something to hide. Not letting that show was a good idea.

Varina seemed to be taking forever to consider my remark, so I forced the issue, to take the initiative away from him. I said "See you," and moved toward him. Getting by him without banging shoulders would be impossible, so I pulled mine in half-way. If he didn't do the same we were going to make serious contact. And it can take less than that to make a cop decide he has to defend himself by beating you to a pulp. Slinking by him was out of the question, however.

Our shoulders were touching before he eased his back. When I saw he was letting me pass I said "Excuse me" with minimum meaning and went up the driveway.

It is amazing the number of sophisticated games people play with each other every day, and even more amazing that almost everyone seems to know and abide by their rules, and can readily discern winners and losers. We both knew I'd won, and that there'd likely be a rematch.

Exiting nonchalantly was what I had to do, and that meant it would be impossible to look back and gawk as the cops went about their business. I walked slowly and listened carefully. When I was out of sight behind a tree on Harlan property I stopped to listen to the two policemen ring the doorbell and talk. One of them went to the car and got on the radio. It was Varina, and he had good projection. He asked the radio dispatcher to get on the phone and tell the Harlans he was waiting outside. The other cop yelled to Varina that the door was open. I moved away as fast as I could without looking like I was fleeing and kept the tree between us.

It seemed like a good idea to become unreachable as soon as possible, so I quick-stepped back to my house and leaped into the Golf. Its tires gave a little squeal when they hit the street pavement. The noise made me aware of what I was doing: I was hurrying, but to where? Nowhere definite. The sense of aimlessness made me feel guilty; I could not hide from myself the fact that I was on the run, from the police and maybe Paul Lacosta.

I'd been around some, but nothing in my experience quite compared to this. I had no idea what to do. That didn't mean I wouldn't be able to come up with a course of action. I just needed time to work something up.

Seeing no sense in just driving around, I stopped in at a small bar on Yonge Street that I visit when I need the trappings of other people but not the other people. It was quieter than it normally is when I visit, yet it imparted a sense of calm through its the-hell-with-'em-and-have-a-drink feeling. I often feared for the place's existence, since it did not adhere to the reigning trend in Toronto bars and look like a plant nursery with tables.

The waiter treated me like he recognized me when I placed my order from a stool next to a stack of newspapers and magazines on the bar. Out of habit I reached for something to read, the way a kid absentmindedly goes for his teddy bear. Elizabeth used to rib the shit out of me because of my reading. One night I pushed her over the edge. It was late, and naturally I was reading. She was bustling about getting ready for bed. She said, "I'm going to bed now." I grunted. A few moments later she said, "I'm in bed now." I nodded behind the book. I still can't believe I missed the tone in her voice. Some noises in the room did penetrate my skull but I didn't bother to look up to see what was going on. So when Elizabeth tapped the book with the end of a cane it took me by surprise.

I dropped the book onto my lap and stared. Elizabeth was standing in front of me wearing a loud plaid suit and a straw boater to go with the cane. They were souvenirs from a college show she'd been in. Anyway, she looked like Gene Kelly in the scene from *Singin' In the Rain* where he plays a hick just arrived in New York because he's "Gotta Dance."

Elizabeth warbled, "Gotta read. Gotta read. Gotttaa ree-aaddd."

The effect was startling, especially when she dropped to her knee à la Jolson and threw her arms wide, making the jacket fly open to reveal that she was wearing nothing but the plaid suit.

I stared at her mutely. My silence caused her expectancy to turn into mock frustration. In a much louder voice she sang, "Gotta ball. Gotta ball. Gotttaa baallll."

The book went back up in front of my face before I said, "Let me finish this chapter, hon, there're only thirty-eight more pages."

Even if I'd wanted to keep reading I wouldn't have gone three words before Elizabeth forced the straw hat down onto my skull.

At that point in my reverie the waiter appeared with my beer. He smiled quizzically in response to the sappy grin I had on my face. "I was just thinking about the time my wife pulled a hat down over my ears," I said. He kept his smile as he nodded understandingly, but I saw his eyebrows go up as he turned away from me.

A glimpse of the front page of that day's *Globe* brought me back to earth. I had a couple of big swallows of my Budweiser before pulling the paper in front of me. The story was still there about Lucille Braverman's murder. Seen in a second copy of the paper it seemed more of a public crime than a private one directed at me, the way it had earlier. It still made my insides ache, however.

I leafed through the rest of the *Globe*'s front section the way I might have traversed a minefield—with a weather eye out for trouble. It wasn't exactly trouble, but the picture taken the day before at Sean's memorial service did not make me burble with glee. The photographer had caught the Harlans leaving the church surrounded by a half ton of beefcake wearing four dark suits and matching looks. One I recognized as Hank Graff, the guy who'd stood silently behind Norris throughout the service.

The story that surrounded the photo was a good newspaper version of what had been said at the service. Nothing there to interest me except that the Metros had scheduled an unusual day-before-a-game practice for 2:00 P.M. that afternoon. It was about 2:30 when I read that. It seemed Coach Baird was not happy with the team's state of readiness for Sunday's game with the Montreal Habitants.

I downed the rest of my beer and stopped at a pay phone on my way out. The phone at the other end rang once before a brusque man's voice said "Yeah?" I did not speak so he said, "Who is this?" I wanted him to be quiet so I could listen to what was going on in the background. A lot of people were bustling about in an excited manner. When he spoke again Sergeant Harry Varina was very angry, but I cut him off before I could hear any more of what was going on in Norris and Leslie Harlan's house.

**21** FROM THE REALITY-BATTERING DISTANCE of the pressbox, the practicing Metros looked like oddly dressed mice learning tricks through repetition. From just behind the players' bench at field level they looked quite different— they looked like oddly dressed gorillas learning tricks through repetition. It was a "light workout," which means no trying to maim your teammates in an attempt to impress the coaching staff. Usually it's important to impress the coaching staff, since they're the guys who decide if you're going to earn and please millions, or if you're going back to the farm where you earn and raise peanuts. "Break his arm, coach? Whatever you say." "Break my arm, coach? Which one?"

There were a lot of people there, enjoying the spectacle and the midafternoon sunshine of early October, but neither of the two I wanted to see: Norris Harlan and Paul Lacosta. I especially wanted to see Lacosta on the field. That way if he came after me there might be enough muscle in the forty or so players standing around to stop him from killing me. I stayed out there for about thirty minutes, ignored by everyone except Eric VanKaspal, who pretended to ignore me.

So much for the safety of being assaulted in public. I set off for the Metros offices in the basement of the stadium. One old security guard looked at me as I passed, not bothering to ask if I belonged there. I looked like I did and that is usually enough.

I walked along a hall that was about twice as wide as it was high, and curved gently along between bright rectangles of natural light at each end of the stadium section. Except for the pair open beneath the ugly Toronto Metros logo all the doors were shut, and the only sound was the tuneless clatter of some electric typewriters.

Then someone yelled "Fuck that shit!" and you could have heard a pass drop. The silence was deep but quick, with the typewriters soon resuming their clatter, louder now to hide the fact that their operators were listening. I stopped ten feet from the doors and looked uninterested.

Bob Baird, ex-quarterback, current coach and perennial hardass, burst out into the hall. Back in the office Norris Harlan struggled to be reasonable and asked for the same in return. Baird was having none of it. Two steps outside the door he turned and looked back. Even though his Georgian accent was pleasingly melodious, Baird wasn't exactly Gaylord Ravenaugh. "He's got no goddam reason for missing practice today, and you ain't gonna wipe his ass for him this goddam time. He's out. I ain't eatin' this shit any longer."

Baird saw me standing up the hall from him a ways and

fixed me with a malevolent look. I gave him back my best smartass grin.

"What the hell's so funny, boy?" Baird demanded of me. Inside the Metros office someone shut a door.

"Nothing's funny. I was just smiling because I was grateful that I never played for a redneck jerk as big as you." Until that moment I hadn't realized that I'd always disliked Bob Baird. There were stories I'd heard about what a bully and a bigot he was that I hadn't put much credence in because I like to see for myself. Now that I'd seen for myself, I knew the worst I'd heard didn't match the worst he'd done. One look at his face in that hall told me that.

Baird's face became as red as his neck, so I tensed, expecting an attack. It came, but in an extremely original fashion—Baird took the clipboard out from under his left arm and skimmed it at me across the ten yards between us, with my face as its obvious target.

What I should have done was make the maximal avoidance move. What I did was the minimal avoidance move, leaning my head and shoulders slightly to the left so that the clipboard passed by inches from my ear. It hit the wall with a nasty thump before crashing to the cement floor and skittering further up the hall. The stupid macho games men play.

I looked toward Baird, ready to give him one of my favorite looks, the one that says "You sad, silly son of a bitch," but he was walking away. He didn't seem fearful that I might return the fire or come after him. He didn't seem anything but mightily angry with the world. I felt sorry for the poor bastards out on the practice field.

A man's face appeared timorously in the doorway and looked in my direction. He asked the standard question under such circumstances—"Are you all right?"—but made it seem professional rather than sympathetic.

Before I could answer a female voice from behind him explained why the question sounded different coming from him. "Mr. Harlan says you can go in now, Doctor Cooper."

He observed me to make sure I wasn't hurt before returning to the office. By the time I followed him through the
double doors he was out of sight. The only people I could see
were two women sitting behind typewriters. One was saying
to the other, "What an awful man." She blushed when she
realized I'd overheard her. Then she closed ranks and put up
a businesslike front; it was okay for people inside the team to
know she'd been driven to exasperation by the coach, but I
was an outsider.

"Would you please tell Norris that I'm here to see him?
Richard Cane."

"Yes, sir, in a moment. He's busy right now."

"With Dr. Cooper."

If she heard me she did not let on. "Have a seat, please,
Mr. Cane."

Before I sat down I had a look around the office. There
were two desks, seven filing cabinets (one of which held up a
TV), a coatrack, a teletype machine and a squat, rolling file
tray. The place was one of those fast disappearing old offices;
there wasn't a computer or a work station in sight. The paint
scheme tried to duplicate the Metro colors, green on blue,
and looked worse than it sounds.

On the back wall was a single door that read: NORRIS
HARLAN, OWNER, PRESIDENT, AND HEAD CHEERLEADER.
Dare to be cute. I hadn't seen anything to compare with it
since a sign at a Vermont motel informing potential burglars
that the chief of security there was named Laddie. His as-
sistant was Tuffy the Cat.

I mentioned the sign on Harlan's door and told the two
women about Laddie and Tuffy the Cat, figuring it was the
kind of thing they'd like to hear. They both commented on
how cute that was and I couldn't argue.

Dr. Cooper let himself out, closed the door, and exchanged
bright good-byes with the two ladies in the manner of strangers who see each other fairly regularly. Me he looked at to be
sure I hadn't started dying when his back was turned. I
smiled my appreciation for his concern.

150

The older of the two women reached for the phone on her desk, only to stop just shy of touching it. She gave me a helpless smile. "He's on the phone now, Mr. Cane."

"What I have to see him about is very important."

"I'm sure." She managed to sound slightly sincere.

Typing resumed on both fronts, but the older one kept a practiced eye on the phone. She stopped typing after a couple of minutes and reached out her hand again—and stopped short again. This time to look at the door. I was annoyed until I noticed the look of surprise on her face. No wonder. A pair of uniformed police officers had just come through it. Her surprise faded and she looked the way innocent people always look when two cops approach them—nervous and guilty. I tried to look calm and innocent.

My worst fear ebbed when they ran me through their mental mug books and then turned away toward the older woman. One of them kept his eyes moving around the room to make sure none of the filing cabinets made a break for it. The other one did something truly remarkable—he took off his cap. It was clearly a sign of deference, and quite unnerving.

"We're here to see Norris Harlan. Police business." The officer without the hat spoke. There was apprehension in his brisk voice.

The older woman had recovered from the presence of the policemen. She picked up the intercom and spoke calmly into the phone. "Mr. Harlan, there are two policemen here to see you. On police business. Yes, sir."

Very carefully she lowered the phone into its cradle, waiting until it was secure before she spoke. This gave Harlan enough time to make her "He'll be right out" redundant as she said it.

Harlan was wearing a track suit in Metro colors, with the team crest and the word *Owner* on the jacket breast. When he caught sight of me he seemed surprised and upset about my being there. He seemed to have taken the presence of two uniformed policemen much better, which was of much interest to me at the time.

He duplicated my curt nod.

Harlan turned to the cops and came almost to attention before staring them down. The second officer took off his hat.

"Norris Harlan?" It was a formal question; they knew who he was. Harlan didn't bother to reply in any way.

"What is it?" he asked. He seemed quite calm. But, then, maybe he was used to cops arriving on his doorstep, probably to pick up game tickets for their chief.

"Sir, there's been an accident. Will you come with us, please?"

"Go with you where? What sort of an accident?"

The young officer doing the talking seemed very uncomfortable. He looked at me and at the two secretaries, who were trying to hide behind their work. "It's personal, sir. Would you please just come with us?"

But Norris Harlan was not the kind of man to do anything unless you convinced him there was a damn good reason for it. He stood his ground, even looking a little angry with the cop. It was a bloody good reason or the cuffs, if they wanted Norris Harlan to go with them. I wondered what life was like when you never let anything just go by you.

"It's your wife, Mr. Harlan," the young officer said quietly, humanely.

Something flickered on Norris Harlan's face, and something moved in my stomach. I wouldn't be able to ignore the truth gnawing away in there much longer. I thought about what I'd felt as I stood in the open doorway of the Harlan house and rang the bell. Bad vibes indeed.

Quite calmly, Harlan asked, "Is she dead?" and I shivered. They were exactly the same words I'd used with Elizabeth's father when he'd called to tell me there'd been an accident.

Wilfred had said, "Of course." He'd meant "Of course, why else would I be calling?" but I couldn't let the phrase alone. Probably never will. "Of course."

152

The young policeman said, "Please, sir, will you just come along?" but it meant the same thing—"Of course."

I couldn't even stand to look at Norris after that. I was afraid that if I looked into his eyes I might see a reflection of my own pain.

No one made a sound for several seconds. I tried to get my feelings in enough order so that I could at least communicate my sorrow to Norris, but before I could get a word out he spoke in a tight, strained voice, quickly working out the logistics of the situation. "Mrs. Carmody, would you cancel any appointments I may have today? If anyone has to talk to me I'll be at home, but only if it's very important. If you have to come along," he said to the policemen, "one of you can drive me home in my car." It didn't sound like he needed to be driven.

The cops exchanged a funny look, like they knew they'd been duped into wasting their sympathy and understanding. Both put on their caps and followed Norris Harlan out.

I watched him as he left, but he did a good job of not looking my way.

"My God," the older secretary said.

"It's horrible," the other replied, "but isn't he taking it well?"

Isn't he though? I thought, then chided myself for being suspicious. We all handle shock and grief in different ways. Norris's life with Leslie was different from what mine had been with Elizabeth. She'd been unfaithful for a long time. Most likely he had been as well. He had a right to his own life, to his own reaction. Still.

 **22** THIRTY FEET BELOW WHERE I SAT NURS-
ing my third bottle of budweiser a yellow
police cruiser drove slowly east on Queen
Street. The one cop I could see was looking
out the window at the people on the sidewalk.

I wondered how near the top of his list of people to look
for I was. Probably the top. After all, in three days three
people had been killed and I knew them all. Most likely I
was the only name those three murder victims had in common. If that didn't qualify me for top suspect status, I
couldn't imagine what did.

This had not occurred to me right away. Not much had.
I'd left the Metros' office in a daze a few moments behind
Norris Harlan and the two cops. "Another murder," was the
only idea I could grasp. That it might be something other
than murder had also not occurred to me.

Even when my muddled mind moved on to "Who'd want to
kill Leslie Harlan?" my own name did not come up as a suspect.

I was working from a privileged position here, of course,
because I knew I didn't have anything to do with the
murder, or murders. When, finally, the penny dropped and I
realized I might be a suspect, I was offended. Me, a murder
suspect? How could they suspect someone of my taste, refine-
ment, charm and humility? What cheek.

Driving along Lakeshore Boulevard I actually had it in
mind to go straight to police headquarters and give them a
piece of my mind. I got as far as York Street before I came to
my senses, so I cut across a couple of lanes of traffic and
made a left. I thought about parking near the Royal York
and looking up Alison Denby. But by then I'd regained my
usual level of paranoia, so I realized the police might be
watching her. I continued up York to Queen, made a right,
and parked in the Four Seasons Sheraton underground lot.

I left the Golf crouching in the dark and made my way to the
light. It only took me a few minutes to walk to the hotel's Long
Bar, which runs along a good stretch of Queen Street and

provides quite a nice view of city hall, the old home of Osgoode Law School, and Toronto in general. I sat at a small table along the window and ordered a Budweiser. The waiter brought it without comment, and did not look at me suspiciously.

As I drank I thought about how I was going to play this. By then I knew I had to be the chief suspect in all three murders. Had to be. I was the only known thing all three victims had in common; I'd been seen at the latest murder site by—unbelievable luck—two cops; and I didn't have a decent alibi for any of the murders. That was the part that really made me uncomfortable. Sure I'd been in Detroit when Sean had been killed. I just couldn't prove it. After the conference ended for the day I'd gone to dinner and a movie—by myself. I'd also been my own company in bed, unless you counted Kathleen Turner, but you couldn't because she was only in my room courtesy of the late show.

Most innocent people in my situation would have hurried off to the nearest police station and told all, out of a strong belief in the basic fairness of our justice system. Because I'd written and followed the news for years, I was not burdened with that opinion. The history of wrongful arrests and convictions is a long and lasting one in Canada. Or anywhere, for that matter. It is constantly being updated around the world, on purpose in certain places, and by mistake in others. Notwithstanding the reasons, the results are the same. The police force that was looking for me had, for example, recently been involved in a classic case of wrongful arrest. A series of murders had the city in an uproar. There was a small group of suspects under consideration, and all but one loudly proclaimed their innocence. The one who didn't preferred to speak to a lawyer first. Almost exclusively for that reason she was arrested. The media held the woman up to public display, leading the country to presume she was guilty. Some months later when a judge got a look at the case he threw it out of court for its profound lack of evidence. The media, ever adept at bandwagon-jumping, then milked the story for all the sympathy it was worth: "Woman spends fortune to prove innocence; government refuses to pay compensation." If the three Toronto papers turned over the profits her story had made for them her legal debt would be gone and she could afford to start a new life. Her old one, after all, had been pretty well ruined.

No, I did not like the idea of turning myself over to that police department.

I ordered another Budweiser instead. As I drank it, I tried to figure out who was the killer, or killers. My personal favorite for the role was Paul Lacosta, since I figured he wouldn't be able to finish the job he'd started on me the night before if he was in jail. At the same time, I had an irrational desire to see Norris Harlan guilty too. It was irrational because no matter how hard I tried I couldn't come up with any evidence against him. On the other hand, maybe the cops would be luckier with such a case this time out. No. Reluctantly I put the idea of Harlan's guilt out of my mind, and worked on the problem of making the case fit Lacosta.

That's what I was doing when the cruiser went by on Queen Street and reminded me of the necessity of coming up with something soon. I had it in mind to solve the case, get it gift-wrapped at Creeds and deliver it to a surprised but grateful Inspector Hurst. Guys on TV did that all the time.

But by Budweiser number five the thing still did not hang right from Paul Lacosta's shoulders. Or Norris Harlan's. Or Eric VanKaspal's. Or Max York's. Or the waiter's. I had spent a few hours trying to put a puzzle together, but it wouldn't jell. It didn't occur to me that I just wasn't smart enough to put it together; the fault lay in the number of missing pieces. My self-esteem was on its way to a full recovery.

Dusk was closing in and Toronto was putting on its makeup for the night. Noise from the traffic on Queen Street started to penetrate the Long Bar's shell, and for the first time I was more aware of the traffic than I was of the people in the bar. Reality had come a-calling again.

Probably from the start of my second beer I'd known what I had to do to turn up something for Hurst: I had to go back to 81 Duke Street and Sean's house to look around. I was brimming with ennui over the idea, so I'd tried to come up with an alternative—and failed. As a final stalling tactic, I decided to think about it until the crush of homebound shoppers had eased, at seven P.M., thirty-five minutes away.

I coasted through the fifth beer, settled the tab and stood up at 5:55. Out in the hall I stopped at a phone and called my own number.

Busy. I looked at the pay phone like it was broken. I'd never gotten a busy signal at my house, partly because my housekeeper was only ever on the phone to take messages for me, but mostly because I still had the four phone lines my father-in-law had had installed. I tried again and it rang, but it rang over a dozen times. When Melinda's son answered, his greeting was abrupt: "Mr. Cane is not here."

I got the impression he was going to hang up, so I shouted "Gene."

"Yes." He was back to his usual timorous self.

"Gene, it's me. It's Mr. Cane. It's Richard."

"Boy, everyone's been calling you. Where are—yes, it's Mr. Cane."

There was a muffled exchange between mother and son before Melinda said, "Mr. Cane, the police have been here looking for you."

"I thought they would be. Are they still there?"

"Yes, in a car outside the house. What should I do?"

"You might offer them coffee and the use of the washroom." She did not respond because she thought I was just being smartassed about a bad situation. "I'm serious, Melinda. No reason they have to be put out because of me." I didn't think the cops would be too uncomfortable; I'd made the suggestion so that Melinda would think better of me.

It worked some, but there was still reserve in her voice when she said, "What do they want, Mr. Cane?"

"They think I'm involved in a murder. Maybe three."

"Are you?"

"In the sense that I have some information about them, yes. But don't worry, I haven't killed anyone." Melinda

157

didn't even bother with a pro forma denial that she hadn't thought that for a moment. I didn't hold it against her; if I were the mother of a young son I'd be suspicious of everyone on general principles. I heard another phone line ringing in the background. "Did anyone else call?" I asked.

She snorted. "Who hasn't?"

"Skip the police and media calls. Who does that leave?"

"Just a minute." She put the phone on hold for a minute, presumably while she sorted through my messages. I started to get antsy, the way I always do when I'm put on hold. The idea crossed my mind that maybe she was calling the cops on another line. Maybe they had a way of tracing the call. Maybe they were on their way up the hotel escalator right that second. Guns drawn. Jeez, I hate being put on hold. "Mr. Cane, your father-in-law called—"

"Did he offer to take me to the station and turn me over to the chief?"

"He left no message. Also, an Alison Denby called; please call her as soon as you can. And a Mr. Amory. He—"

"Julian Amory, the gambler?"

"The way you've been going, I think the odds are good that it'd be that Mr. Amory." Her distaste was palpable. I half expected her and Gene to be gone when I got home.

"Did he leave a number?" He had, and she gave it to me. There were no other non-media messages, so I said, "Melinda, please don't tell anyone you've been talking to me. Especially the police. And Melinda, please don't leave. There's no need. I'll be able to straighten this business out soon. I won't come back there until you're satisfied I had nothing to do with the murders. That sound fair to you?"

Not right away, apparently, because she thought about it for a while. "Okay," she finally said, not sounding very convinced.

"If the phones are bothering you, pick up the lines that aren't busy, get a dial tone and push the hold button. Do that for all four lines and anyone who calls will get a busy signal. I'm sorry about all this."

She did not reply. Before I could say anything else she said,

158

"Please be careful, Mr. Cane. Good-bye," and hung up.

I called the Royal York and was quickly connected to Alison Denby's room, where she answered on the fourth ring. "Hello."

"Hi," I said flatly, not sure how to handle it. The last time I'd seen her I'd kidded her in front of strangers about needing the services of a gigolo. Since then I'd become a murder suspect.

"Well, if it isn't David Janssen."

"David Janssen?—Oh, right, his TV show, 'The Fugitive.' Got any one-armed men in the room with you?"

"Just a minute while I look around. . . . No. So how are you?"

"Hot."

"Me, too. Come right over."

"Not that kind of hot. Hot as in on-the-lam. Jesus, you're relentless. I'm surprised your second husband, the goalie, could ever do the splits."

"He loved doing that. The ice helped with the pain."

I had to laugh. "Can I stay with you tonight?"

"No. There's two cops in the hotel watching me."

"Are you sure?"

"Absolutely. They have a look about them." This was not good news; they must be real serious about bringing me in.

"Okay. I'll call later. Maybe we can work something out. You can give 'em the slip and meet me someplace." I tried to sound confident.

"Sounds good," Alison said, also trying to sound confident.

I'd no idea what Julian Amory wanted but I called him anyway. When a man answered "Amory residence" I thought it was a joke. I couldn't believe anyone but a TV butler would say that.

"This is Richard Cane, is Mr. Amory there? Julian Amory."

"Hold on please, sir." The guy did not have the English accent I thought he had when he answered. Maybe you can't say "Amory residence" into the phone without sounding English.

A less comical voice came on the phone. "Cane, this is Julian Amory. I have to talk to you. Now." His voice was so full of emotion I couldn't sort it out. It was forceful enough to make me go along with his request, however. Turning him down would have been an act of cruelty.

Still, I was rather busy. "You must know the cops are after me," I said. "I'm not sure how much mobility I've got."

"That's one of the things I want to talk to you about. I should be able to help you with that problem." He was trying to be grimly determined, but the erratic note in his voice was unmistakable.

"Okay," I said.

"Where can we meet?"

I looked north and thought about what was nearby. "You know the clock tower at the end of Hart House, by the U of T's war memorial?"

"When?"

I looked at my watch. "How's seven P.M. sound?"

He said "Seven P.M." and hung up.

SATURDAY NIGHT IN OCTOBER IS THE best time possible to prove that the design of Toronto's University Avenue is not attractive to people on foot. It's a great way to go either north or south from Bloor to Front Street, about three miles, if you're in a car. Three, sometimes four, wide open lanes see to that. But if you're on foot it's totally unwelcoming. The buildings are imposing and cold, running as they do to embassies, legal offices, and hospitals, including the city's saddest place, the Hospital for Sick Children.

Despite this, I walked north toward the University of

Toronto and my meeting with Julian Amory because I needed the air and because driving a bright red sports car seemed like a good way to attract police attention.

There was no reason to hurry, but I found myself walking fast anyway. It seemed appropriate. On my left a blur of cars raced by on its way north. The buildings on my right loomed silent, empty and hard. I don't think I passed an unlocked door, except for the guarded entrances to the hospitals, which are never welcoming places at any time.

I hustled across University—with eight lanes and a median you have no choice but to hustle—at College Street on the south side, making sure to keep my head down as I walked. There were people on the southwest corner, and they were a refreshing touch of humanity, even if they were all just waiting to take a streetcar someplace else. I looked into their faces and kept my mind off of what was behind them—Hydro Place, the most unapproachable building in Toronto, with its mirror windows running from College to University like twenty-story sunglasses. Home to Ontario Hydro, it's a fitting monument to a public corporation whose deficit is the only thing bigger than its ego.

Beyond that, however, College Street takes on human trappings. For one thing, it's the southern boundary for the St. George campus of the University of Toronto, one of my favorite places. Whenever I step onto any campus I feel safer, nobler, worthier, smarter—whatever contributes to exaggerated contentment. I have never been able to explain this feeling to myself, and do not intend to think about it lest I break the spell. It's a hearty enough spell, having survived the recent change in public attitude that took universities from being the seats of higher learning to job-training centers, but I don't want to put more strain on it than I have to.

I walked slowly through the mostly deserted campus to kill the ten minutes left before I was to meet Julian Amory, but when I turned the last corner he was already waiting under the clock.

Amory saw me a second after I saw him. He dropped his

cigarette to the gound and overdid that *en pointe*, heel-swinging move peculiar to smoke-butting. When he was done with that Amory jammed his hands into the deep pockets of an exceedingly long double-breasted overcoat and grabbed onto me with a determined look. Up close the look was being held on like a mask, covering the pain and sadness behind.

I nodded a greeting.

Amory lit a cigarette, took a big drag, tried and failed to move the cigarette from his face, then took another big drag. "Cane, you know all that shit you heard about Leslie Harlan being Sean Denby's lover?"

Him knowing about that surprised me. "Yeah. What of it?"

"It's just what I said it was—shit."

"You think it's not true?"

"I know it's not true, Cane."

"How's that?"

"She told me."

"Why?"

"Why what?"

"Why would she tell you that, Amory? She told me yesterday that she was having an affair with Sean."

Amory looked over my shoulder and registered confusion at what he saw. I kept my eyes on his face. He looked back at me. "I know she told you that. She told you that on the way to Denby's memorial service."

While I took this in Amory took another pull at his cigarette and looked over my shoulder again. Over his I noticed two middle-aged men in white single-breasted raincoats coming our way, looking even more out of place than Amory and I. They were looking at us. I knew then what Amory was looking at over my shoulder—more out-of-place guys in raincoats.

"Couldn't she have been lying to you, Amory?" The idea wounded him. He blinked, swallowed and looked away. "We don't have much time," I said. The men were fifty yards away and closing quickly. "So tell me."

He just looked away and stayed silent. But I had to know, and right away. "You were her lover, weren't you?" He answered with his tears. "It was you she was seeing when she was supposed to be working as a hospital volunteer." When he nodded it made the tears run down his face.

"Who'd kill Leslie, Cane?" Amory's voice was out of control. He pawed at his tears with the wrist of his expensive coat.

"Probably the same person who killed Sean and Lucy Braverman." Amory looked blank at the second name. "The hospital volunteer who told me about Leslie," I said, and he nodded in recognition.

The white raincoats were getting very near. "Amory, why would Leslie lie to me?" I spoke in a quick hush. "I believe she was telling you the truth, but why would she lie to me?"

It was a question he'd already asked himself, and I could see the pain of hopeless confusion in his eyes because he couldn't answer it.

The white raincoats were slowing as they came up behind Amory. I saw one of them exchange a look with the raincoats scuffling to a stop behind me. Amory shot me a look that said he was sorry. I pulled myself to attention and looked right at the men standing behind Amory.

But they didn't look back at me. They were watching Amory.

"Julian Amory," one of the cops behind him said.

Amory was confused about being spoken to, but looked over his shoulder and said, "Yes?"

I looked over my shoulder and saw the two cops behind me looking at Amory. I could understand his confusion.

"Mr. Amory, would you come with us, please?" The same cop spoke again, but this time he had his hand on Amory's elbow.

Amory might have been confused, but his experience as Canada's foremost gambler came to the fore. "What's the charge?" he demanded.

"We're arresting you for the murder of Leslie Harlan," the

policeman said. His partner took Amory's other arm at just that moment—luckily for Amory, who would have fallen over from shock if he hadn't.

I don't know who was more surprised, me or Amory. For a mad moment I thought the cops didn't know who I was, and that if they did they'd have taken me along on the same charge, or for murdering Sean or that poor hospital volunteer.

But they knew who I was, all right. One of the cops standing behind me said, "Mr. Cane, Inspector Hurst would like a word with you. We'll give you a ride to the station." He was polite, but left no room for refusal.

I nodded dumbly.

One of the cops took up the point position as the two guys herded Julian Amory away. The fourth man stayed behind me. While we walked more policemen came into view, so by the time we got to the bank of squad cars on Harbord Street we were a nice little parade.

I HAD A NICE NEW PUZZLE PIECE, COURtesy of Julian Amory. For over two hours in a small grim room at the main police building I considered it. I turned it over. I turned it sideways. I turned it upside-down. I held it up next to other pieces I already had. I stared at it. I tried to imagine it in a different shape. Finally, I threw it away in disgust.

As well as being frustrated, I was bone-weary, but no matter how I squirmed or perched in any of the room's straight-

164

backed chairs I couldn't get comfortable. So I walked some of my stiffness off and picked out the softest looking corner of the floor and dropped down onto it. That felt better. Good enough to let my mind slip into neutral as I deep-focused on a wall spot across the room. That spot was still the center of my universe when Inspector Ian Hurst and Sergeant Harry Varina came through the door.

Varina seemed deeply offended by the fact that I was sitting on the floor. He glared silently down, wanting me to know he was pissed off at me but deferential to Hurst's feelings.

Hurst didn't seem to care at all that I was on the floor. It could have been that showing an emotion of any kind would require more effort than he had left. Hurst was so beat he actually got comfort from one of the straightbacked chairs. He swung one of his big legs up onto the scarred table and said quietly, "Let's have it."

I gave it to him. Everything but Eric VanKaspal's sexual preferences. He said nothing; it was purely a monologue. I closed with, "That's about it."

He considered my speech before replying. Finally, he said. "When you were here the other day, did you see a scoreboard in the squad room?" He stopped, obviously intent on waiting for an answer of some sort.

"I don't . . . unnhh . . . I don't . . . ."

Hurst cut in on my banter. "How about a referee? Some cheerleaders? Bleachers full of fans?"

I looked down at my hands.

He stood up, anger overcoming exhaustion. "Well in that case, how in the flaming fuck did you get the idea that this was some sort of a game?"

That was his opening blow in a series of cuts designed to make me feel like a pile of minced dogshit. He would have been more successful if he'd relied more on the disappointment he felt in my actions and eased up on the moral indignation. Still, he did manage on a couple of occasions to make me feel like a bigger jerk than I actually was, and when he was finished I meant it when I said I was sorry.

In a final burst of emotion he laughed at my apology and then slumped into the chair again.

"Have you charged Julian Amory?" I asked him.

Hurst looked at me disbelievingly; I guess he'd expected me to speak only when spoken to. Then he said, "Yes."

"For killing Leslie Harlan?"

Hurst nodded. "And maybe Denby."

"He might have killed Sean, but he didn't kill Leslie."

Hurst's look was pitying. "Why's that?"

"Because he loved her too much." It sounded hokey and hollow when I said it, so I wasn't surprised when Hurst laughed.

Varina joined in, but quit before Hurst and said, "Cane, you think people don't kill the people they love? Shit, man, they do it all the time. I'm surprised they don't do it more often. Especially when they're fucking around behind their backs."

"You think Amory killed Leslie Harlan because she was sleeping with Sean Denby?"

"You got a better reason?"

"No, but I also don't believe in that one. Amory's convinced Leslie wasn't Sean's lover. And if he doesn't believe that why would he kill her?"

Varina dismissed my comments with a shake of his head. Hurst's wheels turned in thought.

Nobody spoke for a few moments. I got the idea that my immediate future was being worked out by Hurst in the silence. During his lecture on the stupidity of my actions it'd seemed that he might be considering crucifixion as a suitable punishment. I was expecting a couple of charges related to obstructing the police, or maybe even acting like a fool without a license. Something to show me who was in charge here. But in a very tired voice, Hurst just said, "Get out of here, Cane."

Varina almost exploded. "Inspector," he said, but stopped

when Hurst looked up at him. Obviously Varina'd hoped to have the pleasure of charging me, during which time I'd try to get away from him and four other cops while standing at the top of a flight of cement stairs.

I got quickly to my feet and headed for the door. My exit was made without eye contact of any kind by any of us, which suited me.

In a couple of minutes I was going through the station's main door onto the street, where I took some long, deep breaths of the crisp night air. I hadn't noticed how crummy the air inside the station had been until I'd stopped breathing it.

Saturday night was getting up a full head of steam by then, so I had some trouble getting a cab. Eventually I did and we shot down Jarvis toward the lake, made a right at Front, and pulled up at the Royal York.

At just past eleven P.M. the Royal York's lobby was firmly in the grip of the stuffy gaiety suitable for the grande dame of Canada's hotels. Some of the guys from the Ugly Suit Society were trying to be just raucous enough so that someone might notice without actually taking offense.

I escaped all that by taking an elevator to the twenty-fourth floor and Alison Denby's room, where I knocked sharply on her door and then leaned against the sill. Through the door I could hear her approaching. The fish-eyed peephole went black for a second and then locks were undone. The door swung open and Alison was standing there looking delighted and concerned. I didn't move for a second, so she reached out both arms and pulled me gently inside. It was the single most loving thing anyone had done to me since my wife had been killed. When I heard the door close behind me, the tension, stress, worry and fear fell off my back like so many capes. I got as far as the bed and threw myself down on it to listen to Alison pour a drink. The bed jiggled slightly when she sat down next to me.

She put the drink in my hand and said, "Tough day at the office, dear?"

I drank the contents of the glass in one long swallow by way of an answer. Then I reached out for her, though not the same way she'd reached out for me in the doorway. I had something more physical in mind. She went along, but I could sense that the encounter would not make her Ten Best list. Mine either, for that matter. It was pure release. Release of what I don't know, but when it was gone I felt better for the loss of it.

I propped myself up on my elbow before speaking for the first time since entering the room. "So what's for dinner, hon? I'm starved."

She tossed a room-service menu in my face and we looked through it while we had another drink. Alison hadn't eaten either, so we placed a rather large order for food, a bottle of wine, and a robe. The person on the other end of the phone was as surprised by that last bit as I was, so Alison repeated the order for both our sakes. "That's right, a robe, a big one."

Alison hung up, came back to the bed and pulled me to my feet. Then she took off the odd items of clothing I still had on and pulled me to the bathroom. She peeled off the remainder of her clothes, started a shower, and told me to get in. I wasn't in the mood for protesting, so I went along with her orders while she stayed just outside of the bathtub enclosure. The water was very hot, hotter than I normally like, but I went along some more. Alison put my head under the spray, and when my hair was wet enough applied bloody big dollops of a strong herbal shampoo.

"What is that stuff," I asked, "garden salad shampoo?"

"Shut up," she explained.

I went along some more. She used the excess suds to clean the rest of me, all the while leaning in from outside the tub. I put my hands up on the wall beside the shower head as Alison kept working. I was really going along now, so much so that when there was a knock on the door I suggested ignoring it. But she left the bathroom, stopping only long enough to put on a towel. I rinsed and turned off the water in time to hear a man say "Thank you" with so much feeling I knew it had more to do with the way Alison looked in the towel than with the tip she'd given him. The waiter was still in the room when Alison pushed open the bathroom door, tossed me the robe and said, "How about it, you want to spend another thousand dollars?"

We had dinner before I spent another thousand—or at least I would have spent it if need be.

When we were done Alison said something I took to be "Good night" and fell asleep. The sight of the blankets gently heaving above Alison's chest reminded me of that Richard Pryor line: "If you're done fucking and your woman's still awake, you got more fuckin' to do." For a time I lay in the bed of that beautiful, sexy woman, staring into the darkness, drinking wine and feeling smug. Then I thought about where another beautiful woman, Leslie Harlan, might be lying and what her embrace would be like. I did not feel smug any longer. I thought about lying with Leslie and was afraid.

I grabbed Alison and hugged her so tight she woke up. She turned into my arms, gave me a drowsy kiss, and drifted back off to sleep. I held onto her warmth to forget Leslie's cold embrace until I could reach sleep. But in the night I slipped out of Alison's arms into Leslie's more than once, and woke with a shudder each time. With dawn came relief. I am one of the millions who stupidly believe there is more to be afraid of in the night than in the light. I got out of bed and pulled back the curtains enough so that the room was completely lit. Alison moaned slightly and rolled over away from the window. I eased myself back into bed next to her and enjoyed almost three hours of solitary sleep.

When consciousness got hold of me again at nine A.M. I was alone in bed. I listened for Alison but could not hear her. I thought about calling out to her, but decided against it. Better to lie there quietly until she announced herself. So I did, until lying there quietly became a ridiculous response.

I got out of bed and went to the bathroom. I knocked and called out her name before easing the door open. It was empty. At least there was no Alison, just proof of her: a brush, some makeup, a travel bag, that kind of thing. The travel bag was on its side with its contents spilling out. A brown pillbox caught my eye. I looked around the room to make sure Alison wasn't hiding behind the toilet tank or the folded-up towels before I picked the pillbox up, opened it and looked inside. Pills. They didn't look like any kind of pills that I recognized—they were sort of yellow. But, then, the only pills I'd recognize would be the aspirins with the trademark cross on the top. People in movies and on TV can always tell what something is by licking it. No use to me, since I couldn't be sure I'd spot aspirin that way. I put the lid back on the pillbox and went to great lengths to get it back in exactly its right position in the travel bag. Not that Alison would ever notice. I felt ridiculous and left the bathroom.

I was flicking off the light when Alison put the room key in the door. I pulled open the door so fast it startled her. She stood there holding a coffee bag and some newspapers. "I'm glad to see you, too," she said, ogling my nakedness. A couple passing in the hall reacted differently.

 ALISON DENBY AND I HAD COFFEE AND A roll while she flipped through the newspapers and I looked out the window at the view. I preferred the view to the newspapers. To her credit, Alison said nothing about what she was reading, even though it was of very direct interest to both of us.

When she was finished I offered to take her out to brunch. She jumped at the idea. She'd gone outside for the coffee and the papers and reported that it was gorgeous out. I suggested Fenton's, a popular restaurant just off Yonge Street that's designed to let a lot of the "gorgeous out" in.

We walked from the Royal York to the Four Seasons where I learned that's it's almost as expensive for a car to stay overnight there as it is for a human being. I eased the Golf along Adelaide to Jarvis, where I headed north. Alison did a good job of talking for both of us without mentioning what was uppermost in both our minds. Only once did she falter—when we passed the main police station. I seemed to be going by it all the time. I looked straight ahead but Alison considered it in silence. When we were past it she said, "Ugly place."

"You should see the inside."

"Pass."

From there we were quiet until I pulled the Golf into the driveway of my house. In a too-even voice Alison said, "Nice place."

"It's a bloody mansion," I said. "That's what I called it the first time I came here, and I haven't changed my opinion."

Alison looked at me askance. "You sound sorry that it's yours."

"Not sorry, exactly. Awkward. Embarrassed. I think it's easier if you're born into it."

Alison opened her arms, closed her eyes and took a deep breath as she moved toward the house. "I think I can learn to live with it." She caught my reaction to the comment. "I haven't told you yet, but in the next couple of days I'm going to have to start dealing with a similar problem. Sean left a lot of insurance money. I get most of it."

"When did you find out?"

It was a clumsy question under the circumstances, so Alison shot me a look that told me as much. "Norris Harlan told me Friday. Why?"

"I don't know why. I guess I'm just suspicious these

171

days." That did a good job of dimming Alison's glow. I needed to work on my people skills.

She sat downstairs while I went to the third floor to change. The house was empty, as it always is on Sunday because my housekeeper takes her young son out for the day. In minutes I was back to where Alison sat, quiet and still. I could see corrective surgery would be necessary to remove my foot from my mouth.

We were driving toward Fenton's before I'd figured out what to say. "I'm sorry, Alison. I didn't mean anything personal by my question. I mean, I don't suspect you. The whole thing's got me shook. I was gonna ask a few questions, turn up a couple of clues and put the guilty party behind bars. Instead the whole thing's turned into a fetid cow patty in my very hands. I have a feeling I've played a part in two deaths, Lucille Braverman's and Leslie Harlan's. And the wrong man's in jail for Leslie's murder, and maybe Sean's. It's not working out and I'm grasping at straws." When I was done I put my right hand out toward her. She took it and gave it a squeeze.

Fenton's wasn't as busy as I expected, so we got a table after only a short wait. The food and the service were first rate, as always, but it was almost all ruined for me by the group next to us. Their very existence grated. I couldn't begin to guess what the men did. The women were wealthy anorexics, exposed to Mrs. Wallace Simpson's maxim at an impressionable age. They were Noel Coward characters without his wit and charm, terminally superficial. I was overreacting to them like crazy; it certainly wasn't their fault about the way things were working out. I was angry because I was spending my time near them rather than doing something worthwhile, and because Lucille Braverman was dead and they were still posing their way through life.

I declined the waiter's suggestions about coffee and dessert on our behalf. Alison looked disappointed but trusting. "I know a better place," I said, trying to sound mysterious and masterful.

Alison sat up in the Golf like a kid on her way to visit Santa.

172

When Santa's place of business turned out to be a Tim Horton Donuts she was not thrilled. "Do I laugh now?" she said.

"We have to go somewhere right away and we can eat and drink these as we drive," I explained. "Black coffee, right? And a donut?"

"Black coffee, and whatever has the most calories."

Alison didn't ask where we were going until I pulled the Golf onto the westbound Gardiner Expressway, and when I told her all she did was take another bite of her eclair and flare her eyebrows.

At first the going was slow because we were battling the traffic going into the Metros game, set to start in about an hour. But once we were past the stadium exit the pace picked up so I pushed the Golf hard, zipping in and out of traffic to show everyone what German engineering could do. I felt the need to hurry, though I don't know why. I was saving some time, but the primary benefit was psychological—I felt like I was doing instead of being done to.

When the road widened and flattened at the beginning of the Queen Elizabeth Way, I let the Golf loose and held it at about 160 kilometers an hour all the way up Highway 427 to the Burnamthorpe exit. If a cop had caught me going 60 kilometers over the speed limit I'd have been out a couple of hundred bucks and half of the demerit points you're allowed before they take your license away. I wouldn't have cared; waiting for the ticket would have been the only thing that hurt.

My memory of the route to 81 Duke Street was sharp so it took me only a few minutes to get Alison and me there. No preliminaries this time, just right along Duke and into 81's driveway. I gave Alison a don't-worry smile, she gave me a brave smile in return and we both got out of the car.

I pounded on the door hard enough to alert anyone dead inside that we were there. When no one came to the door after a split second I had the key in the lock and was moving the tumblers that sounded as loud in the daylight as they had at night.

It was stuffy inside the house, but quiet, and bright. The soapstone carvings still lay on the living room floor, the only obvious victims of the battle that had taken place in there two nights before. No other evidence of what happened was to be seen.

I sniffed the air for liniment but found nothing. That was a sign of what was to follow.

Nothing was what I kept finding all through the house. It might as well have been a guest cottage at a large hotel, waiting for its next visitors. Someone less forgetful maybe, since the previous guest had left some clothing and toiletries, but no books, papers, receipts, magazines, bills, nothing. Nothing on the first floor, nothing on the second.

Okay, so there were no obvious clues; I'd just have to be creative with what there was. Toothbrushes, shaving equipment, underwear, socks, shirts in dry-cleaner bags, and a raft of handkerchiefs, no monogram. Basic gear for the complete philanderer.

I sat down on the double bed on the second floor and waited for what was there to speak to me. There was no sound in the house, not even from Alison, who'd stayed downstairs.

I looked at the night table next to where I sat. A small reading lamp, a clock radio, and a large jar of Vaseline. None of this said anything to me either. Then I thought I heard something clearing its throat.

I went back to the four-drawer dresser I'd gone through a few minutes before and pulled open the top drawer. Men's socks and underwear.

I closed that drawer and opened the second one. Men's socks and underwear.

I closed that drawer and opened the third one. Men's shirts in dry-cleaning packages and handkerchiefs.

I closed that drawer and opened the fourth one. Men's shirts in dry-cleaning packages and handkerchiefs.

Very softly, the stuff finally spoke to me. "Different dry-cleaning packages," it said. Indeed, all the shirts in the bottom drawer were from one laundry, and all the shirts in the third drawer were from another.

I went back to the drawers with the socks and underwear. The top drawer had white briefs and executive wool hose. The second drawer had white briefs and cotton-polyester calf-length socks. Everything had mass-produced labels.

I closed the drawer and hurried back to the bathroom. In my mind was the memory of Sean Denby tossing something to me from the door of my room at university one night. Something he'd been given as a gift at some sports banquet. Something he couldn't use himself. An electric razor.

"Just like this one," I said to my reflection as I held up the shaver I'd just taken out of the cabinet behind the bathroom mirror. My reflection looked excited.

I put the razor in my jacket pocket instead of back in the cabinet next to the can of shaving cream, the safety razor, a package of blades and the two bottles of aftershave.

I should have twigged when my first look around failed to turn up any items obviously used by a woman.

You could argue that Sean and some other guy shared expenses so they'd have some place to bring women, but the big jar of Vaseline next to the bed had me convinced that wasn't right.

A lot of things were starting to come clear now. Many voices began to speak out at once, demanding my attention. There were so many it was hard to understand any of them, but I knew I would in time.

Alison was outside when I got downstairs, but not near the car. She looked tense, and when I closed the door she stepped away even further from the car. I took the Golf's keys out of my pocket and tossed them to her. She caught them and gave me a confused look.

"Take the car if you want. I understand. I'll catch a cab."

She looked at the keys, at the Golf, at the house, and at me. She tossed the keys back. "My turn to be sorry." She faced the house and shivered. "That's not a nice place. And women have to be more careful." At the mention of the word *careful* she tightened up again, probably wondering if I was conning her into getting into the car.

"When you were married to Sean, did he ever use an electric razor?"

Alison watched me for a minute to see if any marbles were falling out of my ears. When she saw none she said, "No, he had a skin condition."

"Then he couldn't have been using this." I held the shaver up.

"No, I guess not." Brief pause while her mind worked. "Then who did?"

"I've got a theory about that. I'll tell you about it as soon as it makes perfect sense to me," I said and headed the car toward Sean's house.

The window Paul Lacosta had smashed two nights before was still broken. I was surprised at this, since I'd mentioned it the day before to Inspector Hurst. Either he'd forgotten to do something about it, or the police carpenters didn't work on Sunday. Strangely, this lapse in police procedure seemed more significant to me than their having arrested the wrong person for Leslie Harlan's murder.

Alison was slow to join me at the door. She stood back, eyeing the house the way people do when something they own has been damaged, only this damage was psychological, not physical, and probably permanent.

"You shouldn't have much trouble getting it ready for sale," I said. "I looked at the police photos and there wasn't any damage I can remember." Alison nodded. "And I wouldn't worry about any loss in market value; some people would pay extra for what happened here, others wouldn't care, and most wouldn't even know." She nodded some more. "You going to wait out here?" This time she smiled thinly and nodded.

In the daylight Sean's home looked a lot more inviting, so I didn't bother to knock. I reached through the broken window and undid the lock. A little more glass got crunched when I stepped into the hallway. The living room was neat, though dusty. Same for the dining room and the kitchen.

176

The bedroom was dusty but not neat; there were wrinkles on the bedspread, and the thick carpet was flat from too many police boots. I crossed the room toward the bathroom, which was neat, though my memory of it was messy. Looking at the toilet Sean had been drowned in was a mistake, so I turned away from it. Out of sight, almost out of mind.

In the medicine cabinet I found only one kind of safety razor, one kind of aftershave, one kind of everything.

I went back into the bedroom. The one night table I could see held only a lamp, so I walked around the bed to look at the other table and found a jar of Vaseline in a drawer.

All I had to do, I figured, was lay my theory at Inspector Ian Hurst's big flat feet. He could do all the grunt work proving it for the resultant trial. I'd be too busy wallowing in self-congratulation.

I sat down on the bed to use the one-piece telephone on the night table. Probably Hurst was at headquarters, making life miserable for the detectives who'd rather be at home watching the football game. Maybe Hurst was at home, preferring the violent order of football to the violent disorder of murder. A detective told me Hurst wasn't in the office but he could be reached if it was important. I told the detective it was and he took my name and phone number in a very casual manner. When I mentioned important evidence in three murder trials the detective's interest level went up, but not enough to fill me with optimism that the detective would bust himself getting my message to Hurst.

I wanted to get it off my chest and maybe get Julian Amory out of jail. What exactly I was going to get off my chest was another matter. The time waiting for Hurst to call could be well spent getting my thoughts in order, so I sat up straight on the bed and looked over for a spot to focus on while my mind went to work.

The room looked familiar from the police photos Hurst had shown me. In real life it was much better. For instance, the odd painting from the photographs turned out to be a stunning, stark Inuit work of a bear loping over the ice. It had no menace; instead the animal looked tense, as if it were running away from something rather than at it. I wondered if Alison would sell it to me when she disposed of the house and its furnishings.

I stood up and went over to have a better look at it. It was large, maybe four feet by six feet, and looked even better from up close—except that it was a little crooked, a little high on the left. With my left hand I tried to straighten it, but it didn't straighten. It closed. Like a door swinging shut, with a click.

I stepped back and stared at the bear, as if I expected him to move or maybe even to explain. He stayed the way he was, silently fleeing.

If a painting closes, I reasoned, it also opens. So with the tips of my fingers I searched the left side of the bear painting. I couldn't feel anything and I couldn't see anything, right down to the bottom of the left side of the frame. But on my knees, from less than a foot away, I saw a piece of dark brown frame molding that was slightly irregular.

Gently, I pushed and pulled on the piece of molding. It moved slightly but nothing happened until I pushed the molding toward the wall and to the left, and the bear picture unlatched with a click.

The picture swung rather easily then. I stepped back to move it all the way open, and the phone rang.

It was Hurst. "Cane," he said when I answered it, "where are you?"

"At Sean Denby's place." There was an ominous pause; Hurst had advised against my coming back here. "I'm here with the new owner."

"Cane, nobody owns a murder scene." He was royally pissed off at me.

"I know you told me not to come back here, but I have, and I've found something here you should see. And something to tell you—maybe."

"Maybe?" Hurst was more incredulous now than angry. He took a breath that was so deep I could almost feel the suck of air over the phone. "I'll be there in less than ten minutes," Hurst said. "Don't touch a thing. Don't even pick your ass." The phone went dead.

I stood up and went back to examine what I'd found, wondering what their significance was. I could guess, but it would take lab work to prove it. They had driven my theory about the Vaseline and the electric shaver right out of my head. This was hard evidence.

But how best to present them to Hurst? I imagined him bursting through the bedroom door, pissed off enough to bounce me around the room. I'd cool him off by swinging the painting open and displaying what was behind it with a flourish. "Inspector," I'd say, "wait'll you see this cache of empty shelves I found."

Right. If that was the best I could do, he'd offer to show me his cache of empty cells.

 **26** WHEN HURST ARRIVED, I WAS STANDING out by the Golf, trying to impress Alison with my discovery of the empty shelves behind the bear painting. I wasn't doing too well.

He'd got there in less than ten minutes because he'd come from home, I guess. He certainly was dressed for home—checked shirt under paint-splattered denim coveralls and large safety boots that crushed gravel as he walked up the driveway to where I was standing.

"Ms. Denby," Hurst said evenly to Alison. "Let's see it,"

he said not so evenly to me. He had a "Go ahead impress me" look on his face.

Without speaking I led him through the house to the bedroom, where he waited behind me quietly as I knelt in front of the bear. I fumbled with the latch for a second, but then it moved. I stood up and swung the painting aside with the flourish I'd planned. *Ta-da:* empty shelves.

I kept my eyes on the shelves, away from Hurst. For a few seconds there was a silence, a silence I was afraid might be a dramatic pause before Hurst said, "So?"

When he said "Jesus H. Christ" I knew I was laughing. Actually, it was the tone he used—angry surprise—that relaxed me. He hadn't known the shelves were there, and he sounded a lot more impressed with them than I'd hoped he'd be.

"There's some white powder in the corner of the bottom shelf. Here," I said, pointing with my finger. I'd taken a quick look after talking to him on the phone.

Hurst was over his shock and back to normal. "I hope you didn't touch it," he said.

I didn't even acknowledge his comment.

"How'd you find it?"

"It was slightly ajar when I came in here. When I went to straighten it, it shut. I found the latch, opened it and you called."

"Good," Hurst said without any clue as to what he was referring to. He went to the phone beside the bed and called his office. Someone was going to catch shit over this, but not until he knew who really had it coming, so the call was only terse.

"Stay here," he said as he went past me toward the bedroom door. He was back in a few minutes, looking determined.

"At the risk of pointing out the obvious," I said, "I figure it was a hiding spot for drugs. I further figure it was what Paul Lacosta was looking for when he came here on Friday night. When I was here."

Hurst did not respond in any way. I took his silence as agreement.

"You haven't been able to find him yet?" It was an assumption on my part, but a reasonable one since Hurst was a good, thorough cop.

"Not yet. Maybe if we'd known about his visit here a little earlier . . ." It was a rebuke, mildly delivered but powerful. And fair. We both knew it, so I didn't bother replying.

"There's a Metros game on today," I said. "All those people, it'd be a good time for him to slip into his office at the stadium unnoticed."

"You figure he has to go back there?"

"Yeah. It looks like him and Sean were in business together, dealing dope. Or maybe they weren't; maybe just Sean was, but Lacosta knew and came here to clean out Sean's supply."

"He must have known where it was," Hurst pointed out, "so maybe they were partners. But why would he go to his stadium office?"

I looked at the empty shelves. "This is the warehouse. One of the stores would have to be the stadium. A football team makes for a good, stable supply of customers."

Hurst turned on his heel.

"I want to come along," I said to his retreating back. When he didn't even admit that he'd heard me, I added, "You owe me that."

Hurst stopped by his car door and laughed at my presumption. But he said "Okay" as he got into the car.

Alison had shown no signs of wanting to come along. When I asked her straight out she was quick to pass. I gave her the Golf's keys and said I'd talk to her later.

Hurst honked at me so I ran to the car door and got in. He hit the gas as soon as I was seated and we roared out of the driveway.

On the way along the street we passed a yellow squad car going the other way. Hurst waved it to a stop, and said, "Don't worry about the woman who's there now in the red car. From then on, nobody gets in until the squad gets there." He pulled away while the uniformed officers were still nodding their understanding of his orders.

On the way down Highway 427 Hurst called police dispatch. He told them to order the officers already at the stadium doing security and giving out parking tags to watch for and detain Paul Lacosta. I could see in his eyes and his voice that Hurst hoped Lacosta didn't show himself until we got there. I felt the same way.

We made good time going to the stadium, thanks to Hurst's unique driving style—he went where he wanted, when he wanted. Bolstered by the car's *whoop-whoop* siren and portable flasher, it worked very well.

When we arrived at the parking lot reserved for team personnel Hurst roared right in, ignoring the surprised looks of the lot's security guard.

The guard had the courage, if not the presence of mind, to come chugging along after us. "You can't park here, buddy," he yelled. Hurst had stopped right in the middle of the lot's only exit.

"You know Paul Lacosta?" Hurst asked as he got out of the car.

The guard clung to his assumed authority. "You can't park here," he said, appreciating the need to be reasonable and polite as he looked up at Ian Hurst.

"Do you know Paul Lacosta?" Hurst was losing his patience.

"Who wants to know?"

"Metro Police."

The guard was transformed before my very eyes. "Yes, sir, I know Mr. Lacosta."

"Is he here?"

"I think so. That's his Mark over there, so I guess he's still here."

I noticed Hurst's confusion and said quietly to him, "His car, a Lincoln Continental Mark VI. The big green one over there."

Hurst looked over at the Lincoln in disgust. "The pimpmobile?"

"That's it," I said, and took off with him for the Metros' private door.

At the door a young man with oily hair, uneven sideburns and bad teeth put his uniformed 175 pounds in our way. Hurst brushed him aside with his left arm, a lion dealing with a house cat at dinner time. "Police," Hurst said. "Paul Lacosta come out here yet?"

"No," said the security guard, putting aside his manhandling and warming to the thrill of talking to a real cop.

"If he comes down here, don't let him past," Hurst said.

The guard blanched, reconsidering his career path right on the spot. In an honestly disbelieving voice he said, "How?"

Hurst smiled at the question. "He'll help you," Hurst said, nodding at me. To me, he said, "Keep an eye outside for a cruiser. Maybe the four of you can handle him." His voice dripped sarcasm.

Feeling offended I said, "You don't know him."

"Whatever happens, just don't let him get in his car." With that Hurst was off, presumably to take on Lacosta himself if he found him. I wanted to follow, to watch that encounter if it came off.

I stayed where I was, though, trying to fool the rattled security guard into thinking we could deal with Lacosta if we had to. Before I got a chance to consider just how we might do that, a cruiser came along and stopped behind Hurst's car. I got to it just as the two cops got out of it, both adjusting their riot sticks as they stood up.

"Inspector Hurst wants you to make sure Paul Lacosta doesn't get away," I said.

"Just a moment, sir," the officer on the passenger side said in that snidely polite manner cops are so fond of. "Who are you?"

"Richard Cane. Listen, Inspector Hurst wants you . . ."

"Just a moment, sir. Is this Inspector Hurst's car?"

"Yes," I said, testily. "He wants you to—" I stopped wasting my breath. Neither cop was paying the slightest bit of attention to me. I took a second to calm down before saying, "Hurst said your ass would be a star if you let Lacosta get away." I figured Hurst was well known on the force.

The cops looked startled and exchanged a quick glance from beneath shiny new hat peaks.

"Who is this man the Inspector wants us to detain?"

"Paul Lacosta." I turned to lead them to the door. "He should be coming out—shit. That's him."

Lacosta had run unemcumbered through the door; there was no sign of the security guard, or of Hurst. He had a slight limp, but he moved very quickly, covering half the distance to his Lincoln before the two patrolmen and I could get untracked. So Lacosta was in his Lincoln while we were still about thirty feet away and had it running before we reached its rear end. He backed it out quickly, and the three of us scattered. The one cop, the one who'd done the talking, was not quite fast enough. He'd tried to leap out of the Lincoln's way, but it caught his butt. He slid along the trunk until his hip hit the rear window with enough force to spin him off the Lincoln and onto the car parked next to it. He took another good bump there before he fell heavily onto his hands and knees.

Lacosta, oblivious to all this or just not caring, narrowly missed clipping the young man with the front of his huge car.

The second cop didn't know what to do. His eyes went from his injured partner to the Lincoln to his injured partner. When Lacosta braked the Lincoln before going forward, the uninjured officer finally decided to run toward it yelling "Stop, police," and other useless things.

The cop, who apparently trained under Mack Sennett, chased Lacosta on foot around the small lot, narrowly missing being run down at least once. The rest of the pedestrians wisely took cover so they could stare in open-mouthed astonishment from positions of safety.

I went to help the injured policeman up, since I had a

good idea of what Lacosta might do when he saw that the only exit was blocked. The officer was woozy and hobbled some, but grateful to me for leading him to the end of the car he'd been bounced off.

Toronto is essentially a peaceful place, and Canada has tough gun control laws, so unless there's evidence to the contrary the police assume the citizens are unarmed. Cops are therefore trained not to go for their guns automatically. Lives have to be at stake. You could have argued that lives were at stake, but the young officer did not pull his service revolver. He followed the Lincoln as well as he could, assuming that, like most Canadians, Lacosta would succumb to his respect for authority and stop.

Lacosta was not burdened in this manner, however; he kept on driving, and dinged Hurst's car as he passed the exit. Without pausing he bulled the Lincoln around the lot and headed back for where it had been parked, so I moved the injured officer further away. Lacosta was going to make his own exit, and I did not want to be nearby when he did.

Lacosta was hindered by the poor entry angle into his parking space, but still he had the Lincoln doing at least fifteen miles an hour when he hit the six-inch curb with its front wheels. There was a bang, some grinding, crunching and crashing, and then a bigger bang when the Lincoln's rear wheels hit the curb. End of undercarriage.

The Lincoln was wounded, but not mortally. It chewed up the grass on the far side of the curb as Lacosta fishtailed it toward the four-foot-high chain-link fence separating the stadium from Lakeshore Boulevard.

If you're going to try to run a steel fence down, a four-door 1981 Lincoln Continental Mark VI is one of your better choices for the job. Including Lacosta's body weight, it meant that there was almost 4,400 pounds of ramming power aimed at that fence. Crunch, snap, end of fence.

But the Lincoln was slowed somewhat by the fence as Lacosta neared the next curb, the big one separating the grass from the road. Also he was going at it from a bad angle, almost parallel to it. He tried to correct but couldn't do it in time, so there was more metal-gnashing as its undercarriage got pounded some more. The Lincoln went over the curb like a giant green turtle on ice skates, and by the time Lacosta got it pointed along Lakeshore Boulevard it was down to five miles an hour and staggering badly.

Those people who get their idea of a car's durability from watching the Duke boys bash the General Lee around Hazzard County are not familiar with mechanical reality. You can't treat a car like that—even a well-built, tough and expensive one like a Lincoln—and expect it to just keep on rolling along like always. Lacosta probably knew that, but he was getting an object lesson just the same. His wounded Lincoln was lurching along slowly despite his obvious demands for more speed.

I propped the injured officer up on the car and sprinted toward the cruiser at the parking lot exit. "Come on," I yelled to the mobile cop, who was standing there looking for someplace to stick his finger.

Moving toward the car, I got my first look at a very impressive sight: a wounded and deeply angry inspector Ian Hurst looking for blood. He jogged awkwardly across the parking lot, trying not to move his left arm.

I waved at him and yelled, "Come on, come on, come on."

The green Lincoln was limping along Lakeshore Boulevard with smoke spewing out of its ass end and the engine bitching constantly. It was doing about twenty miles per hour and holding. We could catch it easily.

"Where is he?" Hurst said when he got up to his car. His face was knotted with pain as he moved while trying to keep his arm immobile. A trickle of blood dripped down his face.

"Going west on Lakeshore. His car's damaged, though, and he's not making any real time."

"Let's get him. You better drive."

Hurst had trouble getting into the passenger side of his own car, but when he was finally in I backed it out rather quickly. I didn't have the room I thought I had, so I banged the rear quarter panel of the cruiser parked behind me.

Hurst didn't even blink. He just said, "Hurry up, for Chrissakes."

So I did.

## 27

FOLLOWING THE ROADS OUT OF THE STA-dium onto Lakeshore Boulevard would take too long, so I decided to follow Lacosta's creative road-making—slowly. I turned the car onto the grass and drove along next to the parking lot toward where Lacosta had gone through the fence. I had to rearrange the landscaping some, and soon I was rolling the smaller car over the flattened bit of fence. I stopped the car by the curb and babied it over when traffic permitted. There was some grinding under the car, but nothing to match the death-throes of the Lincoln. Once the last tire was down on Lakeshore's pavement and the rear end clear of the curb, I dropped the car's transmission into low and stood on it.

Squealing tires is a juvenile activity I've never gotten over enjoying. I probably never will, and I definitely never had a squeal as satisfying as that one along Lakeshore Boulevard in an unmarked police car lighting out after a murder suspect. I could not enjoy it totally, however, because each bump and roll of the car made my passenger grimace.

If Lacosta's car was as wounded as I thought it was, I knew it wouldn't take more than a couple of minutes to catch him. He didn't have much of a lead, and I was going more than three times as fast, yet there was no sign of him, not even of the smoke I was sure his Lincoln would still be throwing off. Either his car wasn't as badly damaged as I figured, or he'd gone another way. Only there was no other way he could have gone—at least in a car. There was only the exit for Ontario Place, the huge park that filled the space between the lake and Lakeshore Boulevard. It was closed for the season, but you could still get into the parking lot if you didn't care for the niceties of the law.

I slowed the car and craned my neck to search the parking lot that stretched off to my left. Bingo. It was either Lacosta's Lincoln or a small oil dump was on fire.

Using a space that wasn't really there, I pulled the car into the left-hand lane, making brakes squeal behind me and sending a couple of fenders to that great wrecker's yard in the sky. Looking to see what damage I'd caused was out of the question because I was busy steering against three lanes of traffic and through a gate marked Do Not Enter.

I was having a hell of a time. Hurst wasn't; he let out little animal noises once or twice, which meant he was in the kind of pain most people faint from. He was grimly determined to get Lacosta's butt on a plate.

We rounded a corner just as Lacosta abandoned his dying Lincoln by an Ontario Place entrance booth. He started to run into the park, which is a pleasantly eclectic mix of beaches, grass, theaters, restaurants, rides and pathways. It seemed an odd place to escape to. In fact, it seemed almost like a dead end to me.

Not to Hurst. He had thought of something I hadn't—Ontario Place's marina—and was on the radio telling the dispatcher to get the harbor police to close off the marina's exit. He also ordered some cars to seal up Ontario Place itself. He did not specifically ask for any help where we were. Bad police practice, I knew, but just fine for Hurst personally.

I pulled up next to the Lincoln and yanked open my door.

"Stay with the car," Hurst said through his teeth as he tried to stand.

"No chance. You're hurt, and I'm not letting you go after him alone."

Hurst wasn't up to arguing the point or doing much else, especially running. I held back to stay with him, but I caught sight of Lacosta twice and knew that, despite his slight limp, he was rapidly getting away.

"I'll see if I can catch him," I said to Hurst over my shoulder.

"Cane, you stupid son of a bitch, come back here. Cane!" Hurst was yelling in frustration. He was genuinely concerned about me.

I slowed enough to explain what I had in mind. "I'll just get close enough to see where he goes. Maybe I'll try to slow him down some."

Hurst shook his head. He didn't like it, but he didn't have another choice. "All right, just stay the hell away from him," he ordered. There was no need to worry about that, since anyone who could get past Ian Hurst and hurt him in the process was way out of my league.

I quickly found I couldn't run as fast as I once could. The body will do that to you if you ignore it for six months. I figured I could push it enough to catch a guy with a limp, though.

Ahead, Lacosta seemed to be fading after a couple hundred yards of Ontario Place's hilly terrain. That made me push myself harder, because I wanted his butt on a plate at least as much as Hurst did.

By the time he reached the edges of the marina, Lacosta was folding up like an old lawn chair. I was gaining with every stride, and when Lacosta went from a run to a jog I knew I could catch him.

Twenty yards behind him I realized I didn't really want to catch him. My run-in with him a few nights before had come out in my favor because of luck. I knew if we got up close and for real he could deal with me without losing his breath, so I eased up and watched for a weapon as I ran.

When Lacosta looked back and saw that it was just me following him, he slowed to a fast walk. I did too, which annoyed him greatly. I wanted to say something but couldn't think of anything appropriate. What do you say to a man you're not really chasing? I wouldn't catch him and he couldn't catch me. Sort of a Mexican stand-off.

I shot a look over my shoulder to see how Hurst was doing, but he was nowhere to be seen. This was a surprise since most of the path he'd have to come along was visible from where I was. I stopped running and looked ahead at Lacosta, who was jogging out onto one of the wooden ramps that floated in the water to provide docking berths. He had something in mind and I didn't think it was swimming all the way to Rochester.

At the foot of the ramp I stopped to work out what I was going to do. Getting closer as an observer would only give me a better view of Lacosta escaping. And if he was going to get away I'd have to try hand-to-hand combat to stop him. I'd probably die in the process, but if I didn't try I wasn't sure I could live with myself. Neither choice appealed to me. "Damn John Wayne, anyway," I said under my breath. "I wouldn't feel this way if Woody Allen had been making movies when I was a kid."

I looked around in desperation for a weapon that I could use from a safe distance, and there they were lying all around—rocks. Big, decorative rocks that divided the paved walkway and the grass border. Most of them were fairly big, five pounds and over, but I managed to scoop up about a dozen smaller ones that I could carry easily. With the painted white rocks cradled in my arms and my standing lap, I waddled out along the ramp after Paul Lacosta. He stopped beside a long powerboat and turned to see what I was up to. My running awkwardly along with a pile of rocks seemed to take him by surprise, but he overcame his surprise soon enough and began to untie the front of the boat. Only once did he look up at me, when I dropped one of the rocks onto the wooden ramp with a deep *clunk*. We both watched the rock roll off the dock and splash into the water, but he enjoyed it much more than I did. He smiled the way he had outside Sean's, just to show me he had nothing to fear from me.

This pissed me off a great deal. About twenty yards from Lacosta and his boat I stopped and eased the rocks onto the ramp with a rumble, losing only one more in the water.

Lacosta looked up, obviously enjoying the madman's show.

While he watched, I hefted one of the rocks to take its weight and figure the distance. I swung my arm like a pendulum and that tipped him. The small look of concern that escaped him warmed my heart.

My first throw was a disaster—it fell far short of Lacosta and his boat, bouncing instead off the deck of the boat next to it.

Lacosta went to the rear of his boat as I readied my next rock. I figured he was going to untie the rope back there, so that's what I aimed for. A couple of pendulum swings, careful release and—*thump,* the rock hit Lacosta's boat just where it was tied up to the deck, stopping Lacosta in his tracks. He looked over at me with murder in his eyes but that look disappeared when he saw I'd already tossed another rock his way. He watched it for a moment and then stepped out of its way. When it hit, it hit with a very loud crack. Lacosta glared at the boat where it'd been hit, and then started toward me.

Which was just what I wanted. I picked up three pieces of my arsenal and ran back along the floating ramp, having no trouble staying away from him. He stopped a few yards from the small pile of rocks and looked along the horizon. I could see in his face that there was no one in sight, but we both knew there probably would be soon. He went back to his boat and I took a running start and heaved another rock. It was wide, and beyond the mark, but moving faster, so it hit the boat with a crash. Lacosta flinched before leaping onto his boat. He knew I was reloading, so to speak.

I regained my firing line and tossed another rock at Lacosta working to unlock the boat's hatch. It hit the deck just behind him as the door slid open. It made him jump because he hadn't seen it coming, and then he quickly disappeared inside.

With my target gone, I stood around feeling pleased with myself for having held him up for a few more seconds. But when I saw that Hurst was still nowhere in sight, I knew I'd have to do a lot better.

And soon. A large diesel engine began coughing and sputtering as Lacosta worked on starting his boat.

What now, hero? What would John Wayne do? Woody Allen wasn't being too successful.

The engine coughed, sputtered and died. There was a silence and then the engine coughed and sputtered some more. And died again. I dropped the rocks and moved quietly to the boat, reaching it just as the diesel engine gave in to Lacosta's demands and began to run. As he worked the throttle to get the engine to run a little smoother, I scrambled toward the rope he'd undone, grabbed it, and looped it back over the cleat on the dock. The engine idle leveled out and I hustled back to my little pile of rocks. I didn't want Lacosta to know I'd been close to the boat. He appeared in the hatch just as I picked up another rock and tossed it in his direction. He watched its arc long enough to see it was going to fall close to him, so he ducked his head. When it hit the boat he barged right out and went to the front of the boat to untie the forward line. While he was bent over undoing the rope I got another shot off and it hit him on the back, just below his neck. He made a noise that was equal parts pain and anger. For a second I thought he was going to come after me again. That would have been fine, since I knew I could keep away from him until the cavalry came to the rescue. I ignored the fact that the cavalry was still nowhere to be seen.

Maybe because he knew it was what I wanted, Lacosta

didn't chase me. He went for the hatchway instead, and I tossed my third-last rock. It missed badly, but I didn't much care, since it had distracted him from seeing that I'd retied the boat. Woody Allen wasn't doing so bad.

Lacosta moved the boat away from the dock backward until the front end was clear, put the motor into forward and opened up the throttle, expecting to move away from the dock.

Only the boat stopped with a clunk when its stern rope ran out.

Lacosta strained the boat against the rope for a couple of seconds before easing off on the throttle and dropping it into neutral.

When I saw him coming out of the hatch I launched my penultimate rock, which he saw as it fell toward him. If he hadn't been an athlete I'm not sure he could have ducked it, but he did, so it dropped in front of him and fell inside the boat. He was nearly apoplectic at that, but, incredibly, his anger grew when he realized I'd tied his boat back up.

He stood in the hatchway glaring at me, another good reaction, since it would give the world's slowest cavalry more time to show up.

I hefted my last rock to toss at him as he untied the rear rope, only he didn't come up onto the deck. He disappeared inside again instead.

I figured he was going to ignore the knot and power away, preferring to lose some rope and the boat's cleat rather than any more time.

No sign of the cavalry.

And no more options. I trotted toward the boat, planning to jump on before Lacosta pulled it away from the dock. So I was only about ten yards away when Lacosta appeared in the hatchway cradling a huge rifle.

Hey, Woody, what's your next move?

The one rock I had left was small enough to toss like a baseball. I don't know how close it came to hitting Lacosta because I started running up the ramp to shore right after I let it go. All I could do was get away—there was no cover along the forty yards of ramp. And it was a straight run, meaning no zigzagging. Sure I was a moving target, but the only kind of moving target that's easier to hit than one running away in a straight line is one running toward you in a straight line.

When I heard the rifle crack I ducked instinctively, uselessly, since the bullet would have passed me before the sound did. They say you never hear the bullet that kills you and that's why.

I knew that if Lacosta was an experienced hunter, and if he was using the right kind of weapon, he'd get three, maybe four shots at me before I made shore, and countless more then. I couldn't see how he could miss if I kept on doing what I was doing.

So I did something else. I angled to the left, slowed some, and leapt off the ramp.

There was another crack behind me.

My intention was to land with my left foot on the deck of a sailboat that was about halfway along the ramp to shore, get my balance, and dive smartly into the dark, choppy waters of Lake Ontario. Only I was moving too fast and the boat was bobbing a bit, so my left foot went out from under me when it hit the top of the cabin. It was like falling on a patch of ice. My legs went up and my butt went down. I hit the deck with a crash and slid painfully to a stop.

There was another crack and an explosion of noise beside me as the bullet hit the boat next to where I was sitting.

Where the hell was the cavalry?

I put my legs over the side of the boat's cabin, struggling to get my footing on the boat's nylon rope railing. I couldn't get a purchase, so I just slid off the boat into the water. As I went into the water close to the boat I thought I heard another rifle crack.

I stayed under water to calm myself before I surfaced, and maybe to fool Lacosta into thinking I was dead, so he'd quit shooting at me and take off. But when I broke through the surface the first thing I heard was someone running slowly along the ramp.

Lacosta would not be able to see me from the ramp if I hugged the outside of the boat. He could just shoot blindly through the boat, of course, but I didn't think he'd do that. At least I hoped he wouldn't do that.

As I waited for Lacosta to make his move I noticed for the first time how bloody cold the October lake water was. I didn't know enough about hypothermia to guess at how long I could survive in the water, but I could tell from the way my body was already reacting that it wouldn't be long.

I managed to forget how my body felt when a more immediate danger to my life stepped onto the boat above me, making it creak and sag.

Using the noise of the boat for cover, I took a deep breath and pulled my head underwater. It had to be a smooth, silent submersion or Lacosta would know where I was. That made it harder and slower. I kept close to the boat, to hear and feel it react as Lacosta moved around on it above me.

Lacosta was probably expecting me to be roughly where I'd gone in the water, which made coming up away from there a good idea. So I pulled myself gently under the boat and up the side next to the ramp, looked up to see where I was, plotted the distance to the underside of the floating ramp, and swam for the surface. The idea was to get to the surface with enough air in my lungs to save me from gasping for breath. I didn't make it. The surface was further up than I thought, so when my head came out of the water I made a gasping, sucking noise they probably heard clear across the lake. Certainly Lacosta heard it. He was soon clambering over the boat toward the ramp.

I gasped down as much air as I could and went under again.

As I dropped deeper into the water, it exploded in front of me, leaving a bullet's foamy wake. When that cleared I saw Lacosta step onto the ramp a few feet above me.

Helplessly, I watched his distorted, wavy image aim the

rifle at me. I didn't know if he could see me, but I couldn't take the chance. I flailed my arms and legs madly, hoping to cloud his view with the churned water while I got out of the way of his bullet. It was hopeless, of course. Even if he missed me this time I'd be an easy shot when I went up for air. Easier than fish in a barrel because they didn't have to surface.

I was braced for the bullet's impact, so when there was a loud thump I shook involuntarily. But there was no pain, no bullet's wake, nothing.

I looked up and saw that the gaps between the ramp boards were blocked out in a very distinctive pattern—the figure of a man lying. At first I thought Lacosta was doing it to get a better look at me. But I couldn't see him or the gun moving, and I was running out of air.

When I surfaced I was right under the figure. Above my gasps for air I could hear someone walking slowly along the wooden ramp. That would be the cavalry. Their arrival didn't excite me at all; I was too sleepy.

The only thing I was clearly aware of was something hitting the top of my head, *drip-drop, drip-drop*. I tilted my head to look up. Whatever it was hit my forehead a couple of times, and then my lips. Instinctively I spit it out, but not before getting enough of a taste to know it was blood.

Moving away was hard because the water had suddenly gotten thicker. Then the gyroscope in my brain reeled out of control and my arms and legs went leaden. I opened my mouth to say God knows what and got a swallow of water that startled me to consciousness. Time to get out of the water.

At first I was too busy sucking in air to answer Hurst, who kept calling my name. Then I didn't care much about answering him. Going to sleep seemed like a much better idea.

"Cane," Hurst yelled. It sort of woke me, but I was too far gone to do anything about it. Only when I felt a big hand grab the shoulder of my coat did I grudgingly try to help myself by latching onto the ramp as Hurst used his one good arm to pull me out of the water. I dropped off to sleep just as my feet left the lake. The last thing I noticed was Paul Lacosta's life dripping from his head into a large red spot in the blue water.

**28**  WHEN I CAME TO I WAS ON THE RAMP not far from Lacosta's body. Hurst sat next to me using his good arm to shake, jostle and rub me back to life.

Back on shore about half of the Metro Toronto police force was arriving on the scene. "Now they show up."

"What?" Hurst said. I hadn't realized I'd spoken out loud.

"The cavalry," I said. "Now they show up."

Hurst didn't answer, but I felt his body go stiff next to mine.

"By the way," I said angrily, "what the hell kept you?"

"I'm sorry, Cane. Sorry I took so long." He really was sorry, and really embarrassed.

But I'd almost been dead, which I figure ranked over embarrassed. "So tell me why you took so long," I said.

Hurst looked up and down the dock before speaking. I mimicked his action, but he missed that. "I left the car without my gun," he said very quietly. "I always wear it except when I'm at home, then I leave it in the glove compartment. After what he did to me in the stadium . . . well, I wasn't sure I could take him without it. Especially with this." He hiked up his injured arm. "So I went back for it. And I called it in . . . and running was difficult."

His embarrassment was gruesome, so I let him off the hook. "Don't worry about it," I said. "It was close, but close only counts in hand grenades, horseshoes and slow dancing."

Hurst grunted a laugh. "You must be better. Can you get up?"

I didn't answer because I didn't know. It didn't help that about thirty cops were running up the ramp, but we managed it and I went without comment when he guided me over Lacosta's body to the end of the ramp.

When I was on Lacosta's boat Hurst left me and went back to issue orders to the arriving officers. He had been rubbing me constantly as we walked, the strength of him making me shake. I found that on my own I was also able to shake, though it didn't feel as good.

I didn't realize how cold it was outside until I lurched through the hatchway and out of the wind. Perversely, I shivered at the loss of the wind. I shucked my clothes and rolled up in a blanket, but one wasn't good enough so I went searching for more. There were a couple of bunks under the hatchway. They helped, as did closing the hatch. But what really saved me was the bottle of scotch I found in a cabinet. Normally I would rather drink camel urine, but scotch was all there was going, so I drank it—quickly and steadily. Combined with the effects of my little swim, it had an interesting affect on my body. I had to lay it down right away.

Sleep again seemed like an attractive option, but something went clank in the back of my mind. In movies, the heroes always keep the other people from going to sleep when they're cold. I didn't know if it applied, but I do know that as long as you're conscious you aren't dead.

I stood up and staggered around the small cabin some more. When I came to a chest of drawers I opened it and found some of Lacosta's clothes: underwear, socks, a pullover sweater, and work jeans, all of them too big for me. I looked at the underwear for a minute and then put them back. Wearing a dead man's jockey shorts seemed a little tacky.

After removing my own shorts and toweling myself dry, I

pulled on Lacosta's clothes, then shivered my way back under the blankets and onto the couch.

I was lying there staring at nothing when the hatchway opened to reveal the young cop from the stadium. Even though he tried to hide it, I could see his service revolver in his hand. He looked to be about twenty-one years old, and he may have been. He stood outside peering in, checking things out before he committed himself.

He looked worried, so I offered him a few kind words: "Come in or stay out, will you? You're letting in a draft."

He did a bad job of nonchalantly putting his revolver away before he came in. He closed the hatch behind him and put his thumbs in his belt gunslinger style before saying, "The inspector says I'm supposed to keep an eye on the boat."

I sat up and he took his thumbs out of his belt. When he saw that I was only picking up my wet clothes he relaxed . . . some. After I'd emptied the pockets I rolled my clothes up in one of the blankets and put them beside me on the floor. I took a long pull of the scotch and held the bottle up to the young cop.

He looked surprised, like he didn't know what I meant, then shook his head firmly.

I lay back on the couch. "Hurst want me to go to the station?"

"Yeah, probably," he said, obviously unsure but unwilling to admit it out loud.

"I'll go and ask him." I had no intention of doing that; I just wanted to jerk the young cop around a little. I don't know why.

"No," he said, slipping into the mindless authority mode cops get so good at so soon. "Just wait here, sir."

I turned away from him and took a slow sip of scotch. I was more jealous of the cop than angry with him. He could slip into an attitude that would get him through this situation, and I was totally at loose ends. I wanted someone to tell me how I should feel, other than cold and scared and generally shitty. And I wanted to stop tasting Paul Lacosta's blood.

Some time later two detectives arrived. "Mr. Cane," one of them said, "the inspector wants us to take you to the hospital, and get a statement."

He was very polite, and seemed concerned for my health, so I gave him a generous smiled as I stood up. He smiled back warily. As it turned out he was quite nice, and ignored the bottle of scotch I took with me to suck on gently all the way to the hospital.

At the hospital they checked me over with the casual attitude they reserve for people who walk into an emergency room under their own steam. With one eye on the hovering policemen, a young East Indian doctor said I seemed okay, but did I want to stay in overnight for observation? My flat refusal pleased everyone. The best medicine I got at the hospital was a package of clothes my housekeeper sent over in a cab.

It was after seven P.M. when the two detectives and I arrived at the main police station squad room where things were hopping and the relief was palpable, almost a physical presence. They figured Hurst had solved four murders with one bullet, the best kind of justice. I could understand their elation: no months of preparing for a trial that a simple slip-up could lose for them. Except for the cheering, it was all over for them.

A search of Lacosta's boat and apartment turned up a nice big supply of cocaine, speed, uppers, downers and marijuana, making Lacosta a veritable Avon lady of drugs. The traces of dope in the cupboard of Sean's house made him a likely candidate for inclusion in the drug ring, which meant, to the cops, that his murder was the result of a partnership gone wrong. There were various theories about Leslie Harlan and Lucille Braverman, but nothing everyone could agree on. A consensus was forming, however, around the idea that it was just too damn bad we'd never know for sure. Even the chief, Lawrence R. Herkimer, was drawn to that. He had

arrived just after Hurst got back from the hospital with a
sling to protect the repairs to his separated shoulder. The
chief back-slapped his way around the room for a while and
even nodded to me, just in case I might be someone worth
nodding to. Hurst glowered during the chief's visit, but his
heart wasn't in it. His heart didn't seem to be in anything.
Maybe killing a man does that to you.

When Hurst came over to ask me how I was, I asked him
what had happened with him and Lacosta. It seems Lacosta
had been so busy trying to kill me he hadn't seen Hurst come
up the ramp behind him. Lacosta had declined Hurst's suggestion to put the rifle down, so Hurst had to shoot him.
Hurst was so uncomfortable with the subject I didn't say
anything about what Lacosta had done to him at the stadium.

I wanted to tell Hurst and the chief and everyone else that
they were getting the champagne out a little early on this
case. But I couldn't. They'd want to know why I thought
that, and I'd feel ridiculous saying, "What about the big jar
of Vaseline and the electric razor?" They'd put it down to
my being in the cold water too long. I wasn't sure then that
they wouldn't have been right to do just that.

So I kept my mouth shut for a long time. Finally it occurred to me nobody was taking my statement and it was
almost nine P.M. I called Melinda Holt, who was relieved to
hear I was all right and more relieved to hear I wasn't under
arrest—yet. Alison Denby was not even as enthusiastic as
my housekeeper, but she did volunteer to bring the Golf over
and leave the keys and directions to its location with the cop
on the desk. Listening to her being so reserved depressed me
into action. I walked over to where Hurst was sitting with a
couple of detectives, and ignored the fact that they were deep
in discussion.

"Inspector, if you don't want to take my statement I think
I'll just go on home."

Hurst looked startled at the very idea. He looked at his
watch and said to his men, "Give me a few minutes, will

ya?" He got up and led me to a small room along the wall behind his desk. He didn't offer me a chair and I did not take one.

"Uhh, Richard, about what happened today . . . uhh . . . I'd . . ."

I took the bit in my teeth. "I will tell them exactly what happened, including how you told me not to chase Lacosta. And how you were badly hurt and how you saved my silly ass anyway. I will not make any mention of time elapsed, and if I do I'll shorten it. And I will not mention that you had to go back for your gun. Okay?" I am not good at pussyfooting when I am tired, but I know when I've gone overboard. Ian Hurst had become an angry statue as he listened to me. "I'm sorry," I said. "I'm here being short which shows I've got no complaints about the way you handled yourself."

Hurst's jaw loosened enough to let him speak. "I guess you were worth the trouble."

I took it for granted that he was kidding me and laughed at that. Then I said, "Can I see the medical reports on Sean and Leslie Harlan? Before or after I give my statement."

"Sure. Why?"

"I'm not sure." It was the truth.

Hurst shrugged and said, "Sure, I guess so. I'll get it for you now. You want some coffee, or some more of that scotch?"

I'd forgotten all about the bottle of scotch I'd taken from Paul Lacosta's boat. "Shit no, no more of that scotch. Coffee, please, black."

Hurst was back in a couple of minutes with some files and some coffee. "Varina'll be here in a couple of minutes."

I nodded, but kept my eyes on the report. When Hurst closed the door, I was already halfway through a speed scan of the first page of Sean's autopsy. It only took me a few moments to find the section where his active dose of VD was mentioned. I turned to Leslie Harlan's medical report and turned to the same spot. No mention of VD. Just to be sure,

202

I very carefully waded my way through the report twice. Still no VD.

Either Leslie had been very lucky or Julian Amory was telling me the truth about her not being Sean's lover. As a youth I'd been taught you could get VD by standing too close to someone who had already had it. That was a crock, of course, but VD is a highly communicable disease that's usually found in both parties who are communicating like rabbits, the way Leslie and Sean were supposed to have been. So I leaned toward believing Amory, but where did that get me?

I didn't have any chance to work on that just then because Varina and a stenographer came bustling through the door. The three of us spent a very stiff and very formal hour hacking out a statement I was comfortable with. Something occurred to me just as I was about to sign. I looked up at Varina, who made no attempt to hide his impatience. "What now?" he said.

"What happens to Julian Amory?"

The question surprised him. "They released him a while ago."

"They? Didn't you arrest him?" Varina looked uncomfortable, which was what I wanted. People in authority need to have their mistakes pointed out regularly; it's their only lifeline to a sense of humility.

"You can go, too," Varina said, sounding like I should be grateful.

"I know that," I said in the perfect tone to make his teeth grind. I enjoyed listening to them all the way out of the office.

**29** FINDING THE GOLF WAS EASY ENOUGH
thanks to the directions Alison Denby had left
with the desk cop, but finding something worth
eating was not. So I settled for one of those
charcoal-broiled hamburgers people say are so much better than
the chain-produced kind. Half of it left me wondering how bad
chain burgers could be. This might be a little unfair, since I could
still taste Paul Lacosta's blood in my mouth. It was no fun to
wonder how long that would be with me.

I drove further down Jarvis Street and retraced the route
I'd taken a few nights before, when I'd followed Eric Van-
Kaspal. His BMW was home, but he wasn't. His friend answered my knock, and was not delighted to see me. "What
do you want?" he said.

"To talk to Eric. I have something to ask him."

"He's not here."

"When will he be back?" It was just after 9:30 P.M.

"I don't know. He's filming a TV commercial, and he'll be
there till they get it done."

"There can't be too far away," I said. "His car's still
here."

The man glared at the traitorous car, but said nothing.

I gave him a chance to be reasonable. "If I don't talk to
him tonight," I said, "I'll see him tomorrow, or the day after
that. It'd be better for everyone if I saw him tonight."

The young man looked at me with newfound contempt.
"They're filming over on the boardwalk," he said, "near the
foot of Kew Beach park." Then he closed the door in my
face. I hadn't meant the threat he'd heard in my voice.
While I was sorry he'd imagined it, I was grateful that it had
got me what I wanted.

It was hard to blame him for his attitude—he probably
figured I'd do VanKaspal some harm. The way it looked, I
didn't think I'd have to. I certainly didn't want to.

I drove the few blocks to Kew Beach Park and left the Golf on
Queen Street while I walked the hundred yards to the commercial location. It wasn't too hard to spot, thanks to the extra

lights, the piles of sound and other equipment, and the curious crowd standing around looking fascinated by the boring work of filming.

Finding VanKaspal was not hard either. People were fawning over him, over a striking brunette next to him, and over the fur coats they were both wearing—but mostly over the coats. I staked out a spot on the edge of the crowd and watched a bearded young guy in a safari jacket, jeans and sneakers talking to VanKaspal and the girl. He was, as they say, giving them direction. When he was done, VanKaspal and the girl got ready to do the scene. It was real tough— they had to walk along the boardwalk about twenty yards holding hands. No wonder they needed direction.

After the fifth take (I said it was tough, didn't I?) a guy in some earphones said something that made the director throw his arms up in despair. When he'd recovered, the director told the cast and crew to take five—but not to take them too far, ha ha, since time was money.

The young woman in the fur coat took the opportunity to come on to VanKaspal, employing all of her spectacular charms in the process. I watched his response carefully, wondering if I was the only person who could see he was carefully feigning interest. Showing no interest in that particular woman's sexual advances could mean only one of two things: you were dead or you were gay.

In a low voice I sang, "It's hard to be a football hero, and get away from the beautiful girls." VanKaspal probably had to spend a lot of time showing some interest in women. Here was a bit of irony Lucille and Leslie Braverman would have enjoyed.

I wondered how little VanKaspal enjoyed the situation as the model rubbed her body against his and put her head in his neck. The parallel situation for me, I guess, would have been pretending to enjoy it while a man did the same to me. The very idea made me shiver. I couldn't imagine how hard it was to pretend it wasn't repugnant. Was it just as hard for homosexual men to respond to heterosexual women? How is

205

it for lesbians with heterosexual men? Is it easier for gays of one sex to pretend with gays of another sex? When is a transsexual comfortable, if ever? How many of those love scenes actually feature the best acting in the movie? And where is Dr. David Reuben when you have questions about sex you're not afraid to ask?

I stepped out in front of the curious crowd far enough to catch the star's attention. VanKaspal gave me a cool look but acknowledged my signal for a quick chat. He disengaged himself from the clinging model by pointing my way and giving her a "What can I do?" shrug.

We went off to one side and he said, "What do you want?" His tone matched his lover's for warmth.

His being so suspicious and snippy was starting to bother me. "For the last time, VanKaspal, I couldn't care less who you sleep with. I want you and your friend to know I can't imagine ever telling anyone what I know about you. I also don't care if you believe me, so this is the last time I'm going to tell you. No one. Ever. Okay?"

He thought about it for a moment and then nodded.

Having promised VanKaspal that, I'd given up my best method of getting information from him—faked extortion. I had no stomach for it anyway, so I said, "By the way, your friend only told me where you were because he thought I was extorting him. Tell him that I'd never do that."

My concern for his lover's feelings softened VanKaspal appreciably. It seemed like a good time to ask the question I'd come to ask, so I did: "I need to know if Sean was gay. It's important."

VanKaspal looked away from me, past the film crew to the blackness that was Lake Ontario in the light. He looked back at me and said, "Why? I hear on the radio that Lacosta's been shot by the police for killing Sean. Isn't that enough for you?"

"Was Lacosta gay?"

"Latently, if at all. He hated gays, and I don't think he was doing it as an act of self-repression," VanKaspal said. "He was a natural hater."

206

"If that's true—if he wasn't gay—then his death isn't the end of this. I think Sean was having an affair with a man, and I want to find out who it was. Sean was gay, wasn't he? I'm pretty sure he was."

VanKaspal seemed very sad when he spoke. "Yeah, Sean was gay."

"Do you know who with?" It sounded stupid. VanKaspal laughed at me and I joined in. "I mean do you know who his lover was, or his lovers?"

I found out why VanKaspal had sounded sad. "I'd wanted it to be me, but it didn't work out. There was someone special, though."

"Just one? Couldn't there have been others?"

"All gay people are not promiscuous, you know. They can be just as sexually faithful as straights."

I let a beat pass. "That's not much of a standard to meet."

This time it was VanKaspal's turn to join me in a laugh.

We stood silently for a few seconds before the director said, "Eric, we're ready for you now."

VanKaspal nodded to him and then said to me, "Is that it?"

"I guess so." I put out my hand. "Thanks a lot, Eric, and good luck."

He considered my hand for a second before shaking it. In another second he was gone.

I walked to a phone booth and looked up Julian Amory in what was left of the phone book. No listing. I called police headquarters and surprised Harry Varina with my request for Amory's address and phone number. He surprised me by giving them to me.

Fifteen times the phone rang before I gave up on Amory answering. I tried to place the address from memory but couldn't, so I went into a nearby variety store and bought a street guide for Toronto and area. That showed me that Amory's house wasn't far from where I was standing, maybe a mile east and slightly less than that north.

Amory's street was called Crescent but was actually

shaped like the Greek letter omega (Ω). There were six or seven properties on the outside of the street, but Amory's place took up the entire inside. The house was at the end of large expanses of lawn and garden and mostly hidden from the street by hedges, a gazebo, a wrought-iron fence, and trees. When I got close I saw that it was a big place, maybe five thousand square feet spread around fifteen rooms. Out of habit I felt envious, until I remembered my place was just as big and worth more on the open market. With that in mind I felt entirely comfortable walking right up to the house and knocking on the first door I came to. I could hear music playing inside, but there was no answer. I stepped back to take a better look at the house. It was totally dark, save for a dull light deep in the house. I went back to the door and listened to the music, waiting for it to soften. When it did I began to knock on the door. As time passed and no one responded, I increased the tempo and strength of my knocking until I was pounding. Still no response. I began to feel uneasy, remembering what had been inside the Harlan house when no one had answered the door there. I pounded the silence away.

Then everything went white. I backed right off and blinked my eyes rapidly to adjust to the brightness from the two big floodlights shining down on me from above the door.

There was a few moments' silence and then locks tumbled open. When the door opened Julian Amory was behind it. He still looked elegant, but ragged. There was a glass in his left hand and he used his right to brace himself against the doorframe to minimize his body sway.

"Cane." His surprise was obvious. "Come in." He moved as far out of the way as he could without letting go of the door frame to let me pass. He closed the door behind me and said, "You want a drink?"

"Great."

"Come with me." He led me through the dark house, using the furniture we passed as guides and as crutches. He walked the way he had talked—deliberately. As we moved through the house the music got louder and the light brighter. Finally, we went into the house's only lit room.

It wasn't a very big room, but it was packed with entertainment equipment: stereo, TVs, VCRs, and so on. There was a large, green wing-back chair in the room facing the TV screens and in perfect position for the two big stereo speakers. I couldn't see any other chairs. Neither could Amory, who looked around the room as if seeing it for the first time.

"Stupid of me," he said, and then led me into an adjoining room with seats for eight. We both sat, but he wasn't down for a second before he said, "Oh, your drink. Stupid of me. What'll it be? I'm having scotch."

"That sounds good." It didn't, but I didn't want to confuse him.

"Will Chivas do?"

I had to laugh to myself; I could still be surprised by the habits of the wealthy. "Chivas'll do," I said.

Amory poured me about eight dollars' worth, retail, over ice, and topped up his own. He handed me the drink and a compliment. "I heard about Lacosta's death. I also heard you were involved. Well done." He raised his glass in a toast. "And thank you on Leslie's behalf."

I was embarrassed by the toast and acknowledged it humbly. His feelings were not going to make what I had to ask him any easier. Nothing about this was easy, as far as that goes. I took a big drink of the scotch and found myself looking for the taste of blood. It was there, but I didn't know if it was real or imagined. Either way . . .

"Did he suffer?" Amory asked.

"Suffer?" I was confused. "Who?"

"That bastard Lacosta."

"No, it was quick."

Amory was very disappointed at that. "Too bad. I wish I could have had a hand in it, I would've drawn it out."

"That wouldn't have brought Leslie back."

"I wouldn't have done it for her, Richard, I would've done

it for me. To make me feel better." He was slightly amused that I hadn't seen that.

"You sure it would have?"

He was about eight feet away, yet I could feel the pain coming out of him in waves. It was a pain I knew. "Anything has to be better than this," he said. It was a feeling I knew also. I didn't tell him that, though, since it's a feeling you cannot imagine anyone else sharing.

For a minute we sat quietly drinking, until I was ready to pose my questions. "Julian," I said, "what was Leslie like just before she died?"

There was a hint of suspicion in Amory's voice when he replied, "What do you mean?"

"I'm not sure. I guess I mean was she different? Was she happier, sadder, what?"

"Why?" There was more than a hint of suspicion now.

"No one's explained the murders to me yet in a way that makes sense. If Lacosta did them, why did he do them? Okay, maybe he killed Sean because their drug business went wrong or something, but why Leslie, and why that poor hospital volunteer? Can you think of a reason?"

"Isn't his being a maniac enough of a reason?"

"It helps, no doubt about that, but you don't believe there was no pattern to the murders, do you? Granted, he had to be a maniac to kill anyone, but why did he think he had to? What was his reason?"

Amory chewed ferociously at a corner of his lip. I could see he didn't like the idea that it wasn't Lacosta who'd killed Leslie, since Lacosta's villainy was the foundation of his shaky grasp on sanity. But he wanted to know the truth. "I see what you mean," he said. "Leslie was different just before she died." He paused again to give his thoughts shape.

I helped him out. "She seemed to be buying things for the first time in a while. Clothes, I mean."

Amory was impressed with this. "How'd you know? Yes, she was."

210

"I saw her getting a delivery of stuff from Simply Devine. Like a six-year-old on Christmas."

He smiled at a memory. "She was getting new clothes for the first time since I met her. And she had money. She never used to. I thought maybe she just wasn't used to spending money because Norris always paid for things. But I came to understand that she just didn't have money, that Norris never gave her any." Amory was getting excited by his thoughts. He was picking Norris Harlan as his new villain, a tailor-made choice for him. "In the last couple of weeks she had money and wanted to spend it."

Amory's face lit up and I hoped something significant had come to him. When he spoke again he didn't disappoint me. "Just before Leslie died she talked about divorcing Harlan. She seemed so certain that he would. Until the last few days she was always sure that he wouldn't, that he'd make any divorce case a nightmare for all of us. I was so happy that she'd changed her mind I never asked her why she had." Amory's spirits dropped again. "I should have," he said into his glass.

Silence would have been my best bet, but I wanted to make him feel better. "Maybe we can find out what changed her mind," I said and stood up.

Amory jumped on my comment and followed me to his front door, pressing me for an explanation. I said it was just a half-baked idea, but I'd let him know if it worked out. He badgered me all the way to his door before accepting that that was the best he was going to get out of me for the time being. There was hope in his eyes when he shut the door, however.

Back at the Golf it was an effort for me to heave my body into the driver's seat. Once there, all my muscles gave out and I slumped in the car to enjoy a few minutes' peace and quiet. Considering my usually self-indulgent lifestyle, I'd had an overwhelming day.

The next day didn't look very promising either. I was

going to see Inspector Hurst and try to convince him that Paul Lacosta's death was not the end of this mess. In fact, the mess was just about to be made. And I'd be standing there in the middle of it all, doing my bit.

The thought depressed me no end, so I braced myself for the effort of driving home. When I got there fifteen minutes later, my sense of relief at being home was great. For the first time I thought of the place as my home, since home is where you feel safest.

My body relaxed, leaving me with just enough energy to put the car in the garage and drag my weary ass upstairs to bed.

I was so tired and distracted I had to think for a moment to recall the code to open the garage door. While I was doing that, the tree I was parked next to moved. Not only did it move, it pointed a very big gun at me.

As I stared at the big black hole at the end of the shotgun, a breeze came along and blew an unforgettable odor into the car. Liniment.

So when Hank Graff stepped out from behind the tree with the shotgun in his hands I was not surprised.

**30** "HOW LONG WERE YOU SEAN'S LOVER?"
At first I didn't think he was going to answer. The only sounds I could hear were the discreet noises the Cadillac limousine made as it rolled along in the opposite direction to the way I'd just come.

212

When Norris Harlan finally answered my question it was in a world-weary tone. "Does it really matter?"

"No," I said, "I guess it really doesn't matter." I knew what did matter, however: "Where are we going?"

Harlan firmed up his grip on the pump-action shotgun in his lap and smiled at me from across the backseat as he spoke, obviously pleased with his clever turn of phrase: "We're going to hide a tree in a forest."

"The Purloined Corpse, is that it?"

Harlan hooted at my joke and nodded his admiration for my sangfroid. The admiration was misplaced, since I was being comical only to push reality aside. I'd been resisting reality, but now I was rapidly running out of ways to do that. Reality is sometimes overwhelming, and this time it pointed in one inexorable direction: Harlan and Graff were going to kill me. They'd killed already and had their own damn good reasons to kill again.

I said to myself, slowly and calmly, "They're going to kill you. They're going to kill you. They're going to kill you." I said it over and over to drown out the chorus of "No they won't" that was coming from every fibre of my body. Deep down, everyone believes he's going to be the one that doesn't die. It's a universal lie that stops us all from going crazy with fear. There's no harm in it, except when it comes hard up against reality and stops you from doing whatever you have to do to keep living. A little desperation can be a handy weapon. I tried "They're going to kill me" a few times, but it lacked the sense of detachment I needed. Everything in moderation, including desperation.

"They're going to kill you. They're going to kill you. They're going to kill you."

I looked out the deeply tinted side window next to me. No sounds got in because this was Harlan's famous bullet-proof, armor-plated security limo, the one waggish critics called the Madillac. We were stopped at a red light waiting to make a left turn from Castle Frank Road onto Danforth Avenue. Less than a mile away was police headquarters. Twenty-five feet away was a subway entrance. None of this counted; what really counted was the three feet from the snout of the shotgun to my chest, and the quarter-inch Harlan would have to move the trigger to bridge that gap.

Still, I felt better because of our nearness to other people, like the two young couples babbling gaily in the car next to us. I had to fight that feeling.

"They're going to kill you. They're going to kill you."

Hank Graff pulled the limo out onto Danforth as soon as the light turned green in his favor. We were soon crossing the six-lane bridge that spanned the Don Valley with its roads, its meandering, dirty little river, its train tracks and its open spaces about two hundred feet below. As I often do when crossing that bridge, I felt my vertigo nudging me in the subconscious. I pushed the feeling away. What a time to be irrational.

I'd often wondered why people who know they're going to die so often go meekly along with their executioners. Why don't more of them strike out and try to stop the inevitable? Do they hope their docility will be contagious and infect their killers? Are they waiting for a better time to fight back? Are they afraid to fight back? Are they so in love with life they won't gamble with the extra moments fighting back might cost them? Is it just that they don't believe death will happen to them? Is a lack of desperation what sends so many of them to an easy grave?

"They're going to kill you. They're going to kill you."

Why was I waiting? Maybe I should make a grab now for the gun in Harlan's lap. I turned away from the activity on Danforth Avenue toward my would-be murderer. He was watching me steadily, quiet and still. The shotgun he held so securely now hardly moved from level, even when the Caddy floated with the street bumps. That's why I was waiting: I'd be dead before the last pellets hit my body. And out on the street no one would see or hear anything, thanks to the construction of the car. The Madillac was designed to keep bul-

214

lets and noise out, but I assumed it would do just as well at keeping bullets and noise in.

At least if I died in the car it would cause Harlan some inconvenience: "I'll splash my insides all over his leather upholstery. That'll show the smug bastard." All right, making my move then would be inconsequential, but the idea was worth bearing in mind.

The situation had to change before I had a good shot at saving my life. And if I'd guessed right about where we were going, that meant I had about ten minutes before the situation would change. Meanwhile, I could do two things: hope Graff would have a high-speed collision with a police car, and put straight in my mind what my death was all about. My proposed death.

"What did you gain by killing Sean?" I asked Harlan.

"It wasn't just for me," he scolded, offended by the question. "I did it for football. And for Sean, of course."

"You killed him for his own good?"

Harlan missed my sarcasm. "Look at the way he's remembered now," he said. His eyes narrowed on me and his hands tightened on the gun before he added, "And will be forever once you're gone."

"I'm to die so Sean's name and the game of football will not be sullied, is that it?"

Harlan smiled that I was correct.

"I tell you what, Norris. You shoot our big friend up there and then kill yourself, and I promise never to say a word to anyone about any of this. What do you say?"

For all Harlan responded, I might never have spoken. Graff did take a quick, nervous look over his shoulder, however, giving me some pleasure.

"I figure Sean was going to come out of the closet," I said, "and bring you with him. Is that it?" Harlan stayed silent, but I knew from the way his body tightened that I was right. "Being gay isn't the stigma it used to be, Norris. Lots of people have admitted it."

"I'm not lots of people."

"You couldn't talk Sean into keeping you out of it?"

"Maybe I could have, probably I could have. There was more to it than my good name, though."

"The name of football, you mean."

Harlan nodded. "Sean also wanted to tell his sordid stories about his drug dealing. He wanted to tell how drugs had a hold of my sport and how we weren't doing anything about it. I couldn't let him do that. The league's best player admitting he was a queer drug dealer? Are you mad?"

I wanted to tell him "No, but you are." Instead I said, "I see what you mean" in a tone of dawning enlightenment. The pretense of student listening to teacher had worked with Harlan before, and should work again. Especially with the stress he was under. We were under.

I couldn't help showing off a little, however. I thought maybe that if he knew how much I'd found out he'd be less sure of himself. A little insecurity on his part might be helpful to me. "When Leslie found out about you and Sean she threatened to expose you. So you bought her off with clothes and money and the possibility of a divorce. All she had to do was keep quiet about you and pretend to have been having an affair with Sean Denby at the Duke Street house. You were the one he was meeting there. That was your Vaseline, your . . ." I was going to say electric razor but thought better of it, so I added coyly, ". . . lubricant."

Harlan did not seem impressed or concerned that I knew this, just annoyed. But not with me. And of course not with himself. With Leslie. "I couldn't believe that she was being unfaithful to me," he said angrily, "and with that person Amory." He calmed down some before going on. "I have you to thank for my finding out she couldn't be trusted."

"Me?" I didn't like the way this was going. "How?"

"She hadn't been too helpful until you showed an interest in the Duke Street house. She told me you wanted the address, and that she couldn't see any harm in your going there. Neither could I, so I gave her the key to give to you.

Something about her—her nervousness, I guess—made me nervous, so I sent Hank there ahead of you." Harlan shot a quick look at his driver before saying in a low voice, "If we had more time I'd get you to tell me how you got away from him; he's been unwilling to discuss it." He took another look at his driver and then spoke in a normal voice. "After his run-in with you, he paid that hospital volunteer . . . what's her name. . . ?"

"Lucille Braverman," I said, angry that he didn't even know her name.

"Yes, he paid Mrs. Braverman a visit, to ask her what she knew about my wife and about you."

"How'd he find her?" I asked, even though I knew the answer. I hoped he'd contradict me.

"He followed you to the hospital, saw who you talked to, got her address, and paid her a visit. Unfortunately for her, Hank felt he had to kill her once he was there."

Exactly what I didn't want to hear—that I was the one who'd caused Lucille Braverman's death. I had to turn away from Harlan; I couldn't stand the sight of him right then. I felt like shit, but there was no time for that now. We were passing Greenwood Avenue.

"They're going to kill you. They're going to kill you."

I looked back at Harlan. "You and Graff both killed Sean. And Graff killed Mrs. Braverman. Did you actually kill your own wife?" I knew I was projecting my own emotions on the idea, but I couldn't help it.

Uxoricide did not seem to trouble Harlan overly. "Not only was she unfaithful," Harlan said, "but she was becoming insistent about an immediate divorce. When she found out about the woman from the hospital she went right over the edge. I had Hank deal with her. I was having lunch with the police chief at the time." Harlan smiled at his cleverness. He liked to do that. So had I, but I couldn't imagine doing it much any more.

Thinking about his cleverness must have made Harlan

consider his mistakes, because he asked me, "What made you suspect all this?"

Whatever I told him he'd cover up, so I gave him a disbelieving look.

He nodded his understanding of my position. "It doesn't matter," he said, "because you haven't told the police anything, not even about Sean giving me a case of VD and not Leslie. You saw on the medical report that she didn't have it and you saw me get shots for it twice. I'm betting that whatever you know you've kept to yourself." I tried to make a poker face look significant. Harlan looked at me closely for a moment and then added, "Unless you told Alison Denby."

"No, I didn't tell her anything," I blurted out, angry with myself for putting these monsters on her trail.

"Sure," Harlan said with a knowing smile.

I had to look away again. Now there were two lives to be saved, mine and Alison Denby's.

My mind swam. What else did I want to know? What else did I want to say? It seemed important that I didn't die confused.

"They're going to kill you. They're going to kill you."

I put my mind to the task of figuring a way out of this madness. Whatever I came up with would have to happen soon—Graff had just turned the Caddy south onto Woodbine Avenue. I was right about where we were headed: St. John's Cemetery, Norway, the sight of Leslie Harlan's funeral the next day. Hide a tree in a forest, indeed. I couldn't resist a feeling of admiration for the idea of where to dispose of my my body—in the earth under where Leslie Harlan would be buried. I thought of my recurring nightmare of the night before in which I'd lain in her cold, dead arms. If I didn't do something soon it was actually going to happen.

"They're going to kill you."

We drove under a passenger train on the CN bridge and just caught the yellow light at Gerrard. I looked around for a cop with a grudge against people in limos running lights, but of course there was none around. I had to shake off the urge to let someone else save my life.

"Harlan, let me go. I won't say anything." It was a lie made in desperation and we knew it. "People will miss me. They'll be suspicious."

He actually seemed to look a little sorry for me when he said, "Not that many people will miss you." It was an unnecessarily cruel remark, though true. "Lots of people will be suspicious, but they won't know where to look or what to think."

The Caddy accelerated to run another orange light and there it was—St. John's Cemetery, stretching and rolling off ahead of me on the right.

"They're going to kill you."

The first gate we passed was locked, and right next to a house that belonged to the cemetery superintendent. I wondered if they spent much time at night looking out at the graveyard.

We slowed in front of the large red brick church, and Graff swung the big car into the outside lane to get a better angle into the narrow driveway. The church was on our right as we went up the driveway, and a part of the cemetery on our left. There was no gate at the end of the driveway. Graff turned off the Caddy's headlights, leaving its parking lights on. Beyond the church we rolled into darkness. The amber parking lights and the red rear lights lit up the narrow roadway and the nearest tombstones, making the cemetery look like a set for a rock video.

I looked out the back window in time to see a large stone angel turned blood red by the car's brakelights. Beneath her sad silent face her arms were stretched wide in welcome.

"Kill you."

 **31** IT WAS ALL GRAFF COULD DO TO GET THE Cadillac through a couple of places—people unwilling to move aside in death the way they would have in life for such a car. Death as the great leveler.

Despite Graff's problems with the big Caddy, we were soon where we were going, which was on the down side of a hill about as far from the street as we could get. All I could see were a few acres of blackness between the car and the backs of some houses to the north. I wondered how many of a graveyard's neighbors look out on it around midnight on Sunday, and what they'd do if they saw a Cadillac limousine parked there.

Norris Harlan was barely visible in the glow from the car's dimmed lights, but I was more aware of him than ever—we were wired together by what he wanted to do to me. So we both jumped when the trunk popped open behind us. Harlan was so startled it almost ended for me right there.

A second later Harlan and I were both blinking in the lights turned on when Graff opened the driver's door. I saw Harlan's face in good, direct light for the first time that night and searched it for something human I could try to reach. There was nothing human there, and I was glad when Graff closed the front door and returned us to darkness.

Graff moved along the driver's side of the car to the back. He clattered around in the trunk getting out a shovel and a flashlight that he turned on before lowering the trunk lid.

"Get out," Harlan said.

I did as he said and stepped into the glare of the torch.

If Harlan were slow getting out of the car with the shotgun I might have my chance . . . but he wasn't. He had the barrels pressed in the small of my back before I'd completely straightened up. "Step away from the car," Harlan ordered in a flat voice.

I'd only taken one small step when Graff gripped my right arm in his huge left hand and pulled me down the hill away from the car. The shovel was tucked under his right arm and

220

the flashlight was in his right hand. He pointed it ahead of us so we could see to step carefully, but nothing more. Norris Harlan followed a few paces behind us.

We walked between the tombstones and over the grass, leaves, markers, and graves for thirty yards. We stopped when the light fell on the ends of four planks and the edge of a pile of dirt. Graff let go of my arm, stepped back, and played the torch all across the top of the empty grave.

"Move the planks, Cane," Harlan said. His voice wasn't flat any longer; he knew the climax to our evening was coming up fast.

So did I, and I couldn't see how I could stop it right then. I moved carefully to the brink of the grave and got on my knees. The planks were two-by-tens, maybe eight feet long, and impossible for me to lift by myself, so I flipped them sideways to the edge, one at a time. As I worked I kept my eyes well above the ground, staring at the dark beyond the grave.

When I stood up and stepped back to where Harlan and Graff stood waiting for me I kept my back to the empty pit. Graff pointed the light right at me, so all I could see was the handle of the shovel he held out.

I took it without comment and looked over to where Harlan was standing. Turned away from the light, I could barely see his outline. He and the shotgun were looking right at me, and both were motionless, just like the momuments all around us.

I couldn't stand to look at him any more so I turned back to the grave.

"Get in and dig," Harlan said, "about three feet."

All along I'd known his plan was for me to dig my own grave, but hearing it spoken still hit me hard.

Graff started to move toward the grave, and Harlan inched closer behind me. Both expected any play from me would come now, which meant I had less than no chance then. I made a little sobbing noise and shuffled forward, using the shovel to support myself as I moved. We were right at the lip of the grave when I stopped and looked down into forever. The doorway to eternity. For a long time I just stared and thought about getting into my own grave while I was still alive. I couldn't and wouldn't do it, which meant I made my play now or died.

I kept my head down but glanced sideways at Graff. He had been watching me, but now he too was looking down into the grave. Probably thinking about his own eternity and when it might start. If Norris Harlan's mind was on similar thoughts, my eternity might be delayed.

Without warning I pivoted on my toes and swung the five-foot shovel like a baseball bat. Graff reacted first and turned the light toward me, but my back was to it so I could see pretty well. What I could see was not reassuring—Harlan was about ten feet away from me and instinctively leaning back to avoid the shovel. That meant my primary target—his head—was well out of my reach, but it also meant he wouldn't be firing the shotgun right away. So I made a mid-course correction on the shovel and sent its whistling head lower, toward the gun barrel.

If Harlan hadn't tried to pull the gun up out of the way of the shovel I probably would have missed it entirely. As it was I caught the shotgun a good one with the metal shovel head, bouncing a *clang* off the nearby tombstones and shooting a bolt of pain up the shovel handle to my arms.

The blow must have been worse for Harlan because he let out a grunt of pain and tried to take his hands off the shotgun without really letting go of it. He couldn't manage it, of course, so the shotgun hit the ground.

I didn't see it land because I was too busy keeping the shovel head from doing the same. Hank Graff's head-down charge had to be dealt with. When I was facing him I knew it was hopeless, that he was too close for the shovel to do any damage. Any damage done would be to me if Graff caught me flat-footed, so I did what I'd done a few nights before—I stepped back and to the side. Luck was with me and it worked again, except that once again Graff managed to hit me as he swept past. This time it was with the heavy metal torch, not his fist. It hurt about as much.

Off-balance and in pain from Graff's blow, I let the shovel head fall to the ground, where it would do me no good at all. I lifted it up, pulled it back to my left, and swung it again.

Graff was crouched and turning toward me, throwing the flashlight beam all over the place. For a second it fell on Harlan, and he used the light to locate the shotgun he'd dropped. To help his boss out, Graff kept the light on him while he picked up the gun.

In doing that Graff also helped me. I did one quick hammer throw turn to get up some speed and let the shovel go when it was pointing at Harlan.

I knew I'd made a good throw when I saw the look on Norris Harlan's face—the slack-jawed, goggle-eyed stare people wear when something is suddenly flying right at them. Harlan pulled away to the right, but that served only to make the shovel hit him high up in the shoulder rather than flush in the chest. Because he was leaning away from it, the shovel head caught Harlan on an angle, and didn't cut him too badly. It did strike him hard enough to make him drop the shotgun again and clutch his shoulder.

Then everything went white when Hank Graff turned the light into my eyes. I turned my face to avoid the glare and lost the split second I needed to get out of Graff's way again. Using every one of his 240 pounds and every ounce of his football experience, Graff drove his head and shoulder into me with a fury. I was completely off guard, so when he hit me he lifted me up and carried me back a few yards before slamming me down to the ground. Even though fireworks seemed to be going off all around me, I couldn't see or hear anything. I also couldn't catch a breath, even though I wanted one very badly. Getting up was simply out of the question, so I lay and gasped quietly, waiting for the fireworks and my life to end. The fireworks ended but my life didn't. That surprised me. I took a deep breath and looked up to see what was holding things up.

The light was off me and leading Graff back over to his wounded boss. Harlan was toughing it out, rocking gently from the shock of the blow. He only let go of his shoulder once, so he could look in the palm of his left hand at something that made him angry and dismayed. People are often surprised at the sudden appearance of their mortality. I saw him speak, but I couldn't make out what he said; there was a dial tone in my head.

Harlan gestured my way with his head and Graff swung the torch back towards me in compliance. I closed my eyes, leaned my head back, and pretended I was still in trouble from Graff's tackle. The light shone on me for a couple of seconds, then left me in the dark again.

The smart thing to do was get up and get the hell out of there, as quickly and as quietly as I could. But I didn't because I wanted to hurt them as much as I could. My entire body shook with anticipation, the way it does when you're close to consummating a four-year-old passion.

The dial tone in my head had gone. I heard Harlan say, "I'll be all right. Deal with Cane." Then he added, "No, use your hands, or the shovel." Either Graff was afraid the noise of the shotgun might draw some attention, or he was afraid to give the weapon up, or he preferred to see his assassin work with his hands. Probably all three.

Time for me to fall back on a recent old favorite trick of mine. In the darkness I groped in the pile of fresh dirt that had been dug to make room for Leslie Harlan and me. Too small. Too small. Too small. Perfect.

I got onto my knees and scrambled over the dirt before the light was shone my way again. Graff held the beam steady on the empty spot for about two seconds, as if waiting for me to step back into my spotlight and get on with the show. I used that time to get a good fix on him.

There was a hard *thwack* and a deep grunt when the rock hit Graff. The torch shone up in the air and then fell straight down. Before it landed I'd already gone two long steps toward following up on my advantage.

The light rolled a little before stopping with its beam pointed directly at a three-foot-high tombstone with "Walker" chiseled on it. In the reflected light I saw Graff drop to one knee as he clutched his head. Harlan let go of his shoulder as he bent to pick up the shotgun. Noise or not, Harlan would use the gun on me as soon as he could.

I was about eight feet from Harlan and the gun when I launched into a dive toward them, four feet away when he got his hand on it, and right on him when he lifted it off the ground. That was the perfect spot to grab it, so I did, and easily took it from Harlan's weakened hold.

I'd stretched the dive to its limits, and was clutching a shotgun, so my attempt to land and do a nifty little roll onto my feet didn't work out. I landed hard on my arm and hip, losing momentary control of the gun and my reflexes. The gun I kept pointed in the general direction of Graff and Harlan. I figured that in their conditions the business end of a shotgun would dissuade them from doing anything aggressive.

I figured wrong.

Hank Graff was chugging resolutely across the space between us—a little unsteady on his feet, but fast enough to do me some harm.

My sore arm stopped me from getting the shotgun up high enough to shoot to kill, and I wasn't sure I wanted to do that anyway. So I pulled the trigger with the gun aimed as low as I could.

It went off with a roar. Graff let out a yelp, wavered, took one long, unsure step, and threw himself at me. He hit me hard again. The top of his head smashed into my face and the weight of his body knocked me flat on my back. The silent fireworks and the dial tone came back, and I wanted to rest for a while, maybe a year. Then I started to gag as blood drained into my throat. I tried to sit up and cough the blood out, but I couldn't move. Graff's large, motionless body had me pinned to the cemetery ground.

I spit out what blood I could as Norris Harlan stood not

far away, calmly looking down at Hank Graff and myself. His attitude angered me so much I wanted to shoot him for it. The only reason I didn't was that the gun was pinned between me and Graff's body.

When Harlan saw me trying to free the shotgun he walked away.

I wouldn't let go of the shotgun in case Graff was playing possum. The idea was ludicrous, but he'd made two or three astounding recoveries on me already and I didn't want to risk another. So I struggled to lever him off as I kept a death grip on the shotgun. He moved, but not enough.

Then I heard the door of the limousine close behind Harlan. I released the gun and shoved up on Graff with my right arm and leg. I didn't know if he was alive or dead, and didn't care. He slid partly off me and I pulled myself the rest of the way out from under.

The Cadillac was just moving forward when I got the shotgun pointed in its direction. I pulled at the trigger—and nothing happened. I swore at myself and reached forward with my right hand to work the pump action, like I'd seen so many people do on TV. The gun made a rasping metallic sound, but when I looked up to aim at the Caddy it was quite a ways away. This time the gun's roar caused a rash of plinking noises, the sounds of an armored car shrugging off shotgun pellets fired into its rear quarter panel. Whatever damage I'd done, it wasn't slowing Harlan down any. That meant I'd have to do a little legwork.

I stood up and spit out more blood. My nose, bloody and broken, did not hurt much. My mouth hurt badly, however, and was swelling rather quickly.

Still, I could run. And that's what I did, right after I cradled the gun in one arm and picked up the flashlight with the other. I began to retrace the road we'd taken in the Caddy on the way in.

Harlan was taking the big car along the road, which, I assumed, eventually led back to the same place. I was count-

226

ing on that place being the gate we'd come through, and which Harlan would have to use to get out.

Harlan was having trouble steering the big, wide car through all the narrow spots, and as I ran I heard the occasional crash. Then they began to come more frequently and in greater strength. Harlan had discovered that most tombstones are no match for a five-thousand-pound armor-plated limo, and didn't seem to care what they were doing to his car or it to them.

I tried not to care about the pain in my face or the exhaustion in my limbs, and tried to make my body behave like it belonged to a nineteen-year-old running back again. It wouldn't go along, so I was losing ground on the limo rampaging along the southern edge of the cemetery. Harlan was going to get out before I got to the exit. If I kept on the pavement, that is.

I veered off to the left, going cross-country toward the dark church. Courtesy of the sense of order its inhabitants took with them to their graves, a path spread open between two rows of their final markers. I sprinted along it quite easily, enjoying the soft, giving grass after the hard, irregular roadway. My only impediment was the low mound of earth atop a recent grave, but I leapt it with ease.

Two steps beyond the fresh grave I heard a wrenching crash off to my right. I looked over in time to see a stone figure take a sideways dive off a plinth onto the trunk of Harlan's Cadillac. It struck the limo a glancing blow and was quickly buried in a cloud of dust and gravel as Harlan accelerated the car up the final stretch to the gate. My shortcut and Harlan's run-in with the statue gave me the slight edge I needed to beat him there. I burst out of the tombstones onto the road, tossed the torch aside and raced the last few yards up the driveway. Behind me I could hear the Cadillac forcing its way along the remainder of the narrow road.

By the side door of the church I stopped in the middle of

the driveway and turned to face the cemetery and Harlan's approaching car. I raised the shotgun in my best thou-shalt-not-pass attitude, pumped it once to load it, and sighted it on Norris Harlan.

He was about twenty yards away in the Cadillac, going about ten miles an hour around the final sweep in the road. When the road was at last straight he gave the Caddy some gas, aiming it right at me and beyond.

When the car was about ten yards away from me I pulled the trigger and jumped over a curb onto the church sidewalk. The windshield turned into a honeycomb of glass and the limo veered right as it passed me, off the road and into the tombstones. Probably Harlan could not see, or was disoriented. Whatever, the Caddy was definitely out of control and off the road onto the steeply sloping grass on the right side. That slowed it some, but not as much as the first thumping collision between its headlight and a tombstone. The Caddy was listing fiercely and slowing noticeably.

But it was going fast enough so that when it hit one of the largest momuments in the cemetery it rocked the plinth badly before coming to a stop. The Caddy had hit the base of the tombstone I'd noticed coming in, the one with the welcoming angel that had burned blood-red in the car's tail-lights. It was white now in the limo's headlights, and leaning forward. Then, slowly, daintily, the six-foot granite angel dove forward toward the Cadillac. Her descent was short, and she hit face-first into the windshield. When her body hit the hood the force of the landing snapped her neck. I got up beside the car just as her head rolled slowly down the wind-shield, across the hood, and off onto the ground. The body, arms spread wide for traction, rocked gently on the hood.

Sensing defeat, the Caddy chugged to a stop. Norris Harlan, sensing the same thing, got out of the car, walked right by me like I wasn't even there, and sat down on the church steps.

Neither of us spoke until the first of the police cars arrived.

**32** IT'S IMPOSSIBLE TO PUSH A BIG, FAT CAT into a pool of shit and not get some on you and get a little scratched up. The media sees to that. So it was in my case, or, actually, Norris Harlan's. It didn't bother me, though.

When I explained my theories to Hurst he was all for shooting Harlan at the station. The only thing that stopped him was the presence of half of Harlan's law firm, whose defense of their client at first was "He wouldn't do that, he's too rich." In their eyes I was obviously the better suspect. Fortunately, Hurst swung the crown attorney over to his point of view, so Harlan was eventually charged on various serious counts, with me as the principal witness and general dogsbody. To everyone's surprise—but especially Harlan's—he even went to jail to await trial. This was widely seen as an omen that things looked bad for him. Official attempts to build a case against Harlan were made considerably easier by the decision of Hank Graff to tell the truth. Graff rightly saw that he'd probably take a big fall if he didn't.

For my part, as soon as Hurst and his people got tired of hearing me tell my story every day for six to eight hours, I got to work on a little legal matter of my own. The first thing I had to do was find a competent law firm that did not have a direct link to anyone who talked to my father-in-law. This was a lot harder than I thought it'd be, but absolutely necessary if I was to do what I wanted without him finding out. Together the lawyer and I learned that Ontario's fondness for property rights extended right into the grave that I happened—as my wife's executor—to own. This I found morbidly comical, while the lawyer saw it simply as practical. We were soon in court before a judge who granted my request but not before making clear his distaste for it and pointing out that this was one of the times when the law was wrong. Later that day the lawyer, a public health official, and a couple of grim undertakers spent a couple of sunny hours carrying out my request. After a liquid lunch I went into a downtown movie theater showing of *The Big Chill,* where I bought two glutton-sized Cokes and went into the men's room and replaced half of the syrupy liquid with a mickey of rye. Except for shedding a few tears during the funeral scenes at the beginning, I handled myself very well during the film. By the time it was over, my little legal matter was straightened out as well. The results of it even beat me home, courtesy of the thoughtful lawyer who left them with my housekeeper.

The next morning I convinced Inspector Hurst that I needed to go out of town for a few days. It was just as well that he said okay because I already had my bags in a rental car and a reservation for that night in Burlington, Vermont, a nine-hour drive away. The next morning I drove south from there and watched the leaves fall to the ground. As always, the dignity and the beauty of their passing impressed me, and set me to wondering why human beings don't take their leave nearly as well. I never did figure it out to my satisfaction, but I did spend many hours in various Vermont cemeteries thinking about it.

A Vermont cemetery in autumn is one of the world's great wonders, full of color, peace and comfort. One was particularly beautiful, so that's where I decided to leave Elizabeth. Staring into what was to have been my grave had marked me for life, and I swore I'd never spend my death in the ground. Neither would my Elizabeth. After I'd had her disinterred and cremated I'd considered keeping her at home with me, but from the first that had struck me as distasteful and unseemly. So I decided to leave her in the most beautiful spot I could find that had a sense of permanence about it. On a fine Friday afternoon, I stood at the top of a small hill under a bare maple tree with Elizabeth's remains. A breeze came along and lifted her away from me. She flew down the hill and disappeared into the sunlight, where she was reunited with the earth and the sky. Some tears fell but a weight was lifted from my heart that I hadn't known was there.

I said "Good-bye," and turned for home.